Between Breaths

The Seattle Sound Series
Book 2

Alexa Padgett

ISBN-13:978-1-945090-08-0

Edited by Nicole Pomeroy and Sara Peterson
Cover Art by Sarah Hansen of Okay Creations

To Juliette. Without you, Hayden wouldn't have his voice.

CHAPTER ONE
Hayden

"Woo! Second encore! Let's go," Ets said, giving me a high five.

"I love playing Sydney. Nothing like the hometown crowd," I said, scrubbing the towel over my face and hair. "Even midweek, their energy is amazing." I let the tech powder my face again. Waited for the same treatment for Ets, Jake, and Flip. Our smiles grew wider as the raucous crowd screamed for more of us. Ets, my best mate, flung his arm around my shoulder, gripping me tight.

"You're on fire," he yelled. His gray-blue eyes lit up with joy and his eyebrow ring flashed in the stage lights. Sweat darkened his hair to a deep brown.

I stepped back out onto the stage. Blinding lights, the deafening roar of thousands of people excited to see me. To hear me play, sing. I raised my arms over my head and the screams grew louder. Yeah, baby. This right here—this was glory. And I was the high priest of rock.

I loved our fans. Loved that they connected with our music. Loved that I could sit at my piano and play this simple melody that'd run through my head for months to a rapt audience of thousands.

I rode the high as I sang, making sure I winked at the beautiful young woman standing right at the front of the stage, her strawberry-blond hair catching the light when she bobbed her head to the music. As our last song ended I dipped my head in her direction before taking my final bow and heading backstage.

"Fabulous show!" Our manager, Harry, slapped my back, his hand landing right on the sore muscles created from hours of lifting heavy equipment, even though I was told to leave those

1

details to the roadies.

Bloody roadies. The rise in fame these last few months was still surreal.

Harry handed each of us a bottle of water. Sure, I would've preferred a beer, but I was the only singer other than Ets, and while his song skyrocketed us to the top of the charts this past year, my voice and compositions kept us there.

"We kicked arse," Ets said, rubbing my chest. "You were on, Crewe."

"You weren't too shabby yourself, mate. Loved the play up the frets at the end there."

Ets's showmanship onstage kept our concerts fresh, interesting. Selling out.

"So did the fans," Jake said. Ets's younger brother, Jake played bass to his brother's lead guitar. But Ets was flashier than his introverted, stocky sibling. Always close, not just in age but also in appearance, they balanced each other. Or had until Ets's behavior turned erratic. Though he hadn't said so, he was still hurt and angry that his long-time girlfriend ditched him for parts unknown last year.

I chugged the bottle of water, tossing it to Harry when it was empty. "Let's do the meet and greet. Noticed a strawberry-blonde." She was hot. All legs and tits. I grinned, anticipating the next few hours.

"She's gorgeous. So's her friend." Harry licked his lips, thinking no doubt of the mostly nude women waiting for us in the next room.

"Go wild, Harry," Ets said.

"Wait a mo'." I dug my phone out of my pocket. I couldn't hear the ring over the din of excited voices filling the space, just felt the vibration. I didn't recognize the number—international. Seattle area code. My stomach tumbled over, landing somewhere much lower.

2

"Hello," I said, cautious. Anyone with my phone number was here, at the venue.

I plugged my other ear, trying to hear the voice speaking into the phone.

"I can't hear you," I said.

"Your mother…Hospice…"

"Hang on," I said, and turned toward Harry. "Harry, I need to get somewhere quiet."

He didn't ask any questions—good bloke, there—and led me through the back hall to a room. He snapped on the lights, shut the door behind him.

"You 'right, mate?"

I waved him off, unsure how to answer. "Please start again. Who are you?"

"First, this is Hayden Crewe?"

"Yes."

"My name's Kelly Winston. I'm a hospice nurse at the Bevins-Kline facility in Seattle. Your mother was admitted yesterday."

"You sure you have the right person? What's her name?" I asked.

"Miriam Hastings. She asked me to call you to let you know she's here."

"How'd you get my number?" I asked, too shocked by her words to think of anything else. My mum. No bloody way.

Kelly sighed into the phone. "I called your record label and jumped through a lotta hoops. Your mom's in a bad way, Mr. Crewe. She has pancreatic cancer."

My knees weakened and I managed to settle into a nearby chair.

"Pancreatic cancer. So—what? She's dying?"

"Yes. The doctor said she has a week at most."

I dropped my head as my neck muscles clenched. My mum, a woman I hadn't seen in decades, was terminal.

"She asked for me?"

"She's been asking for you constantly."

"But she's so young," I said.

"She didn't receive proper treatment."

My chest tightened as my mind spiraled back to my dad's last request as he'd gripped my hand in his age-spotted one. *Find your mother. If not for you, then for me. I never told you the whole story about her illness, Hayden. I didn't understand it myself. You need to hear her version.*

"Give me your information again." I snapped my fingers, and Harry handed me a pen and a notebook. I wrote down the details, the pen shaking as I tried to press the point to the paper. *Terminal. A week at most.*

"I hope you can see her, Mr. Crewe. Miriam's quite agitated."

"Yeah. I bet. I'll be there soon as I can."

I ended the call and stared at the pad. None of the letters lined up. Bloody fucking hell.

Harry patted my shoulder, all paternal concern. "You 'right, mate?"

My eyes darted around the room. Small. Dusty. Two chairs and chipped linoleum. Five minutes ago I'd been playing Sydney's greatest venue.

"No. I don't think I am."

"What do you need?" Harry asked, voice solicitous. "Who was on the line?" More than a spark of interest there. Ambitious bastard that Harry was, my personal life would be splashed across the Australian Broadcasting Corporation news segment faster than I could blink. The media would go digging into my mum...why my dad moved us back to Melbourne from Seattle.

Which I wasn't sure I'd ever be able to handle. Possibly because I didn't know the answer myself.

I cleared my throat, trying to figure out how to thread the needle. "My mum's in hospice. I need a ticket to Seattle. Like, sooner than now." I stood, ready to put my plan into place. Actionable steps.

Terminal. I shook my head. Crikey, she damn well better not die until I had a chance to ask my questions, get some answers.

Harry pulled at the vest under his tailored suit coat. His wife and three kids lived up in Darwin, a place he rarely went now that we'd hit the international charts. "Hayden, are you sure that's smart?"

No, it wasn't. I sure as hell didn't want to fly halfway across the world to watch my estranged mother die.

"She's dying, Harry. I *have* to go."

I'd promised my dad I'd seek her out and hear her side of their story. He hadn't said why I should after all the intervening years, and I never asked. Nor did I make finding my mum a priority. Now I was out of time.

"We've got a concert schedule."

Shock reverberated through my chest. No wonder his wife stayed tucked up in Darwin. "She's only got days to live."

Harry scrubbed his palms across his cheeks, mouth hanging open. "Right. I'll handle it. You get packed and head to the airport. I'll text you the details."

"I'll be in and out, Harry. A few days, tops."

Harry sighed. "Good. Yeah, good. We don't want to screw over the fans. They bought tickets to these shows months ago."

Tension crawled up my neck. "Do you think I'd choose *hospice* over playing with the band?"

Harry put his hand on my arm. I shook him off, so he tried to placate me with words. "You're right. This is a tough time for you."

"I plan to keep my commitments to the band, to our fans—as soon as my mum's gone."

Harry ran his hand over the buttons of his vest, and I struggled to process my emotions. *Why did we leave all those years before?* Next time Harry spoke, he was all business. Don't know why I expected more from him.

"I'm walking a fine line here, Hayden. Everyone should be happy. The fans like that last tune you added to the LP. We'll offer them the live version you did tonight. Glad you overruled Ets."

Not what he'd said when they recorded the track. In fact, he'd sided with Ets, saying the song was too emotional.

People connected with my songs because they were real. Raw. I hadn't known how else to pound out my fear and frustration after my dad died. So I'd written music. Lots of music. Most of which Dad would've hated, but the process was cathartic. And people responded to it.

"Don't be gone long. Jackaroo is front and center right now. You're at the top of your game, Hayden."

"Got that. Spin us hard, mate. I'll do my part. A live chat or whatever. Get me a piano, and I'll play something for the fans we're screwing over. Will you get me on the first flight that's available? I'll need a day at the hospice facility." To deal with the paperwork and such. To ask my questions. "Then I'll fly back. It'll have to be two days with the time difference and flights."

"There's a plan. We'll smooth this over. No worries." He bent over his phone, fingers tapping. "Oh. Condolences."

"What's going on?" Flip asked, barging through the door. His dark hair lay plastered to his head, same as mine. "You ran off. Bad news?" He wrapped his arm around his longtime girlfriend turned wife. Cynthia, a petite brunette, was rounded with a bellyful of baby. Her light hazel eyes were focused on Flip's face, full of love.

"My mum's in final stages of pancreatic cancer. I'm off to Seattle."

"Earliest flight leaves at ten tomorrow morning," Harry muttered, hunched over his phone.

"Book it then," I said.

"Gets you in during the afternoon tomorrow in Seattle. Benefit of the seventeen-hour time difference, I'd say. I'll sort your hotel and a car."

I clapped his shoulder. "Thanks, mate."

Flip's eyes were darker away from the harsh glare of the stage lights. "You'll be 'right, mate?"

I half shrugged. "I'll ring soon as I can, let you know when I'll be back."

"We'll miss you," Cynthia murmured, pulling me into her arms.

I shuffled back, swallowing hard. I offered my hand to Flip, but he also pulled me into a hug, pounding my back a few times to beat the point home. They wouldn't ask the uncomfortable questions, but at least I wasn't alone.

"Right-o," I said, clearing my throat. "See ya in a few days. My leaving will give Ets his chance to shine."

Flip chuckled low. "We'll crash and burn if we're giving Ets the reins. He's on a quick boat to self-destruction."

I rotated my head on my neck. "Don't make me feel worse about this, Flip. I'm having a bugger of a time leaving."

"It's for family. That's first." Flip slid his arm back around Cynthia's waist, emphasizing his point.

"I'll touch base with you before I leave for the airport," I said to Harry.

Our manager nodded, mumbling to himself. I tore the page from his pad and offered it back. He grabbed it and started making notes, still muttering.

"See if I need to do any promo. I'll talk to reporters you set up in Seattle to get the Yanks excited about our tour there."

I ran my fingers over the short hairs on the back of my neck, wishing for a massage. But I still needed to shower and pack. Just past 1:00 a.m. here. I snorted. My courtesy car would be by to pick me up in mere hours.

I walked out of the room, away from the fans screaming, noting the strawberry-blonde's pout. *Me, too, love. I had grand plans for our night.*

Instead, I climbed into my bus and walked straight to the loo. Stripping quickly, I stepped into the narrow shower stall, the tepid water running over my neck, down my back. The water took too long to warm up all the way, and I needed to wash away the sweat and fatigue before I was buried under it.

Three days tops to get there, say goodbye, and hop on another jet home. I'd be free of old promises and the obligation to a woman I could barely remember. And wished I didn't.

CHAPTER TWO
Briar
Five Days Earlier

"How do you do this all day?" I asked, throwing down my pen. "Freelancing lacks all the social interaction I liked about my job."

"Then go get another one. You've had offers."

The problem with talking to Lia was that she had answers. Over the course of the last month, my sister had gone from grieving the end of her relationship with rock legend Tristan Asher Smith to bouncing through her days with enough joie de vivre for the rest of us. While very un-Lia-like, she'd been due her happy.

Don't get me wrong—I was thrilled they'd worked through their problems. Each time she lit up with this internal glow when Asher walked into a room I had the stomach-clenching realization I'd settled for much less than I deserved. Ken still called me, but the calls were tapering off. Finally.

How he could think I'd want to talk to him after what he did— the man was brilliant and dense all at once. Like Ken, my career mattered to me. I frowned. Or it had. Now...I glanced over at Lia. Seeing her happy, knowing she was thrilled with spending time with Asher's son, Mason, my priorities seemed skewed. Maybe even silly.

In Ken's last message, he reminded me of our shared life. Of our compatibility. He even—finally—apologized, saying he'd been tired of fighting with me about starting a family, but he knew he'd handled the situation wrong.

Wrong didn't begin to cover it.

I wasn't ready for kids. Not with Ken and not because I didn't like them—hanging out with Mason and my niece Abbi was fun. More fun than I'd had in years. But why did me having a child mean giving up my career to stay home and maybe, one day, focus on charity work? For most men, I'm sure having a child didn't mean the wife automatically filled the role of a stay-at-home mom, but for Ken, who was raised by the freaking nanny while his mother was at yet another charity event, a woman's career was over the moment she began to gestate.

I shuddered. My mother was a huge Elvis Presley fan—she even named her third daughter, my half sister, Preslee—but to me Elvis and Ken shared a warped, scary view of a woman's place in the world. One I couldn't accept.

"Do you want me to move out?" I asked. At first, I'd stayed to help Lia through the grief of her imploding relationship with Asher, but now that they were planning their life together, I was restless and well aware of my third-wheel status.

Lia sidled around the kitchen island, gray eyes intent on my face. "I want you here. I've enjoyed spending time with you. It's the first time, really, since Dad died that we've spent more than a few hours together."

"But you have a whole life, and I'm in the way." I leaned my chin into my cupped hands, restless, searching. As I had been since... well, if I was honest, since Dad died.

"You're part of my life, Bri. An important one. But if you want to move on, you should. I don't want to hold you back from any of your goals."

I opened my mouth, ready to tell her I'd go. Out of pride more than anything else.

Asher slid behind Lia, arms around her waist, lips pressed into the side of her neck. They'd built the kind of relationship I craved. I wasn't ready to leave, because then I'd have to face that my years with Ken Brenton were over—wasted. I'd have to start over. Again.

"I'm your house sitter this weekend. My longtime dream is being realized. Who wouldn't want this all to herself?" I gestured around.

Asher chuckled, his hazel eyes dancing with mischief. "You hate to clean more than I do."

"But not as much as Mason. Think how much easier it'll be to keep a clean house without the Legos scattered across the living room like tiny IEDs."

Lia sighed, leaning back into Asher's chest. "Those things hurt. I caught one with my heel on the stairs last night. It used to be a propeller."

Asher stepped back, his sigh gusty. "I'll talk to him."

He squared his shoulders at the landing, calling Mason's name.

"He's so cute when he's disciplining," I said.

"Mmm." Lia set her glass of lemonade on the counter. "So what's this about? You're restless. And unhappy."

I walked to the row of windows at the back of the house, staring at the thick copse of trees, their bright green needles raised to the relentless summer sun.

"I am. Not just job-wise."

I turned back to my sister, thrusting my hands into my pockets. Part of me worried I'd fixated on the idea of disliking journalism once Ken The Asshole planted it in my head.

"The money's fine for what I'm doing, especially with my rent-free, hobo lifestyle."

"We haven't talked much about your break from Ken," she said, her voice careful, her eyes assessing.

"The Asshole fits him better. You know the worst of it."

"He wanted you barefoot and pregnant. He's pestering you. Is that why you're still here?"

A woodpecker drilled its beak into the thick bark of a pine nearby. "I'm relieved our relationship is over. He didn't love me—not the way Asher loves you. The deep, forever kind. In fact, there were times I had no idea why Ken wanted me. What he saw in me. Except that Rosie liked me, and he seems to like to please his aunt."

Lia wrapped her arm around me. I stood inches taller than my big sister. She gripped my waist, her fingers firm on the curve.

"He wasn't the right man."

I tipped my neck so my cheek rested on her hair. "Figured that one out already."

"Once you admit you made a mistake, you'll forgive yourself."

I straightened and narrowed my eyes at Lia. "You think that's what I'm waiting for? Forgiving myself for getting so deep into a relationship I knew wouldn't go anywhere?"

Lia met my gaze, hers steady and patient.

"Why is that so hard?" I whispered.

"Because we're hardest on ourselves."

I put my cheek back on top of her crown. "You got smart."

"I've always been this smart. You just started listening."

If I wasn't feeling so sorry for myself, I would've giggled. Lia was much better with words than I'd ever be. That's why I wrote for newspapers and she wrote best-selling novels.

"You're right. I've been hiding here. I think I should head back to Seattle soon."

Lia pulled back, surprise and concern flashing through her gray eyes faster than mist drifting on an ocean breeze. "If that's what you want."

"I think it's what I need to do."

"I *need* you to be happy."

"Thanks. I've got to face up to the life I left at some point. And I miss Rosie."

Lia smiled. "Ken's aunt is the best thing that'll ever come out of your relationship with him."

"I should call her." I rolled my shoulders, trying to ease the guilt building there. "Soon. We went to lunch when I drove back to Friday Harbor to clean out my desk, but I couldn't tell her about losing my job and the stunt Ken had pulled. When she asked if we were still seeing each other, I totally chickened out and changed the subject."

"Rosie's the best. She'll understand. Give her my love when you call her. If you want to go sooner, we can find someone here to look in on the house."

"It's for a weekend, Lia. Not a biggie. And I think I'll like the solitude. It'll help me think through some of these decisions I need to make. I can't leave my stuff in storage forever. And I'll need closure with Ken."

Lia nodded slowly, eyes never leaving mine. "You know I'm here any time you want to talk."

"Thanks for not pushing."

She raised her eyebrows. "Wouldn't do any good."

I wasn't so sure, but I couldn't tell her that.

"I'm going to help Abbi pack," I said.

Lia smiled at her daughter's name. "Explain to her she doesn't need four swimsuits to go to San Francisco, please. We're touring Stanford, not hitting the beach in San Diego. I'm not getting through to her with her excitement-fogged brain."

"Will do."

———◆———

The emptiness of the house settled over me before Asher finished pulling down the driveway the next morning. I'd never learned how to be alone. I'd always lived with someone—Lia and my dad, then my mom and her new family, various roommates, and finally Ken. That's why I'd wanted these three days. To prove to myself I could be alone.

Less than a month from my thirty-first birthday and just now learning how to be by myself. Sighing, I scooped up another pile of Legos Mason had dribbled across the living room and headed toward the overflowing bin. Not wanting to face the silence yet, I pulled out the vacuum and ran it over the whole first floor.

The kitchen clock read nine when I finished, so I changed into my running clothes. Attaching my iPod to my armband, I shoved in my earbuds. Setting out, I ran toward the trail Abbi had shown me earlier this summer.

As I hit the path that looped around the small lake, a doe slid from the tree line. I stopped. Just before she lowered her head to drink, she raised glimmering brown eyes, her entire body poised to sprint away. I wanted to touch her. To feel the velvet of her nose against my palm. I wanted to stop squelching my desires and actually *do* some of the things with my life that others did so effortlessly.

When I stepped forward, I hit a small twig and she flinched

back. In one leap, she disappeared. I stood there, breathing hard as mosquitoes swarmed my sweaty skin.

I'd always been afraid to look for a man I actually wanted. Like the doe, I was too skittish to let him close enough to find out if we'd be compatible. I could continue to do so and pine for a relationship like Lia and Asher's, or I could stop trying so hard to keep people out and face the fact I was lonely and sad because of my fear.

I turned and jogged back to Lia's house, pondering the changes I'd need to make.

CHAPTER THREE
Hayden

Going straight to hospice would have won me points, but I couldn't care less about scoring points with my mum. We didn't have a relationship, hadn't for nearly two decades. So I chose to focus on my needs, which included some much-needed rest. Sleeping was rare what with the late-night performances and hours-long partying. The thirteen hours of pillow time proved how much my body needed to reset.

I woke up at 4:00 a.m., stretched my arms over my head. Dark though it was, I wanted to get out into the city, go for a run. I loved running on the beach back in Sydney, where the warmth of the sand in summer traveled up through my feet, pumping into my muscles and making it easier to take the next step. Impossible here, so I settled for the popular running trail in the Olympic Sculpture Garden suggested by the sleepy-eyed desk clerk.

I ran down rain-drenched Elliott Ave., marveling at the lit skyline, so different from my dad's hometown of Melbourne, which boasted a low-key city center. This place reminded me more of Sydney but with some extra eye-popping style. Home to some of the world's most well-known brands, Seattle was primed for further success.

The smattering of people I passed moved out of my way as I ran, unaware and uncaring—to them, I was just another driven, success-oriented city dweller. They didn't see that as I ran faster and harder, I slid closer to the demons I'd been fighting for years.

Namely my mum.

Rather, our relationship. My last memory of her was a blurred image of her being loaded into a police car.

My dad was a quiet, introspective man. Almost a caricature of an artist from an era long past. But he'd been dead-set serious about two things: always treat women with respect and never, ever have sex with a woman I didn't plan to spend my life with. He'd learned the second lesson the hard way when he was forced to marry his pregnant college girlfriend.

She'd lost the child two weeks after the wedding, but divorce wasn't common in the sixties, making the marriage much harder to dissolve. He spent nearly twenty unhappy years with a woman he not only didn't love, but didn't respect. Thankfully for my father, his ex-wife didn't like the music-teacher salary and upgraded to a financial executive sometime in the eighties.

Several years later, Dad met my mother when he flew to Seattle for a guest lecture series. She'd been a promising concert pianist, and he one of her teachers. I'd never understood their relationship and not just because my dad was her father's age at least. Neither had my mum, it turned out.

I'd missed her for the first couple of years after my dad and I moved to Melbourne, expecting her to show up laughing as she ran toward me for a hug. Her laugh—that's what I remembered. A fairy's laugh that made me believe in the magic she spoke of so often.

But she never came; she never even called.

So I stayed in Australia, through uni. Dad held on, through one illness after another, pleased with my growing knowledge of music theory and expanded musical capabilities.

I'd hit college hard because I had something to prove after my too-quiet youth spent with a kindly, puttering piano teacher who wore cardigans over his stooped shoulders in the heat of summer.

Even Ets didn't approve of my media-loving, bad-boy-off-the-rails actions during our first small Aussie tour. After one of our concerts, I met Asher Smith, one of my heroes and an all-around fabulous bloke. He'd pointed out I'd fallen for all the vices of fame without the trappings of success. To some degree, I owed Asher a debt.

I'd read in an online paper he'd reconnected with the woman he'd loved years before. The woman we talked about during our late-night philosophical ramblings. I couldn't be happier for him.

I turned back toward the hotel, my sneakers pounding against the rain-slicked pavement. My stride was long, confident—the one thing I could control in this city of my childhood. A small flash of excitement bubbled through my melancholy as The Edgewater, my hotel—one that had hosted a long list of rocker guests—came into my field of vision. I loved the view, the illusion I could reach out and touch the crisp, navy waves so different from the ones in Wollongong, my favorite Sydney beach.

I slowed to a jog, then a walk, shocked by the crowds pushing through the narrow streets that led to Pike Place Market. I ducked into a coffee shop, asking for a latte as the crowd eddied and boiled with early-morning commuters stopping for breakfast and a paper.

As a young mother strapped her child onto her body in some sling contraption, a memory bubbled up, breaking past my normal defenses. I stared up into my mum's face, her brown hair swinging forward, covering us both. She'd liked to play outside, no matter the weather. "I breathe out here, Hayden. Don't take the connection with nature for granted. It grounds us."

I'd loved our hours-long rambles, the swish of her skirts through the grass. Her sun-warmed hair when she picked me up and carried me, exhausted, back to the house.

But my mum ditched me. Not the other way 'round. I gripped my latte and trudged back to my hotel.

CHAPTER FOUR
Briar

Going back to Seattle meant facing the reason I'd left in the first place, and the long drive left too much time for my mind to conjure the months-old memories that caused me to break off my relationship with Ken.

Jess had called me more than a month ago at work, something she never did. We'd met in the premed program. I'd ultimately switched to journalism and she chose pharmacy. Now, we were occasional-text friends, not as close these days compared with when we were on campus.

"Can you come in to pick up your script today?" she had asked.

I had glanced at my clock, then at the pile of papers sitting next to my keyboard. "I have a lot to do before I put this edition to bed for the weekend," I'd said.

"Please, Briar. I wouldn't ask if I didn't need to talk to you," Jess had said.

"Can't you just tell me over the phone?"

"No. And don't let your boyfriend pick up your script this time. Please come by. I'm here until nine."

Walking up to the counter two hours later, I'd felt my stomach cramp when Jess had immediately waved me toward the consultation window, ignoring the five people ahead of me in line. But her words had still shocked me.

"Tampered with them how?" I had asked. Much as I'd wanted to think I'd heard Jess wrong, she wouldn't lie to me. Anyway, who would joke about something as serious as altering prescriptions?

"That's why I called you," she had said, leaning out the little consulting counter. "I needed to tell you this in person. Ken wanted me to drop a placebo pack in instead. One he'd had made to fit the usual package. Wouldn't be hard—I mean, he has access to that kind of stuff through his medical practice, and you're on a generic script."

"He picked up my prescription for me last month," I had said. Blood rushed to my head, and I'd swayed.

Jess had gripped my upper arms as her mouth thinned in grim acknowledgment. "I know."

"I was covering a big story." I'd cleared my throat.

"This is the first time he approached me. I can't ask my colleagues about his actions, Briar. This is so fraudulent…" Jess had shuddered. "You need to take a pregnancy test."

"Why would he do that?" This was the part I couldn't wrap my head around.

Jess had rolled her eyes. "Like he was going to tell me."

"Can I dig into this further?"

"If you do, there will be an investigation and that's enough to put me on probation. I didn't report him for two reasons." My stomach had dropped as she said the words. "My word versus his, and I wanted to tell you—as a friend. *And* because tampering with birth control is wrong. But please don't drag me into this anymore. Please."

I had nodded my understanding. Much as I'd hated letting it go, I wasn't willing to hurt Jess. I'd held up the small white bag. "These?"

"Are good. New Rx shipment came in an hour ago. I filled your script myself. To make sure."

"Thanks, Jess. I—I don't even know what to say."

She'd pulled me in for a hug. "Good luck."

I had hugged her back, hard. Then I'd walked dazed toward the pregnancy-test shelf.

I'd picked up two tests, paid for my purchases, and had walked to a coffee shop on the corner. After ordering a light latte, my comfort drink, I had gone to the bathroom. I'd read and followed the instructions—they were the same for both brands. Then I'd waited.

I had picked up both sticks, and I'd taken a deep breath. Not pregnant.

Thank you, thank you, thank you.

I'd leaned forward, closed my eyes, and wondered how I'd managed to end up in a coffee shop bathroom thanking some greater entity that my soon-to-be ex-boyfriend hadn't tied me to him forever through a child. I'd turned on the tap and let cool water pour over my wrists, reviving me enough to come to an important conclusion.

I'd been with Ken three years too long.

Tossing the tests into the trash, I'd collected my coffee and walked back toward my car.

Lia called Ken The Asshole. I'd ignored her dislike of him because Ken was wealthy, powerful in his field.

He had been the kind of man I should want. But he'd proven to be underhanded, manipulative. I had a choice: I could go home, confront him. Or I could go to visit my family and consider what I knew, dig a little deeper into Ken's motives.

Either way, our relationship was over.

I had turned left, heading toward Simon and Ella's house, where Lia had been staying that weekend. While they hadn't been expecting me, I hadn't thought dropping by would be a problem. Lia and I might not hang out or even talk as much as some sisters did, but we had long shared a fierce bond—one forged over the tough years between the time our mother left us to start her new family, our dad's death, and the forced move to Seattle, when we were inserted into our mom's new life.

Ken's number had popped up on my screen, cutting off the song I hadn't been paying attention to. I'd pressed Ignore, dismissing him from my life.

———◆———

I blinked the memories back and focused on the rest of the drive to our once-shared condo. After more than a month of silence, I was finally ready to talk to him about his underhanded method to get me pregnant.

For a man who didn't like PDA, Ken had gone out of his way to woo me back via clichéd gifts—why would he think I needed a *third* Kindle? Or a card that said "You complete me"?—for the past few weeks. When those didn't work, he'd started with the biweekly call. *I miss you. I don't understand why you left. We were so good together. I have an event and want you there.* As his arm candy. I was smart enough to hold a conversation but not ambitious enough to screw up his desire to be *the* oncologist in Seattle.

While I wondered if I'd misjudged his feelings for me, I was sure my feelings for him were deader than roadkill.

None of me remained in the condo. Not my Kindle on the coffee table, which always annoyed him. Not the crisp, apple-green teapot and cups next to the ostentatious six-burner cooktop. My trench coat no longer sat on the hook near the door.

He, like the luxurious space, was neat; not a single one of his short, dark hairs out of place. Clean-shaven. Large hands folded over the chest of his expensive wool-blend suit coat. Blue dress shirt and tie done up tight—even at home. I used to undo that tie, muss his professional persona. I closed my eyes, willing away the memory.

"I've missed you," he said.

"I couldn't tell. Nothing I own is still here."

"Because you asked me to pack up your items. Which I did."

"Thank you."

"If this is about your being fired from that paper, you can use the time to get more involved in charities, plan our wedding." He touched my cheek. "I don't think less of you for losing your job, Briar."

I stiffened. "I was fired because I wouldn't rat out my sister. And that's not why I left you."

Ken waved his hand, dismissing the situation he deemed immaterial. My career gone with a flick of his hand.

"You left so suddenly. More than a week went by with no explanation. We could've talked about what you think happened, Briar."

My back snapped to full attention, but I borrowed Lia's method of coping and met his gaze with mine. Steady and calm, I waited for him to try to make our breakup my fault. "You mean how you tried to bribe my pharmacist to get me off the pill without my consent? That's not something we talk about *after* the fact."

"I made a mistake." His eyes were contrite. He stepped forward, tried to wrap me in his arms.

"Yes, you did." I stepped back, putting the low chrome-and-glass coffee table between us.

"You weren't listening. I've been ready to settle into family life."

I tucked my hands into my pockets. He didn't need to see how badly they were shaking.

"You weren't excited about my proposal, and I felt rejected."

"I was thinking about it," I bit out.

"Rosie told me she counseled you to reconsider, and I worried you would. I mean, my own aunt was telling you I wasn't the right man for you. That's more than a blow to the ego."

"She never said that. She asked if I'd be happy as Mrs. Dr. Ken. And I'm not sure I could have been."

He moved forward again, but I stepped to the other side of the table. "You read people, open doors," he said. "Together, we can own this city."

I rocked back on my heels, eyes fixed on the small mole on his left cheek. Ken's narrow frame was inches taller than mine but no broader. He stepped closer, his pale eyes fixed on mine. Gray, but so different from Lia's. Colder, like steel.

"Aren't you going to say anything?" he asked.

"There's really not much left to say." I spun around. Coming here wasn't a mistake, per se, but Ken was delusional if he expected me to forgive and forget.

"That's it? We were together for years, Briar. I asked you to marry me."

"The answer's no, in case you were still wondering." I opened the door.

"We were good together, both in bed and in our careers."

My neck heated with the anger I'd been trying to suppress since Jess had called me. "You tried to manipulate my body, Ken. My future."

Ken's mouth flattened. "You want financial security. I offer you more money than you can spend. And entry to the top of the medical community. You can write those health articles that are so popular."

"I also want my partner to respect me. If you could take the choice of whether or not to have a child from me, I've never been your equal. You see my work as—" I waved my hand, but the thought was no longer there.

"I respect your mind. You just aren't always reasonable. You're approaching thirty-five. There's a reason you shouldn't have children after that point. Fewer pregnancies go to term and fewer babies are healthy. You're running out of time, Briar."

"This is my time to choose to do with as I will. And I don't want a child now."

"Because you're too busy?" I tried hard not to flinch but Ken smiled. Like a shark, he circled closer. "Or, no, you expected to find true love. Like in your sister's books. That's antiquated. As long as the sex is good and the conversation mutually satisfying, who gives a shit about something as ridiculous as love?"

I turned back and gave him a thorough once-over. "Me." Admitting that out loud was unexpectedly cathartic. I'd spent years being dishonest with myself, pretending I was fine with my current circumstances. I strode down the hall. "Bye, Ken. I'll let you know if anything's missing from the boxes."

"Rosie called."

Dammit. She was the one person we shared, the woman I'd almost married him for.

"She's looking for you. Said she hasn't seen you in weeks. What kind of 'daughter of the heart' does that, Briar?"

He used Rosie's term for me mockingly. I shouldn't have come here. I'd expected…more than I got from him. Less coldness, more actual emotion. But I should have known better: I'd met his parents. My family might not be close, but Ken's was the epitome of dysfunctional. They sure as hell didn't laugh or hug or do anything that makes someone human.

"She's being moved into hospice tomorrow."

My world tilted, and I grabbed the back of the chair to stay upright. She'd said she wasn't feeling well when we went to lunch weeks ago. Told me not to worry. I hadn't, too caught up in my own drama, then Lia's. But I hadn't known the cancer was back, much less the severity of Rosie's prognosis.

"Where?"

"Come back, sit down," Ken smiled. "We can discuss her treatment. I'll do it, pro bono."

His mother's sister, and he used her as he used everyone. We both knew he'd continue to manipulate me, seeing me as a possession more than a person. One he'd tire of eventually. Rosie told me, more than a year ago, that Ken's childhood was emotionally stunted. He'd been sent off to various boarding schools, camps, anything to keep him from spending time with his parents. Now he wanted me to create a child he could do that to. I shuddered, wrapping my arms around my waist. I'd let my need for financial security, for material success, supersede everything I cared about.

"Where, Ken?"

"Let's discuss this—"

I walked toward the elevator. My breath hitched as I realized how much time I'd missed with Rosie. Hospice. She wouldn't have many good days left. My apartment search could wait. Rosie was more important.

"Where?" I snapped back over my shoulder.

"Bevins-Kline."

The elevator opened and I walked in, pulling out my phone.

"We should discuss her treatment," Ken called. "I'm her best option."

She was already on her way to hospice. She hadn't called to talk to Ken herself, something she would have done if she'd wanted to. My knuckles tightened as the metal handrail dug into the skin on my palm.

"Neither Rosie nor I want you there," I whispered as the door slid closed.

CHAPTER FIVE
Hayden

The building was more depressing from the outside than I'd anticipated. The red brick, though well maintained, appeared tired. The blue shimmer of the water behind the building reminded me of the Great Beyond in those cheesy, low-budget movies I'd watched on Sunday mornings, waiting for my dad to putter through his morning routine.

The soil itself must have sucked in some of the emotions of the thousands of people sent here to die, because even the trees and flowers were brown and droopy in an otherwise verdant city.

Crikey. I was supposed to walk in there. On purpose. A place that was nothing less than the yawning maw of hellish, unfinished dreams. A fitting final place for the mother who'd chosen to disengage any inkling of maternal responsibility.

Forget that I'd flown more than fifteen hours to get here. I pulled my key fob back out of my pocket and began to turn back. Harry was right. I should never have left my band. I definitely shouldn't have come here expecting answers. Her years of silence spoke volumes.

As I hesitated, a woman strode toward the doors. Her shoulder-length hair was the exact color of a mink I'd seen in a traveling zoo as a child. That mink's fur was soft, rich, warm. Like my mum's hair when she carried me home after our rambles. For years, I'd thought my mum's hair was more beautiful than anything I'd seen before.

And when I'd seen that mink's fur at the zoo, the color reiterated how much I'd missed her. I'd spent an hour petting the soft,

29

warm pelt, much to my dad's bewildered acceptance. A good man, my father.

The brown-haired woman hitched her large bag onto her shoulder and wrapped a hand around her elbow, head bent down. She passed me without so much as a glance, feet tapping a no-nonsense rhythm that pulled her inexorably closer to the institution of death.

I didn't want her in there. I didn't want my mink contaminated with illness, death, and despair. Two steps ahead, she crossed the threshold into the hospice before I worked up the nerve to open my mouth. I shivered as I strode through the glass partition, following just inches behind her.

Holy hell. The building was worse inside. The smell of death lingered, astringent and too close.

"Hi, there, Briar. Did you bring someone with you today? Welcome to Bevins-Kline Hospice Care Facility."

As I stepped forward, the girl behind the desk stared at me, mouth agape. I groaned.

"You're—"

"Hayden Crewe," I sighed, sidling closer to the desk. "I'm here to see my mum."

"Oh. My. God." The girl breathed, her face pasty. "I. Love. You." Her cheeks flushed an unnatural shade even darker than crimson. While I was glad for the return of color, her comment made me uncomfortable.

"Er, well, thanks. What room is Miriam Hastings in?"

The woman with the beautiful hair—Briar?—stood next to me at the desk. "Stop, Ginny. You're embarrassing him."

Her voice reminded me of blues singers who'd moved beyond

controlled lust and dipped lower into emotional pain. It ripped through my gut in the best possible way. I wanted to hear that voice calling my name as she writhed against me. I blinked back the image. I was in a bloody hospice center. So not the place for sexual fantasies.

Her eyes were blue. The same shade as the native bluebell Dad used to plant in the back garden.

"He's in Jackaroo. He plays the piano and keyboard," Ginny said, her voice rising with excitement.

Briar waited for me to say something. I hadn't caught enough of what Ginny had said, but I'd heard something about a piano. "Piano's my favorite, but I also play the mandolin. Some guitar." Could I sound any more pompous?

"Miriam's in the room next to my friend. We good to go, Ginny?" Briar took two visitor stickers, handing one to me.

I cringed at the bright sheen in Ginny's eyes. Briar leaned forward, placing her hands on the desk.

"Don't, Ginny," Briar said, her voice lowered to just more than a whisper. "Don't make this harder for him. Think about what's happening in this building now, without the extra attention. You told me you needed this job for the summer. If you make that call, tell anyone, I'll be sure to have you fired."

The girl leaned back, annoyed, but she dipped her head once in acquiescence. "Go on through. But would you sign this for me first, Hayden?"

She batted her lashes at me and held up a sheaf of paper. I snagged her pen and scrawled my name on a confidential billing statement. Shaking my head, I followed Briar through another set of doors. "Thanks for that. I think."

Briar's long, trim legs ate up the industrial-carpeted hallway. "You have as much right to grieve as the next person. I'm glad Miriam's got you. I've spent most of the last couple days here, and I was worried she'd die alone."

I cringed, biting back a curse. "We aren't close," I said. My voice was defensive, the gate holding back all my anger buckling under the surging emotions as we got nearer our destinations.

She stopped walking and turned toward me fully. Crikey, she was gorgeous. Thick, dark lashes framed those blue eyes. Pert nose set in the middle of her face, her rounded chin curved into an elegant jawline. Her pink lips were slightly too wide. Today, those soft lips weren't painted, but the natural plumpness of the lower one wasn't something I could ignore. I wanted to bite it until she moaned, then soothe the sting with my tongue.

"Look…"

I was, thank you very much. I'd already stared at the rounded globes of her bum as we walked in. Her waist was cinched by a wide belt, and her blue top, too demure to show off her scant cleavage, was soft, feminine. Her chest tapered into the long, elegant line of her neck. Nice. She ran her hand through her hair and glanced up and down the hall. Her eyes darkened.

"Miriam's close to the end. Whatever you need to say, remember she won't be here in less than a week."

With that, she turned and entered a room behind her. She greeted a woman named Rosie, her voice hushed but upbeat. I slid my hands into my pockets, rocking back on my heels as I sought my mum's name. Next door, she'd said. There, written on a dry-erase board: Miriam.

In all the years I'd played through the moment we met again, I'd been the injured one and she'd begged for my forgiveness—forgiveness I wasn't sure I could give. What kind of woman walked away from her only child? But she was the one hurting now. Briar's words echoed through my head as I braced myself to enter the room.

The door was open. Good. My steps were hesitant as I approached the hospital bed. She turned her head on a pillow, making me feel like an arse for not stepping into her line of vision. Her skin was pale, nearly translucent. Tubes and wires were connected to most of her body, making her look more like a bad sci-fi movie experiment than a person.

Her brown eyes, they were alive, bright. I inhaled sharply, mirroring her breath. Fuck me, they were the exact same color and shape as mine. Much as I might want to, I couldn't deny our relationship.

"Hayden?"

Her voice was tentative. Her eyes filled with tears.

"G'day."

"Are you real, or one of my dreams?"

"I'm real."

She tapped her finger against her lip, her eyes narrowing slightly. "I'd like to hope so. I've thought of you so many times over the years."

We stared at each other for another long moment. Her long, thick brown hair was now a cap of translucent gray. That I mourned; my best memories were lying my head on her hair.

What to say? "Thank you for birthing me" sounded ridiculous. Anything else was much less polite. Especially bringing up the *incident*.

"Will you sit with me?" she asked.

I inched closer to the armchair next to the bed. The padding was thin, lumpy. As uncomfortable as a chair could be. A metaphor for my life. Shit-tastic, as my mates would say.

"You look like George," she said. "I have pictures he sent and others from the newspaper, of course, but you're so much handsomer in person."

"Thanks, I guess." I glanced up at the clock. A quarter hour gone. How was I going to sit through many more minutes if all we did was exchange platitudes and chitchat?

She smiled a little. "Tell me about you. I want to know everything."

I cleared my throat, my gaze probably wide and wild as she talked to me. "Er, well, my band's on tour. We canceled one show in Melbourne, but I'll catch up with them in in a few days when we head to Japan. We're coming to the States in September. After Europe."

Another long pause. I squirmed in my chair.

"Do you like performing? Music?"

I shrugged, unsure how to answer that, really. "Reckon I do."

"What's your favorite song?"

"Not sure," I hedged. "When you write so many, there's lots of choices." Patently false, but I wasn't ready to tell my mum that. I glanced up at the clock. Barely another five minutes scraped off the hour. At some point, I could walk back out, the obligatory meeting over.

She memorized my every feature while I catalogued the lights on each of her machines.

"I've never met anyone as passionate about music as your father," she sighed. The breathing tube hissed, pushing new air into her failing lungs. "His timing was so confident. I loved that about him even as I envied his ability."

"He's dead," I said.

Her eyes slid closed. Out of tiredness or to block my words? "We talk, you know. Now. He looks younger than I do." She smirked. "He's told me so much about you. He's proud of the man you've become. So am I."

We sat there again, me unable to look at her, she unwilling to look away.

"I miss the piano," she whispered. "I miss music."

I glanced at the clock again. I could leave this horrible place soon, after I asked my questions and met with the director.

"Why'd you do it?" I asked. I wasn't quite sure what I was asking. Let me leave? Never call? Hurt me in the first place?

She slid into sleep as I sat in the chair. I bent my head toward the edge of the bed. Her breathing remained even thanks to the steady hiss of the oxygen machine. I willed her to wake, to tell me something—anything—she remembered about my childhood. Jet lag and sadness pulled at the edges of my consciousness.

"You okay?"

I startled at the voice. The woman I'd walked in with earlier stood before me. Briar, the blue-eyed girl with the mink hair that I wanted to pet.

"Sure. Great."

Her lips pulled down in concern. I stood quickly.

"She's asleep," I said, motioning toward my mother. She appeared so small in the bed. Wasted. I scrubbed my hand over my face, trying to get my bearings. "I need to talk to the director."

"He's not in right now."

"How do you know? I have to set up arrangements."

Briar's hand was soft on my bare forearm. We both froze, staring at her pale hand on my tanned skin. The potency of her touch was overwhelming. Awareness flickered between us, building.

Holy hell. I wanted this woman.

"Most of the staff is at lunch. They'll be back in about an hour," she said. "I'm Briar Moore, by the way."

"Okay." I drew out the word, not sure what to do with my desire or her interest. This was a weird place to meet someone, in a building shrouded in illness and death. Getting away from the pretty, dark-haired woman was less important than leaving my mum, but just as necessary. I was on a short time frame to handle my mum's arrangements.

"Come on. I'll buy you lunch," she said.

Did Briar expect more from me? I couldn't quite gauge her.

"I didn't really think about fans and media when I made my travel plans. How crazy going out anywhere would be. I'll talk to the director and her—my mum's—doctor and leave. Go back to my band." I glanced around, looking for inspiration.

She dropped her hand away and chuckled. "You forgot you were famous? You sound like Asher. All wide-eyed when the fans mob him. Like he hasn't dealt with fame for nearly twenty years."

I paused, trying to retilt my world back on its axis. "Asher Smith?"

Briar exited the room. "My sister's boyfriend," she murmured over her shoulder. "He's mentioned you, especially with your band's new album. I've heard so much about you, in some ways I assumed I knew you."

I shoved my hands in my pockets, trying to hide my surprise. "Asher's great."

"He's perfect for Lia, that's for sure."

"Is he in town?" Maybe I could salvage tonight with something more interesting than the self-flaying I was planning on doing.

"No. He's staying with Lia right now. In Idaho."

"Ah. Right. We heard about his new relationship with your sister. The divorce. Ugly business."

"You have no idea."

"Bet I do. That's why I need to get out of here fast. Before the journos figure out where I am and how to turn my mum's dying into a circus." I liked the easy banter we fell into. Not that I planned to share my life history or anything. But if Asher liked Briar, she must be okay. Some of the tension in my shoulders and back eased.

She peeked at me from the corner of her eye. "Marination Station."

"I have no idea what you're talking about."

"Food. Let's go eat at Marination Station. But you need a cap. Sunglasses."

"See this? It's raining. Like it does pretty much all the time in this godforsaken place. Why the hell would I put on sunglasses?"

Briar rolled her eyes. "This is barely a drizzle. You people from sunny places are so water allergic. And the glasses and cap are to make sure you can eat without being recognized. It works. Most of the time."

"Maybe I'm overreacting and people won't recognize me?" I opened the door leading outside for her, and inhaled her shampoo as she walked past me. Sweet, but with undertones of spice. Just as I hoped she'd be.

Behind us, Ginny called, "Bye, Hayden."

Briar raised an eyebrow, showing off the amusement in those big blues. I blew out a breath.

"I have sunnies in the car. Would you prefer to ride with me or in your own car?"

"If you want, we can take mine. I plan to come back and sit with Rosie again this afternoon. You can get your car then."

"She's a relative? Rosie?"

She shook her head, causing her pretty mink-brown hair to slide across her shoulders. Teasing me. I wanted to touch both her pale skin and the silkiness of her hair.

"A friend. I met her through an ex."

"Kind of you, to find her again."

"You'd think that," she said as we stopped at my dull, gray compact. I'd hoped the car would bring me some anonymity. "My ex told me about her earlier this week. He offered to trade oncology treatment for sex. Maybe a child and marriage." Her words trailed off as she seemed to realize the weight of what she'd said. "Wow. His actions sound even worse out loud than rolling around in my head."

I pulled my head out of the little car, one of my hands resting on the car's cool metal roof, the other, now holding the sunglasses, on the door. Briar was tall, her skin fresh and smooth in that healthy, outdoorsy way. Beautiful. Real. I couldn't say that about any of the women in my life except Cynthia, and she belonged to Flip.

"Your ex is a wanker."

"I don't know what that means, exactly, but yeah, I think he is."

She pointed to a red Audi two rows over. "That's me."

"Cute."

"A gift."

"From the wanker?"

"Yes. Before I knew just how devious he was."

I shook my head, unhappy that she drove a car gifted her by the doctor-ex. How stupid was that? Jealous over a woman I'd just met.

I glanced back at the building where my mum lay, dying. She was so frail. Nothing like the photo I'd kept of her—her young face beaming at the camera as her hands cradled her large belly. Before I was born and destroyed her life.

So far, my first trip back to America wasn't going as I'd expected.

CHAPTER SIX
Briar

He insisted on opening my door, something Ken always did, too. But unlike Ken's need to keep up appearances, Hayden's gesture seemed genuine. Maybe. How would I know?

This whole being more open thing might have been a bad idea. I mean, I'd already blurted out details about my life that made me cringe. For Hayden to know them was hide-under-the-covers embarrassing. If he hadn't been so unsure and unhappy when he walked into the hospice center, I would've ignored my desire to help.

Once I settled in my seat, he strolled around to the passenger's side and climbed in. He reached down, fumbling for the release under his seat. Finding it, he pushed the seat back to give his long, jeans-clad legs more room.

"So this restaurant. What do they serve?"

"It's a food truck. To give you the full-on Seattle experience."

"Food truck?"

"Come on—you have to have them in Sydney. Marination Station serves fusion. That's a Northwest thing. Hawaiian Korean. I like the miso chicken."

"Miso and chicken I'm familiar with. Hawaii and Korea not so much."

I drove in silence. The truck wasn't far, and we would arrive at the mobile restaurant after the normal lunch rush. I circled past where the truck was stationed and found a parking space a couple of blocks away.

"This okay?"

"Yeah, sure."

Hayden put on his dark sunglasses and the Seattle ball cap I tossed him before jumping out of the car. It was a good look for him. The cap covered all his sun-kissed hair, and the glasses left only his straight nose and firm, square jawline covered in a couple days' worth of stubble visible. Why did musicians dislike razors?

I'd always liked my men clean-shaven. Put together. A man in a well-fitted suit and wingtips revved my engine better than any half-naked guy. Especially if that suit included a power tie and cuff links. I loved cuff links.

Just thinking about Hayden in a suit made my mouth water. Right now, he was scruffy in that I-slept-in-my-clothes look some men had; his faded Rolling Stones T-shirt was rumpled and his jeans must have been ten years old. He even had a stainless-steel chain against his left hip to complete the look. He wore scuffed brown leather boots that were probably as ridiculously expensive as they were sexy.

Must have been my visit with Ken, who was all buttoned-up and arrogant, this week. Because right now, I preferred Hayden with his bad-boy, casual vibe—a first for me. I finished putting another quarter in the meter, and we turned in tandem, meandering down the sidewalk.

"I'd forgotten how big Seattle is." Hayden said, glancing around. "It's a bit like Sydney, but not."

"Is that good?"

He was quiet for a moment. "Yes. I can see why Aussies like the Pacific Northwest. Colder and grayer, but similar."

I quirked my lips up. "Better music scene."

He hip-checked me. "Careful, love. Those're fighting words. We have our fair share of talent."

"I've heard of Kylie Minogue. She remade an American song."

"I'm appalled. We export greatness. Lenka, Gotye, Hugh Jackman, Nicole Kidman. And I bet you have a thing for the Hemsworth brothers."

"Most of the people you listed aren't singers."

He waggled his eyebrows at me and I sucked in a breath. My lips tingled and my nipples perked up. Lia talked about lust at first sight in her books, but I'd never experienced anything this raw, visceral. I stepped back, afraid of what Hayden Crewe was doing to my body. I needed to get a grip on these thoughts.

I'd already compared him to Ken and found Hayden better, proving I had a serious case of rebound syndrome. Any man seemed a step up from my ex—because just about any man was. I sighed, wishing I'd left Ken sooner.

I'd thought about it, but I loved Rosie too much to risk not seeing her anymore.

"Admit it, you love Aussies. Want to know everything about us."

"Nope. I don't need to even guess."

"Sure you do. C'mon. You know you want to."

I stared at him, meeting what I expected were his eyes through his dark lenses. "Guess about you? Besides the instruments you play and that your band's called Jackaroo. Fine."

"Yep. What else do you know?" he waggled his brows again, and I'd bet his eyes were shining with humor.

I didn't have to think long. "You're staying at The Edgewater, in one of the Beatles' suites."

His lips curled up in a smile. "The Beatles came to Oz, too. I wasn't born yet so I didn't get to see the concert live."

I tapped my lips. "You've already Googled the band list at The

Showbox and The Crocodile. You're hoping to hear a new up-and-coming group of the same caliber as Nirvana or Death Cab for Cutie."

"If I'm on hiatus, the least I can do is support and listen to the local talent. No surprises in your guessing, love."

I shrugged. "Asher likes to pop in at the singer-songwriter shows when he's in town. That's how he and Lia met. Well, met again."

"She's a music aficionado like you?"

I snorted out a little chuckle and began to walk toward the food truck. "Lia actually understands the music and stuff. I just listen and sing along. I'm having the kimchi fried rice bowl."

"A particular favorite?" At my nod, he leaned against the counter. "The lady and I'll have the kimchi rice." He raised a thick golden brow at me before he said, "Hers with chicken, mine with kalbi beef. Thanks." Another pang built. Ken never ordered for me. I was a strong, independent woman. But Hayden remembered my comment about the miso chicken, made sure to order it with my meal.

I resisted the urge to rub my hand against the painful squeeze in my chest. I liked this man. Liked that he wasn't afraid to take care of me. He glanced back at me, and I stood straighter.

"Water," I said, my voice sort of strangled from my throat.

"And two waters."

Hayden paid and we stepped back, letting the other lunch stragglers order.

"I told you *I'd* get lunch."

"You drove. No worries."

"You're good with the American money."

He checked, a scowl building. "My mum's American," he reminded me.

A sore spot—his relationship with his mother. I searched for something else to bring back the lightness we'd shared before, but he beat me to it.

"So music's not really your thing?" he asked.

"I love it. Just never got much of an education in it."

"Aren't all American kids forced to play some instrument? A form of torture for teachers and parents."

I shook my head. "I wasn't. We moved to Seattle when I was ten. My school before, near the army base, didn't have a real music program. Most of the kids here were already all set in choir or band, and I struggled enough to fit in. I refused to even try. Stupid, I know, but in my defense, my dad had just died." I shook my head. "God. I said all that aloud, didn't I? I'm officially embarrassed."

"No need for embarrassment. I've been told sharing is cleansing." He paused, clearly pondering something. "My dad died a few years back. I miss him."

Something else we shared. I picked at my water label, head down. My feelings toward Hayden built into more than a case of lust.

"I miss mine, too. So." I said, flailing and failing to pick a safe topic.

Hayden linked his fingers, his elbows on his knees. "Before you ask—and because I know you're interested—my mum has pancreatic cancer. I didn't find out until a couple of days ago. Her nurse called my record label. Took time for her information to get routed to me."

Something in his voice caused me to pause, consider what I could see of his face behind the glasses and the deep shadow cast by the cap. The woman in the truck called out our order. Hayden hopped up from the rough bench we'd commandeered. Holding the bags, he followed me as I turned toward the park a block or so to the east. We found a spot near the fountain with a view of the Space Needle.

Opening my bag, I started eating. Skipping breakfast was a bad idea. One of these days I'd actually remember to eat it.

Hayden followed suit, making humming noises in the back of his throat as he sampled the various items in his bowl. We ate in silence for a few minutes, comfortable in the quiet between us. I finished and set my empty container back in the sack and relaxed into the bench, tilting my face up toward the watery sun.

Hayden packed up his trash. His arm rested on the back of the bench, inches from my hair. Tension pulled at his mouth, firming his jaw and neck. His glasses faced the Space Needle. He was thinking, hard. He took off his sunglasses, tucking them into the pocket of his T-shirt.

"I didn't want to come here. I plan to head back to the band tonight. After I talk to her doctor, square away the finances with the director."

"You said you and your mother have a rocky relationship?"

"That's a polite way of stating it."

His eyes narrowed as if he considered something but discarded the idea, and I mourned the loss of his openness. It was obvious Hayden wasn't emotionally cold like Ken—he felt deeply, but he kept that part of himself behind a wall. I'd bet his emotional repression started with his mother.

"My mum left when I was little. My dad took me back to Melbourne, where he'd grown up. She never called or wrote."

I sucked in a breath. We were more alike than I'd realized. I didn't think about it, just leaned into his side and gripped his hand, trying to offer what little support I could.

An immediate and desperate craving to get even closer speared through me. Either he didn't feel the attraction or he was lost in his thoughts, because he squeezed my fingers with gentle pressure.

He met my gaze, confusion and sadness mingling in his eyes. "I'm leaving as soon as she dies, maybe before. This is duty."

"I get that," my voice regretful. Like mine, his mother had been selfish, thinking of her own happiness. Never mind her child's suffering.

He shrugged, as if trying to brush off the pain that never quite left. "I keep thinking about how she chose to leave me. I can't imagine making the same choice."

He turned back to look at the fountain. So him being here *wasn't* just duty. He'd been thrust into an untenable situation and was floundering, both with his feelings for his mother and how to proceed as an orphan.

"My mom left my dad when I was six. My dad was active-duty military and she hated the moving."

"Sounds tough."

"Got worse when she started a new family here in Seattle."

"And that was that? For you and your sister?" Hayden's voice sharpened.

My turn to turn away from his all-too-knowing stare. "Until my dad died and she was forced to take us in. Yeah."

I peeked up at Hayden from under my lashes. The sadness was still there, shadowing his lovely brown eyes.

I'd been numb for so long, it's what I knew, how I kept my sanity. But this man somehow wormed through my long-standing ice wall and was already in my head. No way I was going to forget his sad eyes. Ever.

"I just wanted you to know I get it," I said, my voice cracking. "And I'm really, really sorry."

CHAPTER SEVEN
Hayden

I'd tried to warn her I was leaving. Soon. I had to be honest, no matter the awareness sparking between us.

All I could do, I guess. Didn't feel like enough. Not when we shared the same lost look. I recognized it from my own broody eyes whenever I looked in the mirror to shave. The same hitch in her smile I'd developed since I found out my mother had stage-four cancer.

I didn't want to lose my mum. She hadn't been there for me since I was ten, but with her death, I'd have no one left. No one to ask about family history or an amusing anecdote from holidays long past. No one to remember my first step, my first word, my first piano recital.

The idea of walking through the rest of my life solo was depressing. Fear crept up behind the sadness. Thanks to years of distancing myself, I didn't really know how to not be isolated, even in a group of people.

Briar's head settled more firmly against my upper arm. Not an embrace because neither of us was ready for that. Not even with the heat between us building faster than a bonfire. I liked her, though I didn't want to enjoy her company as much as I did. She could easily become my crutch while I was here. Leaning on her was unfair to us both. I was leaving. My life, my career was based on traveling the world. And even if that weren't the case, I lived in Sydney—almost eight thousand miles away.

Yet I sat, enjoying the feel of her next to me, especially the silky texture of her hair on my skin. Her body heat mingled with mine on the damp bench, warming me more than I expected.

She, like me, had been hurt deeply. There was a reservation in her demeanor that I understood. Protective armor, my dad had called it.

"You know what I think?" Briar asked. Her voice wrapped around me, all soft and warm, like one of my mum's merino wool blankets. The one I'd taken to college just because I'd needed some connection to her even if she didn't want me. When I started touring, I'd put the blanket in storage, refusing to carry it around with me like a two-year-old, but I missed its softness, the faint scent of the childhood home I no longer owned. My dad sold the place after we moved back to Melbourne into a modest cottage with a large back garden, not too far from the beach.

"What's that?" I asked.

"You need a friend."

I snorted. "I'm surrounded by people all the time."

"Key word: *people*. I'll restate my conclusion. You need someone you trust," she said, her voice dipping lower than usual.

Like an arrow of lust to my gut, all kinds of fantasies erupted, triggered by her voice. I'd like to show her where to put my…trust. I smirked at the image but then had to shift, easing the tightening in my jeans.

According to a few of the major magazines, I was introspective, introverted, a bit too stiff and formal. Came from spending too much time with my dad's set, many of who were at least two generations older than me. While the media's description bothered me, I hadn't cared enough to change my image. Until now. But I didn't know how to be the man she expected me to be—I didn't know the first thing about trust, or even real friendship for that matter.

I understood my piano. Its hammers and keys and strings. That made sense. I liked to sit, pick out something classical with intricate finger work that my hands remembered well enough for my mind to wander. With this tour, bigger than anything we'd managed before, I hadn't made time for those long, rambling sessions. I'd been busy perfecting our songs, doing press junkets and making appearances.

I missed the intimacy I shared with my piano. The gleaming ebony grand I'd inherited from my father was my confidant, my one true love. And she sat thousands of miles away, probably dusty and quiet as she waited for me to come back to her. But I wouldn't. Not for months yet. Not with a massive world tour to complete. The weight of the responsibility pressed onto my shoulders.

"And you're offering that to me in exchange for what? An exposé to show poor Hayden Crewe whose mum's done the Harry."

She sat up fast, her mouth screwed up in disgust. "What did you just say? I got the tone a lot better than the words."

"She walked out. You going to sell my story to the bloodsucking journos who are every-fucking-where I go? Who gives a shit how that makes me feel, right?"

Briar met my gaze, hers steady and blue. "I haven't mentioned what I do—did—for a living."

My stomach, so recently warm and comfortable from my meal, clenched, sliding deeper into a place it should never go.

"I was the editor in chief for a local paper."

I jumped from the seat, my heart racing. I turned away, ready to run. This woman knew details of my life I'd never shared with anyone, ever. My mum's problems would soon be splashed all over the national media. And I was the bloody idiot that let it happen—all because of a pair of pretty blue eyes and a soulful voice.

"Sit down, Hayden. Everything's going to be fine."

"No. You'll…you'll write about me. Make heaps of cash, all while laughing at my stupidity for trusting you."

She stood, tugged on my wrist, but still I resisted. "Please," she said, her voice soft. "People are going to notice this, you. Sit down. I won't hurt you. I won't write about you. I promise."

I refused with a quick shake of my head.

She sighed, her wide lips pressed tight in a firm, unhappy line. "I was fired from my job, Hayden. Fired. Because I wouldn't rat out my sister while she was struggling with the fallout from Asher's divorce. I've lived through the ugly side of journalism. I'm not about to send anyone down that path."

I collapsed back on the bench and leaned forward, running my fingers through my hair and knocking the cap off. "Tell me to rack off."

"Half of what you say is not in English."

The laugh crept up my chest, unbidden but cathartic. "It's Aussie."

She shook her head, causing her hair to spill over her collar. "You're half-American. Tap your memory for appropriate idioms."

"Maybe I don't like my Yank roots."

"Tough shit, as my dad would say. Doesn't matter if you like where you came from or if it's easy to talk about. Anyway, you're private. That's different from not liking your roots. I am a little offended you think all journalists are paparazzi. Some of us really do enjoy telling the truth."

"I don't want you to spit—er, be angry with me. I'm sorry your boss fired you for sticking up for family. I'm also very sorry I freaked out. Shit." I moaned. "This isn't my day."

"True enough. I'm considering a career change." She sighed, a heavy sound laced with defeat. "Have been for a while if I'm honest. I did some freelance work, but I haven't queried anyone in over a week, and I'm shocked by how little I miss the daily routine and the stories."

"You realized journalism is a vampiric tendency that leeches everything good and wholesome from your body?"

"That would be a no. Ironic to admit this now, but I've always wanted to help people. Ever since we came to live with my mom, I've had this need to make situations easier, better. Probably because I couldn't do that for myself." She laughed, a rueful sound. "Then Lia's husband was diagnosed with Huntington's. It's degenerative, deadly. She and her daughter struggled, and I couldn't make *that* situation better. So, for a while, I quit trying. Stuck to journalism." She murmured, tucking her hair behind her ear. "But I never loved the crazy hours. It's part of why Ken and I broke up."

I sat back, loving that her cheeks were pink from being outdoors and maybe even embarrassment. "Part?"

She smoothed her top, her fingers plucking at a small thread. "I liked my work. Most of the time, anyway. I really liked being the boss. I'd been promoted at twenty-seven to the top spot, the youngest woman in the country." Pride straightened her shoulders. "For a while, I wasn't sure I wanted to be married to more than my job. It was exciting, interesting. But Ken's always right," she said, rolling her eyes. "He's a doctor, which fits his personality to a T."

"Not following you there," I said.

Briar waved her hand. "He has a God complex. He's wanted me to get pregnant for months, sure that the hormones would kick in and I'd get all loving and maternal and give up my job and life outside our home. I'm not sure that'll ever be me."

"Because of your mum?" I asked.

Briar shook her head. "Because I haven't felt the desire to have children." She wouldn't meet my eyes. "I'm pretty sure I lack whatever that gene is."

"So he forced the issue?"

"He tried to bribe my pharmacist into giving me a placebo instead of my birth control."

"Holy shit," I breathed out, barely able to process her words. "That's low."

She glanced up at me from under her lashes and bangs. My blood pumped harder. I liked that look. She needed to look at me like that again. Preferably when we were near a bed, alone.

"It's worse than that. He'd proposed a couple days before. I was considering his question. Until I realized how ruthless he was to reach his goal." She shook her head. "He didn't ask me about something as important as a having child."

Anger slammed into my gut, low and vicious. "I stick to my original observation. He's a wanker."

The bloom of embarrassment faded from her cheeks as she pressed her fingers to her lips. "I can't believe I told you that." She dropped her hand away. "Well, I can. We met at a really emotional time. Hospice is intense. I understand the hurt and confusion. Mine was a different path but we ended up in the same place."

"Because of the arse you dated?"

She chuckled as she pulled sunglasses from her bag and went to settle them onto her nose. A few hairs caught in the edge piece and she paused to work them free. "I didn't just date him, I lived with him," she said, her voice soft, a hint of disbelief at her own admission. She cleared her throat. "No. I mentioned my dad died when

I was ten. That my mom was long gone—with three new children she actually wanted."

She kept her gaze on the fountain, her breathing slow, like she was trying to be nonchalant. She failed.

"My mom didn't come get us for nearly a month after my dad's funeral. Lia—that's my older sister I mentioned before—had to play parent to me the whole time. I wasn't very helpful. And then, I went numb." Her gaze dropped to her lap, her sunnies sliding down her nose. "Some days I still think I am. It's easier than caring."

"I get that. That's the shit of it—sometimes you can't not care." I blew out a careful breath. "Like when people are dying."

"Like then." Briar agreed. "Which is why I wanted to bring you out to lunch. Being there with a person who's working so hard to die, that's a gift. Not only for them but for you, too."

We remained quiet, needing time to soothe the rawness of our confessions. I needed Briar right now. Unfortunately, I wanted more than just her sympathy. I wanted her body and the hours of mindless pleasure we'd glean from each other. In some ways, that would make the trip here more worthwhile than telling my mother, a stranger, goodbye.

"So now you have dirt on me, too," she said. "Secrets that would hurt me if they became general knowledge."

"I would have been your friend without the hoops, Briar." Surprise rippled through me at just how much I meant those words.

"But now when I promise I won't say anything to those 'bloodsuckers' about your relationship with your mom, you know I'm serious. I gave you the leverage to hurt me back."

Did she really think so little of me? I suppose I brought that on myself. My comments before weren't nice. "I have a certain core decency, and I refuse to be considered that much of an arse." I winced at how formal and clipped my words were. Like a runaway train, I'd lost control of my mouth. Fucking fabulous.

"You aren't an ass at all." She patted my shoulder as she rose from the bench. She arched her back, stretching her arms above her head. The sun caught the strip of exposed skin at her lower back, bathing it in a pinkish glaze. I shifted in my seat, shocked by how much that thin strip of exposed skin turned me on.

"Let's get you back to your car."

She didn't say to visit my mum. Just as well. I wasn't sure I could go back in today.

CHAPTER EIGHT
Briar

We drove in silence back to the hospice center, me hyperaware of Hayden. I tried to ignore my growing attraction. I wanted to be angry with him—he'd been a dick to me. I frowned. Problem was, his response came from confusion and hurt.

I wasn't a doormat and had no intention of starting to be one now. Except…his soul-deep sadness called to me. I recognized the emotion, lived it in my own life.

Didn't hurt that his tall gorgeousness was enhanced by his sun-streaked caramel locks and those brown eyes. When the faint afternoon sun cleared a cloud, the light highlighted the golden stubble glinting from his cheeks and chin. He appeared so self-assured, strong, until I met his eyes. Then, he reminded me of my niece, Abbi, right after her father was diagnosed with Huntington's. Hayden struggled to understand the unfairness of life, and he wanted to break out of the anxiety that was his new constant.

I still couldn't believe I'd told him about Ken. I wasn't the emotional-sharing type, but sitting in the warm pool of Seattle summer sun loosened my tongue. And eased some of the hurt I'd bottled up inside.

"Thank you for lunch," I said as I parked the car and turned off the engine.

"Now I can claim to have eaten from the best food truck in America."

"Saw one of the signs, huh? Consider yourself properly indoctrinated to the food truck craze. It's big here in the Northwest."

"You were right; we have 'em in Sydney. Different, obviously, than here." He turned his head to face the window. "Depressing place, this building."

"Death isn't happy," I sighed. "Not for those left behind, anyway. But sometimes it's a relief for the person leaving."

I kept my eyes on the entrance. He ran his fingers through his hair again, making the caramel waves stick out in thick cowlicks. He exited the car, walked around and opened my door.

He looked at the building with abhorrence. "I'll go in and see my mum."

I gripped his forearm, trying to ignore how good his skin felt under my palm. "You don't have to."

"Yeah, I kinda do. That's why I'm here. To hear her deathbed confessions and forgive her transgressions or some other utter tripe."

As he opened the second set of doors, his hand rode the small of my back. I fought down the urge to shiver. Much as I tried to deny it, I'd always been a sucker for the emo loner. Way more than the buttoned-up suits. Those guys—men like Ken—were supposed to be safe. Unwilling to push too far into feelings and my untapped desires. But even power suits and cuff links didn't stop my secret yearning for a man who *needed* love the way I did.

In high school, I'd mooned for hours in my bedroom over the brooding artist and tatted photographer. I'd even dated a documentarian during my sophomore year at U-Dub. He'd been too stuffy for me, using words like *lexicon* and *patristic*. No one talked that way at nineteen. Even then, he wasn't exactly what I craved, which was why I'd spent my entire sophomore year with him—either bored out of my mind or annoyed he didn't seem into our relationship.

Hayden maneuvered down the hall toward Rosie's room. "So I'll see you later?" he asked outside her door.

"You're staying?" I asked, surprised.

He puckered his mouth like he'd just smelled the worst scent. "Didn't you say that was the best gift I could give both her and myself?"

I rocked back on my heels, surprised those were the words he'd latched on to. "I'm sure your schedule's tight," I hedged.

"So it is. Give me your number and I'll give you mine. That way you can text me when you're on your way out. You can take me to some other place I should eat tonight on my whirlwind tour of Seattle."

After exchanging numbers, he gave me a small smile. "See you later, Briar. Thanks for giving me something to look forward to."

Bemused, I shoved my phone back into my purse. "Yeah. See you."

Sitting in Rosie's room, in a whisper I told her about my new, strange relationship.

"Divine accent on that one," Rosie said, her voice raspy from the oxygen forced into her nasal passages.

I smiled a little as I settled into the only chair in the room. I dropped my purse at my feet and leaned forward. "I'm really sorry I didn't come see you earlier. Or call. I was worried you'd be upset. You know, that I broke up with Ken." I grabbed her hand, fighting the building emotions.

"Stop." She squeezed my fingers to gentle the rebuke. "You've already said that. Lots of times. You're here now."

"If I'd known the cancer was back—"

"None of that, honey. You needed some time, and I didn't call you. I knew you'd be here in a flash if I did, and I wanted you to see you'd made the right decision. Ken's sure he knows how to run everyone's life better than they do. My sister's just like him. The apple didn't fall far from the tree. I know firsthand how terrible a trait that is in a person."

I mashed my lips together, gathering my emotions. "Of course I would've come. I love you, Rosie." And I did. Deeply. A rarity I'd saved for just Lia and Abbi—until I met this incredible woman.

She smiled and nodded a little. "And I love you, honey. You're the daughter I never had. And thank God you're not actually becoming a niece by marriage."

I shook my head. "I want us to be family," I said. So much so, I'd almost married Ken.

"We are. The best kind of all. The kind we chose for ourselves."

I opened my mouth, needing to say something, but Rosie released my hand.

"Have you thought any more about what you're going to do next?"

"I actually told Hayden journalism isn't my thing. That's been hard to accept. Especially because Ken always said so."

Rosie wrinkled her nose. "I almost agree with you just to oppose Ken. But in this case, he was right. Just don't tell him I said so. His ego doesn't need any stroking."

I couldn't help but giggle at her. Ken was her blood relative, but that didn't mean she didn't see his faults. She'd finally pried the story of our sordid breakup out of me, unsurprised by Ken's actions.

"Appalling," she'd murmured. She cocked her head, appraising me. "He had the sense to see how great you were. Maybe there's hope for him yet."

We sat for a few minutes while I held her hand and tried to figure out how I'd gotten to my thirties without any real direction.

"You're good at what you do," Rosie said. "But you never loved it."

"I love being here with you. Helping people." I sucked on my lower lip. "I'd thought to be a doctor. I was in the premed department when we found out my brother-in-law was dying."

"Lord," Rosie laughed, though it quickly turned into a dry, painful cough. "You'd make the *worst* doctor. You're too nice. I mean, look at Ken. He's top of his profession because he doesn't care."

"Not really helping." I sighed.

"Well, what do you like to do?"

"Besides chat with you?" I smiled. "I told you, I like having a purpose. Knowing I'm doing something worthwhile."

"That wouldn't be sitting with me, dear." Rosie's eyes sparkled and her lips curved upward just a bit. The hint of a smile. I'd done that—helped her feel better. If only for a moment.

"I disagree," I said, softly. "I think this—helping individuals die," my voice broke, but I held back the sob. Rosie deserved my strength as she lost her own. "Helping their loved ones get through it, this might be exactly what I'm supposed to do."

Rosie considered me for a long moment. "You mentioned this last year when you were covering a story about the new cancer center. I liked the idea then."

I nodded, lowering my eyes. She didn't need to see the hurt in them. She wasn't choosing to die. "I want to do something real. Something that actually makes a difference. For all that Ken's emotionally stilted, he's doing that. He's helping people."

"If you want to, you will. Ken's a good man, just not the right one for you. He'd try to ramrod you into doing things his way and that'll do nothing but make you both miserable. He needs a society wife—a woman like his mother. Now"—she smoothed her hands over her blankets, dismissing Ken and the rest of her family from our conversation—"tell me about Princess. I miss that ragamuffin."

Not wanting to tell her how thin the cat was, I launched into the story about visiting Princess last night. I'd never owned a pet, and after Princess, I probably never would. To say it went poorly was an understatement.

"Then she darted into the living room and used her claws to mutilate one of the sofa cushions. She'd obviously been shredding it for days."

"What? Did she have anything to eat?"

"A bowl full of food." I paused. Rosie waited, too still. Best to simply tell Rosie all of it. "Your neighbor came by last night after work. She couldn't get Princess to eat and she'd tried all kinds of different foods."

"I left her enough money to make sure Princess was taken care of." Rosie's voice rose in agitation.

"It's fine—everything's fine. I'd bought some salmon at the market. Once I gave some to Princess she even purred a little. She sounds like a big dually truck when she gets going."

Rosie chuckled a little, the sound weak but happy. "She likes you. Always has. I'm glad you're watching her now."

"I'll make sure she eats." I didn't tell her I'd shut the bedroom door, terrified the cat would maul me in the night. Some things just didn't need to be shared.

"Good," Rosie sighed. "I'm glad I talked you into staying at my condo."

She slid back into sleep, holding my hand. With slow precision, I extricated myself and stood. I bent to gather my purse.

"Hello, Briar."

I stiffened my back but turned to face him. "Ken."

"I called earlier. The doctor said you've practically been living here." He cocked his head, eying me in that way most people look at a puzzle they can't figure out. "She's *my* aunt."

"She's like a mother to me," I said.

"So you're just trying to worm your way into her fortune? My money wasn't enough for you. You want Rosie's instead."

My jaw snapped closed with a firm click. "I don't want *you* because you tried to manipulate me. I'm here for Rosie because she's my friend. A dear one."

"I'm calling bullshit, Briar. You left us both without explanation."

"Because you tried to force me into pregnancy," I snarled.

"Now you're all cozied up with my aunt in her last dying days. Any will she writes now, my father and I will contest. She's on heavy medication. Definitely not in her right mind."

I stepped closer to Ken and grabbed his tie so that we were nose to nose. "I. Don't. Want. Her. Money." Each word pushed through my teeth like a dart.

He yanked back. "See that it stays that way."

"I'm going to be here this week. All week," I said, staking my claim. "We both know you only stopped by out of obligation."

"Of course it's obligation. She's *my* family."

I narrowed my eyes, but before I could say anything further, Rosie's voice, filled with amusement, drifted over from the bed. "Ken, still being your charming self, I see."

He glared at me before ducking around to press a kiss to Rosie's check. "How are you feeling?"

She leveled him with a look that had him squirming in those perfectly pressed Brooks Brothers trousers. "If you really wanted to know, you would have come by sooner than this."

"Of course I want to know. I plan to talk to Dr. Chin every day."

"Kenneth," Rosie sighed. "You aren't going to win Briar back. I'm not planning to change my will. It's been set for weeks. While I appreciate the visit, we both know you came to antagonize Briar for not being more interested in a life with you. Which, as I told her, would only end in bitterness and probably divorce. Do us all a favor and look for a beautiful but vapid young woman who only wants to be your arm candy. Everyone will be happier."

I stepped out into the hall, unwilling to listen to anything else. Before I pushed through the double doors, Ken stormed past. "I don't know how you've wrapped my aunt so tight around your finger, but you better believe what I told you." He stabbed his finger into my shoulder. "You're not getting any of my aunt's fortune. And my parents have already blackballed you from all the lists."

"I don't care about your stupid high society. Never did." I blinked, shocked to realize that was true. Maybe I'd liked the trappings of wealth, but I'd never felt comfortable with those people, who catalogued my dress and my verbiage, waiting for me to show how out of place I truly was. I took a deep breath, feeling freer than I had in years. "All I wanted from you was an apology."

He smoothed his tie and did up his suit buttons. "You're not getting one. You're a cold, heartless bitch, Briar, and I will expose you as such."

CHAPTER NINE
Hayden

A nurse was in the room with my mum, looking grim. Middle-aged with graying light brown hair and sensible shoes. Her scrubs were a size too small but still managed to work on her.

"Bad as all that?"

"And you are?" the woman barked.

Crikey. Friendly sort.

"My son." My mum's voice was thready but stronger than it'd been earlier. "Hayden."

The nurse's dire look softened. "Glad you're here. I'm Kelly, Miriam's day nurse."

"You're the one who called," I said.

She nodded. "Your mom asked. Cost an arm and both legs by the time I got through, but I wanted to see Miriam happy." Kelly patted my mum's leg gently. "That working better for the pain, Mir?"

"Sure," Mum said, but both Kelly and I frowned. "Leave it, Kelly. I'm fine."

"You're not." Kelly turned toward me. "This is stage four. Her doctor is shocked she's lasted so long. I would be, too, but this woman is stubborn. She's waited for you to show up. Except she wouldn't call you."

Emotions roared up through me, but the one I latched on to was confusion. "But you called me. I'll reimburse you for the calls, of course."

"I already handled the money," Mum said. Her eyes were cloudy with the drugs and the remnants of pain. "I didn't think you'd want to see me. You must hate me, Hayden."

I was silent because there was no way I could refute that. I did hate what she'd done to me, even though my feelings were mixed up with the images, mostly from photographs, of her holding me as a baby, kissing me, snuggling me in close.

"You chose to leave," I finally pointed out.

"George and I decided I should sever contact," she said. I glanced at Kelly, whose face was set, eyes pleading me to listen.

"Without ever asking me what I wanted?" The words wrenched from my throat. This was it—if I didn't ask now I might never know. She needed to explain how she could grab her own child in a viselike grip so tight and shake his teeth near loose. I'd worn the bruises for weeks. She hadn't explained her screaming and hitting me on the head, shoulders, chest, before shoving me through the window. It took me years to fight off the nightmares of that day.

"I was sick. Very sick. I spent nearly two years in that facility after you and George left before I could manage any kind of life on my own. And then only with a pillbox full of prescriptions. I missed you so much, I kept falling back into the depression."

"So, it was fine to move me from my friends, from my life, from you?" I stood, not sure why, just knowing I couldn't sit there and listen to her recounting.

"That was George's decision. He'd missed Melbourne and I—I wasn't capable of helping raise you." The skin around her mouth turned white when she pressed her bloodless lips together. "I'd hurt you enough."

I glanced up and saw a flash of fabric. It was the blue of Briar's top. Shit, she must have heard that as she passed my mum's room.

So many emotions bubbled up, but the strongest was anger. I didn't want anyone to know my mum's struggle with mania and depression. Especially not Briar. She was a bloody journo. No matter what she said, I feared she'd turn my mum's death to her advantage. Except…except she understood the unfairness of parents putting their desires—hell, even their wellness—before their child's. Not fair, that thought, but I wanted Briar to see *me*, not the musician, not the son of a sick woman. More, I wanted Briar to like what she saw.

"Yes, you did." Which was why I'd planned to pat my mum's hand, fix up her bill, leave. Simple. That was more than she deserved after she'd pummeled me in a rage for interrupting her piano practice.

"I couldn't see you again, Hayden." Her voice was full of regret. "What if I had another violent episode? That last one sent you to the hospital for a week." Her lips trembled as a tear splashed over the thin lid.

She'd left me in some noble attempt to protect me? My dad told me to find my mum. To listen to her. Bloody hell. I didn't know what to believe anymore.

"And better to ignore me for the next two decades than to write something? An apology, maybe?"

"I'm bipolar, Hayden."

I'd known she struggled with mental illness thanks to some of the papers my father had locked in one of the drawers in his study. But my dad didn't talk about bipolar disorder or mania or even my mother's depression much, so old-school in his beliefs, he assumed people needed to *want* to change to stop their strange, sometimes dangerous behaviors. The word, *bipolar*, tied a heavy weight around my neck. Mental illness was hereditary, passed down from a parent or close relative.

"Look, I don't know how to deal with my mess of a life. I'm not going to judge how you deal with your problems," she said with a sigh. "I want to spend time with Rosie. She doesn't have much left."

I stared into those beautiful blue eyes. "I'm not saying tomorrow will be better."

Her lips flipped up in a sardonic smile. "It's possible tomorrow will be worse. This is hospice after all."

"I'm expecting worse." I tilted my head back and groaned. "I don't want my mum's death to drag out. Too many people are counting on me."

"You'll do the best you can."

"Doesn't feel good enough."

"Welcome to the club. Speaking of, my sister doesn't believe I met you, Mr. World Famous Rock Star."

I raised my eyebrow. I cradled her shoulders. I liked holding Briar. Wasn't a briar some kind of rose? Sweet but with enough defenses to bloom. I liked that—she'd fight for her chances.

"We'll have to take a selfie. For digital proof."

"Thought you didn't like digital proof and journos, as you call them."

"Reckon I don't. But…I'm making an exception."

Her lips curved up and her eyes sparkled. The weight from my chest eased a little and I could draw a full breath. "I'd like that. Ready to go?"

"Photo first."

I grabbed her phone and positioned us together before snapping a few photos. "For posterity or whatever."

She smiled again. "I know just the place to go."

She snagged my hand, her cool fingers sliding between mine, our palms fusing softly. Something in me clicked, like I'd just latched into a safety belt. I followed behind her as she pulled me toward her car again. After she unlocked it, I opened her door and waited for her to slide in. Instead, she stepped in closer, her body heat mingling with mine.

"I've done a lot of soul-searching these past few months, Hayden. But today, with Ken's comments, my purpose clicked." She closed her eyes, reliving something. "I'm tired of closing off, pushing people away," she whispered. "It's all I've done for years." She opened her eyes, filled with the fire of new determination. "So I mean it when I say I'll be here with you. Through this. As your friend."

I ran my knuckle down her cheek, marveling at the smooth, firm texture of her skin. "I don't know how I got so lucky in the friend department, but I'm chuffed you're here. And such a gorgeous lady at that."

She rolled her eyes, and I winked. Walking around the car, I curled my fingers tight to hold in the fading heat from her skin. I glanced up at the building. Whatever my mum needed to tell me, I needed to hear. I could process her reasons and come to terms with her years of rejection later, but for now, she wanted me to know her side of the story. And I'd listen.

As I eased into the car, Briar's floral scent wrapped around me, cradling me almost as well as her arms had just moments before.

Bloody fucking hell. Bipolar. From what little I knew about mental health, the disorder was serious, on par with schizophrenia.

My mum exhaled hard, struggling against the forced oxygen that was being pumped regularly into her nose. "For me the depression is aggressive, angry. And it's much harder to climb out of that than the mania."

"And I was the easiest target." I pressed my fists to my forehead.

"Because you were there. That wasn't my first episode with you. Just the worst. Your father told me I either got help or he would leave me."

"So you got help and he left you."

"Not exactly," she said. She stopped twisting her sheet in her fingers. "I asked him to take you away. You were a temptation I couldn't resist. I wanted to be with you, not in a treatment center." She gestured to the room. "They weren't as nice as this. I found out later, after years of therapy, the intensity of my love for you also brought about more focused negative emotions like rage and depression. They were focused on you because I loved you. So much."

"You loved me so much you ran away?" I sneered.

Kelly stepped forward, laid her hand on my mother's frail shoulder. The nurse sent me a glare that said "you better calm down" before she refocused on my mother.

I gnashed my teeth. I didn't want to calm the fuck down. I wanted to yell at the nurse. I wanted to run from my mother's comments. My fingers were through my hair, trying to ease the confusion and anger cracking open my chest. "Dad said you needed time. But you'd decided I wasn't worth the effort."

"No! God, no, Hayden. I just...I struggled for years with the depression. Because I missed you. I spent most of that time in and out of facilities."

"Well, isn't that convenient," I scoffed. "For your story."

"George told me that leaving was best for all of us. That I could start over." The machines started beeping.

"Miriam, you need to calm down," Kelly said.

"Why? So I can live longer? I'm dying. Hayden needs to understand—"

"I'll come by tomorrow," I said as I strode toward the door.

"Hayden, I was your age." My mum's voice was edged with panic. "I didn't know how to fight for you. We didn't know then what we know now about the disease."

I stopped, turned slowly to face her. "That you passed along the chance of me being just as fucked up as you are? That's all I know about bipolar disorder. It's genetic. You gave me a life sentence, just like yours."

"I didn't understand how to manage the disorder then," she whispered.

My shoulders hunched inward. "Do you have any idea how hard it was, growing up with a dad old enough to be my grandfather and a mum who ran away?" I asked, my voice vibrating with a fury I'd worked for years to suppress. I searched her face. "Do you have any idea how hard being alone was on Dad? How much I wished for one phone call—just one—where you told me you loved me?" I crossed my arms over my chest, holding in some of my righteous anger. "Of course you don't. You didn't see Dad age overnight or hold me when I cried into my pillow for weeks on end. Because you *left*."

"No, honey. Your move, my leaving…it wasn't like that, Hayden. I always loved you…"

"Not enough to do anything about it."

I strode down the hall and slammed my hand against the release bar of the front door with more force than necessary. I cursed as I stumbled out the door. The cool air slapped me in the face. "Fuck, fuck, fuck."

I wanted to hit something but I wouldn't. I refused violence of all kinds. I still remembered those moments when my mum had slapped me.

I glanced around, looking for some outlet. Nothing. I needed to calm down enough to drive myself away from this place. I pressed my palms against the side of the building, trying to draw in enough air to loosen the tightness in my chest. I needed a keyboard to pound out my frustrations. No one would get hurt if I played out my emotions.

A hand slid over my wrist. I turned to see Briar, this woman I barely knew, thankful for her steady presence. I buried my nose in her neck, my arms wrapped tight around her, and finally I could breathe. She slid her arms over my shoulders and rocked me like mums do their small children. And just as I'd always assumed, there was comfort in that sway, in those warm arms.

"You listened," I mumbled into the soft skin of her neck.

She nodded. Her fingers slid into the hair at the nape of my neck. I liked that she didn't offer platitudes. "Enough to know this isn't our afternoon. I'd just gotten into it with Ken."

"The wanker stopped by?"

"To pronounce Rosie very sick and me very stupid. Cold and calculating." She closed her eyes, trying to mentally shake off his words.

"My mum's always been sick." My voice cracked. I heaved a breath, pulling her tighter against me. I wanted me in her, buried so deep I couldn't feel this anymore. "I knew that, but I didn't know how sick. After my dad died, my anger drove me deeper into music, deeper into myself." I shut my eyes and tipped my head back, swallowing hard. "Now that she's dying, she's trying to take my anger at her leaving me, too."

"I totally get that."

"Will you…I don't want to be alone."

"I'm pretty raw right now, too."

"Because of the wanker?"

"He called me a cold, heartless bitch."

"Didn't know you well, did he?"

"Even when I was with him, I never let him in."

The sound that erupted from my throat was somewhere between a sigh and a growl. "I understand. And in this case, you were right to keep him at a distance. He's a total shithead." I glanced around. "I need to get out of here. I'll come back in the morning, talk to the director then. Keep me company, Briar. We'll do each other some good."

She hesitated, her shoulders stiff. She wrestled with her thoughts while I waited, just as tense. After drawing and releasing a deep breath, she pulled back just enough to cup my cheeks. She stared into my eyes, forcing me to steady my gaze, to regulate my breathing.

"I'll make you a deal, Hayden. For as long as you're in Seattle, you don't have to do this by yourself. I'll be here with you, for you."

I nodded, inhaled deep and leaned my forehead against hers. "I'd like that. I'll offer the same. Get you through your shit-tastic evening and we'll come back tomorrow. I'm sorry you saw me…" I waved toward the front door. "I'm not usually so…"

"Look, I don't know how to deal with my mess of a life. I'm not going to judge how you deal with your problems," she said with a sigh. "I want to spend time with Rosie. She doesn't have much left."

I stared into those beautiful blue eyes. "I'm not saying tomorrow will be better."

Her lips flipped up in a sardonic smile. "It's possible tomorrow will be worse. This is hospice after all."

"I'm expecting worse." I tilted my head back and groaned. "I don't want my mum's death to drag out. Too many people are counting on me."

"You'll do the best you can."

"Doesn't feel good enough."

"Welcome to the club. Speaking of, my sister doesn't believe I met you, Mr. World Famous Rock Star."

I raised my eyebrow. I cradled her shoulders. I liked holding Briar. Wasn't a briar some kind of rose? Sweet but with enough defenses to bloom. I liked that—she'd fight for her chances.

"We'll have to take a selfie. For digital proof."

"Thought you didn't like digital proof and journos, as you call them."

"Reckon I don't. But…I'm making an exception."

Her lips curved up and her eyes sparkled. The weight from my chest eased a little and I could draw a full breath. "I'd like that. Ready to go?"

"Photo first."

I grabbed her phone and positioned us together before snapping a few photos. "For posterity or whatever."

She smiled again. "I know just the place to go."

She snagged my hand, her cool fingers sliding between mine, our palms fusing softly. Something in me clicked, like I'd just latched into a safety belt. I followed behind her as she pulled me toward her car again. After she unlocked it, I opened her door and waited for her to slide in. Instead, she stepped in closer, her body heat mingling with mine.

"I've done a lot of soul-searching these past few months, Hayden. But today, with Ken's comments, my purpose clicked." She closed her eyes, reliving something. "I'm tired of closing off, pushing people away," she whispered. "It's all I've done for years." She opened her eyes, filled with the fire of new determination. "So I mean it when I say I'll be here with you. Through this. As your friend."

I ran my knuckle down her cheek, marveling at the smooth, firm texture of her skin. "I don't know how I got so lucky in the friend department, but I'm chuffed you're here. And such a gorgeous lady at that."

She rolled her eyes, and I winked. Walking around the car, I curled my fingers tight to hold in the fading heat from her skin. I glanced up at the building. Whatever my mum needed to tell me, I needed to hear. I could process her reasons and come to terms with her years of rejection later, but for now, she wanted me to know her side of the story. And I'd listen.

As I eased into the car, Briar's floral scent wrapped around me, cradling me almost as well as her arms had just moments before.

CHAPTER TEN
Briar

His eyes were shattered, but the pieces weren't continuing to break further as they'd been when he first turned toward me. Being more open with others meant I had to feel some of what he was feeling. But helping him made me feel better, too.

The silence built. Maybe I'd handled him wrong. Hayden was so contained, so private. More so, even, than I was. But I could see how worn down he'd become from holding all those emotions in—just like Lia said I did, burying my emotions deep and building walls higher with each heartache I'd faced. I wanted better for him than this slow, grinding sadness. More for me, too.

His fingers tapped, restless against his jeans-clad thigh.

Maybe it was the pain meds, maybe the cancer had eaten away at his mother's ability to cushion her words like it had her organs. Or maybe that's just the way she was. Whatever her reasons, she'd ripped Hayden's heart bare in minutes. Much like Ken did to me.

Seeing Hayden lost and angry…his response now brought back those horrible days when my dad died, and I was too scared to help Lia as she struggled to keep us fed and moving through our routine.

I hated anything that reminded me of that time in our lives, but somehow, sharing this connection with Hayden helped. We were survivors.

The evening commuter traffic had mostly passed. I pulled into the dark parking lot of the studio. Lia had checked for me, and Bill was in town. When I'd called, he'd been more than happy to let us in to the studio space.

"You didn't have to meet us," I said as Bill pulled me into a hug. He was about my height and solid. His hair was shorn shorter than I'd ever seen it, probably in an effort to hide the gray swirling through the flaxen strands. Bill took his appearance seriously. His designer jeans, expensive black leather boots, and trendy Western-style shirt proved it.

Like the rest of Asher's band, Bill treated me like family—the kid sister they loved to razz. But if I was ever in any trouble, they'd be the first to step in and make things right. Hard to believe my sister and I had only been in their lives such a short time. Everything about Lia and Asher just clicked.

I wanted that for me.

I glanced at Hayden, saw the frown building between his brows. With Hayden, I was opening myself up, helping him as he helped me.

"Pass up a chance to play with the Aussie rocker of the year? Like that was ever going to happen."

Bill held out his hand and Hayden shook it—after he pulled me into his side. I beamed up at him.

"So this is Bill," I said.

"Good to see you again, mate."

"Yeah, you, too. Bri said you wanted some studio time."

Hayden glanced down at me, his eyes widening a little as he considered the offer.

"You got a piano?"

"Of course. Wait till you see our baby." Bill chuckled at his joke.

"Excellent," Hayden said. He squeezed my waist, letting me know how pleased he was with the situation.

"C'mon. I want your opinion on the acoustics."

I followed behind the guys, glad to see a bit of bounce in Hayden's step. My jaw dropped when Bill opened the door. The space was big, loft-like. The far wall was a bank of windows with breathtaking views of the sound. While we were miles from the shore, the building was high enough to have unrestricted line of sight to Alki Beach. The Cascades rose, jagged and dark, against the velvet lavender of the night sky. I moved closer to the windows.

"Wow, Bill, this is amazing."

"Right? Glad we brought in the piano. We can bang out some chords, but none of us have anything close to that"—he tilted his head toward Hayden—"kind of talent."

The light from the lamp on top of the ebony baby grand glinted off the caramel waves on Hayden's bent head as he positioned himself on the piano bench. Haunting notes filled the room. His fingers moved with mournful perfection over the keys. I sank into the melody, carried away by his obvious love of the instrument. He didn't raise his head, just segued into the next song with a seamlessness that seemed easy.

"He's amazing."

I jumped, my hand to my heart. I'd forgotten Bill was there; I'd been so focused on Hayden.

"Thanks again for letting us come," I said, keeping my voice quiet. I didn't want to distract Hayden. His notes were getting louder, building to the crescendo of emotion he'd otherwise try to bottle back up inside.

"He needed it," Bill said. "Damn, that's some fine playing. Think we could steal him from his band?"

I shrugged, unsure how much Hayden wanted to talk about his reasons for being here, in Seattle, instead of on tour.

"How long's he in town?"

Hayden dropped his hands from the keys and raised his head. "Until my mum dies. She's got stage four pancreatic cancer."

Hayden's eyes met mine, silently thanking me for keeping my mouth shut.

"I'm sorry, man. That's—wow—no wonder you wanted to play. Helps screw your head on straight, yeah?"

Hayden put his fingers back on the keys. "Something like that. Though, both my parents played piano. It's how they met."

I moved forward, leaning on the gleaming edge of the instrument. With the lid up, I could see all the strings and hammers moving, a juxtaposition to the smooth motion of Hayden's fingers on the keys.

"I've never heard that piece before," I murmured, trying to redirect his thoughts.

"That's because I just made it up." Hayden slid the bench back and stood. "Reminds me of you."

I blinked, shocked, but Hayden's gaze drifted around the room.

"This is a great setup," he said. "The guys and I are playing a show here later this summer. Will you be in town?"

Bill pursed his lips, considering. "We're doing mini-tours this summer, mostly up and down the Pacific coast. Carl's getting Seth settled at Northern University and Asher doesn't want to leave Lia for too long." Bill grinned. "My guess is he's worried Mason will drive her crazy and she'll run screaming back to Iowa."

I rolled my eyes. "Idaho."

Bill shrugged. "Whatevs."

"Mason is Asher's son," I said. "Asher was awarded full custody of him a few months ago."

Hayden nodded. "I met the Supernaturals a few years back in Sydney. Asher showed me a picture. Cute kid. Glad Asher's getting to be the dad he always wanted to be."

Bill narrowed his eyes. "Hayden and his band played a gig at this tiny pub while we were in town. We'd heard all about this piano prodigy we had to check out."

Hayden shuddered. "*Prodigy* is a strong word."

"Bri, have you let Asher know Hayden's in town?"

"I told Lia. I'm sure she's told Asher." I shook my head, mystified by Bill's boundless enthusiasm. Hayden's band, Jackaroo, was growing in popularity thanks to a song titled "She's So Bad," but Asher and Bill were indie-rock royalty. They'd been around for twenty years and wore the scars—both mental and physical—to prove it.

"I'm texting Ash now. He's going to go apeshit when he hears I have Hayden in the studio and he's not here."

"I'd love to meet up with some musicians while I'm in town," Hayden said. "Might make this waiting game feel more productive." His eyes shone, his face more animated than I'd seen it all day.

"I get you. I'm always happiest wailing out some riffs. Yep. Knew it. Asher's excited. He said Lia mentioned you were hanging out with Briar. Said they'll be here tomorrow, day after at the latest." Bill looked to me, annoyed, and asked, "What's the holdup? Ash loves to jam."

"They're settling Abbi's school situation, getting Lia's house ready to sell."

Bill nodded, the frown easing. "I forgot. Seth's glad Abbi's going to be closer." He wiggled his eyebrows.

"I don't want to think about my niece like that," I said.

"Wait—how old is your niece?" Hayden asked.

"Seventeen."

Hayden blinked, then nodded. "Does she play an instrument?"

"No. She refused. Doug—her dad—was a guitar player."

"There's a story there," Hayden said.

"Always is with you musicians," I mused.

"So Asher wants you to come by again and jam with him," Bill said. "Now, show me that melody again. I want to see if I can get the chords."

Bill pulled the strap of his guitar over his head. I stepped back to the windows, looking out into the deep sky and replaying Ken's comments over in my head. I turned back, smiling when the guys laughed at Bill's wrong note. This was what Hayden needed. Maybe what I needed, too.

CHAPTER ELEVEN
Hayden

Part of the reason I'd felt so off today was because I hadn't played the piano. While in college, I'd play for three, sometimes more, hours each day. Between the flight and visiting my mum, I'd gone nearly two days without touching the ivories. Music was my escape. I'd needed it. Briar had known, sought out the opportunity so I could settle my head and my emotions.

Bill had called me a prodigy, and I guess to some people I was. I'd shown talent early and spent most of my childhood in music camps and private lessons. My first big recital was at the age of fourteen at the Enmore Theatre. Granted, that venue was much smaller than Sydney's Hordern Pavilion, where the Supernaturals played a sold-out show when they came Down Under, but performing at the Enmore was still a respectable notch in any musician's belt. And I'd played to a packed-out Pavilion just last month with Jackaroo.

Now, as my fingers moved across the keys, my foot pumping the damper pedal, I was home. Centered.

Briar gazed out the large windows, lost in some deep thoughts. Bill crowed out the worst rendition of Asher's "Let's Do it in the Surf" as he strummed his guitar. No wonder they kept the man away from the microphone.

Crikey, that was painful.

"Now, watch this—this is what we're doing on the new album," Bill said.

His fingers slid upward, a smooth progression across the frets. Nodding, I slid back onto the piano bench and said, "You mean this type of melody?"

"Yeah, man. That's great. Then I could do a layer over it."

I stopped playing on an abrupt chord and stood.

"This has been excellent, Bill. Briar's got to be famished and I could use a bite myself. Care to join us?"

"You sure you don't want to jam more?" Bill kept strumming his guitar, lost in a place I didn't want to follow again. Not with Briar here.

"Not tonight. I need to call my manager, let him know I'm still here. We have to set up some promo, get me back on the tour."

Bill shook his head, eyes far away, lost in his music. "Y'all go ahead."

"Thanks," Briar murmured as we headed toward the elevator. "Bill's great, but I think my ears are bleeding. He really shouldn't sing."

"Occupational hazard."

"So I have a question."

"Shoot."

"What does Jackaroo mean?"

I smiled, brushing my hand down her spine as I held open the elevator doors. "A ranch hand."

"But you don't play country music."

"There are influences, especially from Ets."

"Ets being?"

"Murphy Etsam," I said. "We tried calling him Etso but he wouldn't answer."

"Because that's a stupid nickname," Briar pointed out.

"That's why we liked it."

I urged her from the elevator with a little pressure on her lower back. I was very aware my hand was mere inches from that delectable bum.

"I need to feed Rosie's cat," Briar said.

Hope took root. Was she inviting me back to her place? I'd been trying to figure out how to invite her to my hotel room without sounding like a perv. I didn't want to presume past our friend pact. Her asking me over was just…well, hot.

"All right."

"She's probably trashed the place by now. She's the meanest beast I've ever met."

"Sounds interesting."

"You may be risking your life entering the apartment."

"I think I can handle a tiny tiger."

Her gaze was steady but her lips flattened. "You've been warned."

"Mind if I make a call?" I asked as we got into her car.

"Of course not."

I dialed Harry's number. He answered on the first ring. "So you are flying back. Good. Ets is pissed at the thought of canceling another show."

"Can't come back yet. That's why I'm calling." Hell. I didn't know if this was the right decision. I glanced over at Briar, thinking about her naked. Well…not even Ets would blame me for being late if I was shagging a beautiful woman.

"This isn't the time to go walkabout," Harry moaned.

"Tell that to my mum."

"I don't know if I can spin this. We can't cancel more concerts. Besides the financial headaches, people are asking questions about where you are. How am I supposed to answer them?"

"Get Pete to come in. He's a great session pianist." Even as I said the words, I hated the idea of someone else touching my instrument, playing my melodies in my band.

"Hayden, you've got the world at your feet. Don't throw this away. She's dying. Would she want you to mess up your life?"

"Talk soon, Harry. I'll text Pete. Let him know to expect a call from you for the last show in Melbourne."

"Fine," Harry sighed. "But Ets is going to throw a fit."

I ended the call and stared at the window. Briar didn't say anything, her eyes focused on the road, and I appreciated the chance to realign my thoughts. Only I couldn't get past the question Harry'd asked. Would my mum want to mess up my life?

Briar drove to a nice high-rise condominium complex. After parking in the underground bay, we rode the elevator up to the ninth floor. "This is Rosie's place. The cat's name is Princess."

The place was neat, if a little dusty and neglected. The living room, like the kitchen, was small but functional. The couches, though, were tattered. Both the armrests and fronts were shredded by what appeared to be cat claws.

The first bite of apprehension tickled the back of my neck.

Mrrowww.

"Hi, Princess," Briar said, her voice nervous.

Hiss.

"Don't be like that, Princess. I want to feed you." Briar slunk toward the kitchen, her steps tentative. My amusement turned to shock when the cat leapt from the kitchen counter, batting at Briar's face, claws unsheathed.

Briar stumbled back, hands up, biting off a scream.

"Oi!" I charged forward, stepping between Briar and the fluffy feline hellion. The cat ran pell-mell down the short hall. Probably to hide under the bed.

"She hates me," Briar said, voice shaky. "Rosie says she likes me but that's not true. Animals usually like me. Not even my employees hated me." She rested her head against my back for a moment before heading into the kitchen, where she pulled out fresh salmon.

"You're hard to hate. Wait, you feed the fiend raw salmon?"

"She likes it. It's the only time she purrs."

"Of course she does. Her dinner costs more than most humans'."

"She normally settles down after she's eaten," Briar said, casting a nervous glance toward the hall.

"You're not staying here with that cat."

"I have to. I promised Rosie I'd look after her."

I folded my arms over my chest. "That's a promise you'll have to break for your own safety. Cats carry bacteria in their claws. A scratch can be dangerous."

"I've heard the song," Briar said, laughing. "'Cat Scratch Fever,' right?" She stood and washed her hands before carefully wrapping the food and putting the plate back in the fridge.

"You irritate me, woman."

"Lia will be proud I haven't lost my touch. You want something to eat? I know you're hungry."

"Here? With the spawn of Satan on the prowl?"

"Princess isn't that bad."

I raised my eyebrow and Briar wilted.

"Okay, she is. I think she's freaking out that her mom's gone and I left her alone all day…That's a lot for any dependent to handle."

"You realize you're rationalizing a cat's behavior?"

"We can order some takeout or I can try to cook something," Briar said, looking with nervous anticipation around the kitchen.

I chuckled. "Seeing as how I can't make mac and cheese—I'm talking the microwave kind—I'm not about to complain about your lack of culinary skills."

Briar smiled. "Oh, another domestically challenged person. You have no idea how happy that makes me. Lia's a kitchen whiz."

"Those people are such show-offs."

"I dial a mean Chinese. That okay with you? Or maybe Thai? Hmm, then again we had Korean for lunch—pizza?"

"I love pizza. Anything on it is great. Well, not squid. Or broccoli. Got any beer?"

Briar called in an order. She walked back to the shredded couch with a cold can, which she handed me.

"Asher told me to get this kind. I like to drink lager with my pizza. Reminds me of my dad."

I settled back onto the surprisingly comfortable cushion and popped open the can.

"Cheers." I took a long swallow. Jet lag settled over me.

"When did you get into town?"

"Yesterday. Why?"

"You're going to crash hard," Briar said with a frown. "Your body's still all messed up from crossing so many time zones."

I pulled her down and into my side. "Not till after I eat Seattle's best pizza, though."

───◆───

The beer probably wasn't a good idea, but the talk with my mum lay heavy on my mind. Sucking the cold brew down, I managed three slices of the pie, fascinated by the weird toppings.

"What's on it again?"

"Mortadella, nettle pesto, and pistachios."

"Only thing I've heard of on that list is pistachios."

"They're good," Briar said as she munched her second piece.

"Is this the kind of pizza your dad ate?"

She inhaled to laugh but choked instead. She set the pizza down, struggled to catch her breath. After a sip of beer, she said, "No way. He loved meat."

"Good man, your dad." I yawned hard enough to bring tears to my eyes.

"Yes, he was. A very good man."

"You miss him heaps. Still."

She nodded, her eyes darkening with an old pain. That I understood all too well. I knew I shouldn't, but I couldn't help cupping her far cheek and settling her head onto my chest. I rubbed the ends of her silky, chocolate-colored hair between my fingers just like I'd wanted to all day.

"Your hair reminds me of a mink. I always liked those animals. Like the color on your head more though."

"Flatterer."

"Not so much. Just tell it as I see it."

"My dad used to say that."

She nestled in a little closer, and I could just make out the rapid blinking of her lashes. Damn, she was going to cry. I was very uncomfortable with tears.

"My dad liked to play really esoteric composers," I blurted. "Weird, almost nonmusical music. I hated it, would cover my ears. He told me I didn't have an ear for minor progressions."

"Is that true?"

"I was seven at the time. But I matured and learned the importance of tension in a piece. Just not as much as my dad preferred. Music should speak to the listener, not bash her over the head."

Her chuckle was watery, but I'd take it.

I closed my eyes. When she slid her arms around my waist, contentment and sleep washed over me.

CHAPTER TWELVE
Briar

I didn't have the heart to wake him. I cleaned up our dinner, putting the leftovers into the fridge, then brushed my teeth while I debated what to do with Hayden. He couldn't sleep on the couch. Besides it being too short, half the stuffing was now missing, making it way too uncomfortable for an extended lie-down.

Princess was curled in a corner in the small dining nook. She blinked open an eye when I tiptoed back to the bedroom, hoping she'd let Hayden sleep for a while longer. I put on my shorts and cami set. While not overly revealing, the outfit was soft, and the hot pink was a good color for me.

But when I came out of the bathroom, face washed and hair tied up for sleep, I gave in to the inevitable: he'd stay the night.

I'd only fantasized about it three thousand times today. Thank goodness I'd made time earlier this week for a haircut, waxing, and mani/pedi. I'd stewed in self-pity in Rathdrum, letting every part of me fall into disrepair. The timing for my beauty salon overhaul couldn't have been better.

Not that I expected Hayden to—screw it, I did want him to make love to me. Lying wouldn't change the yearning building in my core and spiraling out toward my breasts.

I padded back down the hall, keeping my distance from Princess. She rumbled from her corner but didn't try to shred my leg. Progress.

I slid my hip next to Hayden on the couch, and ran my finger down his nose and over his firm top lip. His warm breath slid across my hand, and I moaned. He was sinfully good-looking. His lashes rested on his cheeks, as sun-kissed as his hair. I leaned in, noticing a few faint freckles on each cheek. I bit my lip and turned away, barely resisting the urge to fan my overheated cheeks.

Who knew freckles were so sexy?

"Hayden?" I said, keeping my voice soft, soothing.

"Mmm."

"Hayden, come on. Time for bed."

His lashes fluttered, his pupils dark and large, nearly overpowering the lighter brown of his irises as his eyes opened. "Shit. I fell asleep."

I smiled, amused as he ran a hand over his face. "You've been out for a while."

"You should've woken me. I need to get back." His fingers were in his hair, tousling the waves.

"Well, I put on my pajamas now, so you'll just stay here. With me. If that's okay."

"Is there a bed?"

"Yes, I have a bed."

"Great."

He wasn't completely awake so I offered him my hand, helping him up off the sagging couch. He stumbled around the coffee table and bounced off the wall as I led him down the hall to the only bedroom. I bit my tongue to keep from laughing.

"Bathroom's in there," I said, pulling him forward. "I put out a toothbrush for you. I found a new one in one of Rosie's drawers."

He nodded, blinking, then yawned. His jaw popped and his Adam's apple was more visible as he stretched.

"Brush your teeth."

"Right-o."

I clambered into the bed and turned on my e-reader. I listened with half an ear to Hayden's pre-bed ritual, and I wondered what it'd be like to brush our teeth together sometime. That thought led to another: us, getting ready to go out. Ken used a completely separate bathroom—the master one, natch. But with Hayden, I imagined him watching me brush my hair and maybe coat my lashes with mascara, enjoying the sight as we prepared for a night out together.

Thinking like that was crazy. I barely knew the man. Shame built in my chest because I was being ridiculous.

There was a difference between opening myself up to other people, helping them through their time of need, and leaping into a doomed relationship.

Besides, he might have a girlfriend. Crap.

After another couple of minutes of silence, I slid out of bed and knocked on the bathroom door.

"Hayden?"

"Unh?"

"You okay."

"Sure."

"Ready to come out and get in bed?"

"Mmm hmm."

"I'm opening the door."

"Yep."

I opened the door to find him leaning against the counter. He'd brushed his teeth, splashed water on his face if his wet lashes were any indicator. I smiled, surprised he was still so out of it.

"Need to do anything else?" I asked.

He glanced around the room, his eyes unfocused.

"Never mind."

I led him to the edge of the bed and sat him there while he watched me with owlish eyes. I unzipped his boots and pulled them off, setting them next to the door.

"Jeans on or off?"

"What?"

"How do you sleep?"

"In my boxers."

"So jeans off."

"Right-o."

I undid the snap and zipper. I bit my lip as I slid the pants off his lean hips and down his long, toned legs. A rolling line of music disappeared into the waistband of his boxer-briefs. I studied the black ink, my breathing escalating. Holy hell. That was sexy.

"Do you have a girlfriend?"

I folded his jeans into quarters and set them on the chair. I tugged off his socks and then yanked at the back of his T-shirt. He lifted his arms. He was tan everywhere. That sun-kissed look most of us Northwesterners never get because we lack sunlight and vitamin D.

He flopped back onto the bed, rolling onto his side, arm pushing under the pillow. Crap, he was going to be right up against me.

"Hayden, about that girlfriend."

"No girlfriend. No interest. No time."

Well. I'd asked, and he'd told me.

CHAPTER THIRTEEN
Hayden

I woke in the dark hour before dawn. My arm tingled from lack of circulation. A warm body was draped across my chest, hair tickling my nose.

Son of a bitch. I'd slept with some woman, and I couldn't remember any of it. That was low, even for me. I inhaled, trying to stave off frustration. A familiar scent filled my nose. I smoothed my hand down the woman's back, surprised to feel soft cotton over her sleep-warmed skin. A sigh of relief flooded my lungs. Briar.

Though I didn't remember much from last night after drinking a second beer, some glimpses of memories came back to me. She helped me to bed. That was it. Good. I'd hate to have no recollection of my first time with Briar.

She felt perfect, her breasts against my chest. I ignored the pinpricks shooting up my arm. I rubbed my free hand back up her spine. She sighed as she snuggled in closer.

My hand was at the base of her neck, the skin there so soft and delicate under my fingers. I cupped the back of her head, loving the way she fit against me.

Loud purring echoed through the room.

I glanced around, confused by the invisible Harley revving. But no, the noise came from the cat. Princess or Angel or some stupid name that embarrassed the hell out of the animal and gave the cat a complex. The name alone explained half its aggressive pissy-ness.

The cat jumped lightly onto the foot of the bed, and I tensed. Her blue-gray fur ruffled as she walked with all the sedate grace of a runway model up the side of the bed. Her whiskers twitched as she licked her thin kitty lips. I pulled Briar tighter into my embrace before I freed my arm closest to the beast.

We glared at each other, Briar between us. Somehow the purring got louder. Crikey, it was as many decibels as a jetliner.

Eyes still fixed on me, the cat lifted one soft, slightly fluffy paw and touched Briar's shoulder. I waited. The cat cocked its head and pushed with its paw again.

She added a soft *mmrrrooww*. Briar mumbled something, throwing her leg over my hip, snuggling closer.

I bit back a moan. Helluva way to wake up. Soft woman draped over my sex-starved equipment while the rest of my body was tensed against an imminent hellion attack.

The cat leaned its head down, eyes never leaving mine, and licked Briar's shoulder, the rough rasp of her tongue loud in the quiet room.

"What?" Briar cried out, her whole body bowing.

I scrambled out from under her before my dick took a beating.

"I'm feeding the cat."

"It's dark."

I smirked. Not a morning person then. I pressed her head back into the pillow, smoothing the hairs back from her warm cheek. "Sleep, Sweet Briar. I got this."

She settled back into the bed and her eyes slid shut, body relaxing into the mattress.

The cat exploded into a ball of angry hissing and batting paws. I lunged forward as Briar cried out, body curling into a protective posture as the cat pounced, back arched, spitting her anger.

I managed to get my hands under her fluffy belly. I could feel each of her ribs. Poor kitty. She was hungry. Really hungry. Briar said the cat wouldn't eat for the neighbor who was supposed to be feeding her. Even now, she struggled to get to Briar, the kind woman who fed her, talked to her, and probably reminded her of her owner. I ran from the bedroom.

Damn. All of us, even this blasted cat, were just looking for a connection. Someone to love.

The cat continued to hiss and meow until I started humming. I cuddled the cat against my chest as she shuddered, turning those big, guileless sapphire eyes up to me.

Sweet hell, I was falling for a cat. A cat that didn't even belong to the woman I wanted to sleep with. I was in so far over my head.

"Salmon coming up for Her Majesty."

The cat curled around my arm like a python, and purred loud enough to break apart the walls.

I gave Princess twice as much of the salmon as Briar tossed in her bowl the night before, adding some of the dry food I found in the pantry. Of course, smart kitty that she was, Princess munched on the salmon, her tail twitching with pleasure.

"Got it, love. You like a big brekkie. Does set the tone for the day, eh? Now to make coffee for the other princess still in bed."

Only there wasn't a coffeepot, at least not the kind I was used to. After looking through all the cupboards, I found a mesh contraption. A coffee filter? I heard footsteps padding toward me and turned to face the hall.

Hot damn. Briar's belly button, a shadow secret I wanted to take my time learning, peeked between the pink material of her cotton shorts and tank top. When my eyes drifted over the flare of her hips, my mouth went dry. Her legs were long and toned. She clearly enjoyed exercise and taking care of herself.

Briar's toenails sparkled in the dim light and a narrow silver chain circled her left ankle. I forced my gaze back up to her sleep-flushed face, willing my body back under control. Not that she wasn't aware of my interest. It was embarrassingly obvious.

"I was going to make you coffee. There's no pot."

Briar's smile could warm the southernmost tip of Tasmania. "This is Seattle. We take coffee seriously."

She walked right up to me, so close I could feel her hair slide across my chest. She'd let it down. It was pulled up, a few pieces straggling around her face, when she'd helped me into bed last night. I liked her hair both ways. She plucked the filter thing from my unresisting finger.

"I'm from Melbourne. So do we."

She tipped her head back and met my eyes. Hers were dark, almost navy. Her soft lips parted. An unconscious opening, I hoped, seeking my mouth, my tongue. Because I wanted to give her both. I slid my hand over her hip, settling at the curve of her waist, my fingers farther up her back as my thumb rubbed across her ribs.

Her eyes widened, her lips parted fully. "I'd like you to kiss me," she whispered.

Her voice, husky from sleep and need, was the best music ever. I brought my other hand up to cup her cheek, fingers in her silky hair, palm against her jaw. I tilted her head just how I wanted it and brought my head down. Keeping my eyes locked on hers, I waited.

"If I kiss you, I'm going to want to do so again." I drew her closer until her breasts touched my chest. Right where she belonged.

"I think I'm going to want you to do more than kiss me."

"This will take us past the friend agreement we made yesterday,"

I said as I pressed my lips to the very edge of her mouth, pulled back. We stared at each other for a long breath. She slid her arms around my neck.

"What do you want, Briar?"

"You," she whispered.

"I need to know. Exactly."

She pulled back a little, a small furrow building between her brows. Pain built in her eyes, muddying the vivid blue. Then she blinked, coming back to me. Taking a deep breath, she said, "I want to be with you, Hayden. I want you to make love to me, but I also want to spend time with you. I enjoy your company."

I pulled her flush against me, my hand splayed on her lower back, my fingers on the upper swell of her bum.

"I want that, too." I pressed my lips to hers, firm and sure of our mutual pleasure.

She melted into me further, quicksilver seeking its home. I shifted her jaw to give me deeper access, parting her lips with my tongue. Sweeping inside her mouth, I moaned, loving the warmth and hint of mint from her toothpaste. Her nipples pebbled against my chest, and I cupped the side of her breast. Her tongue slid over mine, touching, tasting, learning.

She cuddled closer, her belly cushioning my raging erection.

She grabbed fistfuls of my hair and strained into me. I flicked my thumb over her nipple and she moaned, arching her back into my body.

She pulled her tongue from mine and smoothed it over my bottom lip. Her teeth found that spot at the corner of my mouth and nipped. I dropped both hands to her hips and pulled her up, pressing her warm core to my hard dick.

This kiss was a rip curl thundering toward the beach. I never wanted to stop.

Briar's legs wrapped around my waist. I turned and set her on the counter, needing my hands free to touch all her soft skin. She tipped her head back as I pulled my mouth from hers, trailing my lips across her jaw and down her neck, my tongue and teeth teasing the spot where her collarbone dipped. I rolled her breast across my palm and her thighs squeezed my hips tighter, trying to pull me even closer.

I pulled down the strap of her tank top. I needed that lush little bud in my mouth. Now.

A sharp sting in my calf forced me back, and I yelped. Three red lines of blood dripped near my ankle. The cat stared up at me, all wide-eyed shock, her tail curled around her now-sheathed claws.

"I don't think the cat wants to share you," Briar said, her voice shaking with both laughter and need. "Rosie was just saying yesterday that she doesn't like many people. But she seems to like you."

"I can see why. She's a menace. A hungry menace."

Briar pressed her nose into the side of my neck. "I didn't want to stop."

I pulled back so she could see my eyes. "I wouldn't have if the she-beast hadn't clawed me."

"The heat between us is intense," she said, her eyes showing some of the vulnerability buried beneath the passion.

"Very," I said. I stepped back, putting some space between us so I didn't grab her again. "I've never wanted a woman like I want you."

Her cheeks flushed—with pleasure at my words?—but her eyes remained steady. "I know you're leaving."

"I have to. The less time I'm gone, the better. Not just for me, but for my band. For our fans. This isn't something I can fuck around with. Too many people are depending on me."

I pulled her back into my arms, not caring if the cat scratched me again. Briar tucked her head in, pressing tight against my chest. Her arms wound around me, and while this embrace wasn't as sexy as our kisses just moments before, it was intimate on a deeper level. I wasn't about to study the why too closely.

CHAPTER FOURTEEN
Briar

"How about this?" Hayden asked, pulling away just far enough to brush my hair back, his eyes roaming my face.

I wasn't supermodel material, but at least my features were symmetrical. My eyes and mouth were a bit too big for my narrow face, but my nose was straight and small, my chin softly rounded. I spent way too much money keeping my eyebrows thin and arched. My lashes were long but not as thick as I'd like, my eyes a boring blue. Lia said my coloring was striking, and because I'd never lacked for dates, I guessed that was at least somewhat true.

"I want to take you on a date tonight. A proper one. No hat and sunnies. No eating on the couch."

I nibbled my bottom lip, still plumped and sensitive from our make-out session. Hayden's kisses were addictive. I wanted more.

"If you're worried about the pap, we can eat in my suite," he said, rubbing his hands up and down my arms. "But we'll do it at a table. With candles and real glasses."

I blinked, forcing my train of thought away from all the places I wanted to lick, suck, and nuzzle. "I hadn't thought about the media."

He smiled, tucking a strand of my hair behind my ear. "Says the journalist."

"No, seriously I—"

"You're not much of a yabber either." He pressed a kiss to the sensitive skin right at the corner of my eye. Who knew that spot was such a turn-on? Or maybe I was just turned on because Hayden was touching me.

"So. Tonight?"

"I'd love to, but what about Princess?"

Hayden glanced down, staring at the fluffy ten pounds of fur wending between our legs. "We'll feed her again before we leave this morning and then stop here on the way back to my hotel. Does that work?"

I nodded. "You're sure you want to be seen with me? Written up with me in the media?"

He kissed the other side of my face, in the same spot. I couldn't suppress the shiver. "Yes."

"Then I agree."

"Smart woman."

I snorted. "I want some coffee."

"Then a run. A good ripper to get our blood flowing."

"My blood's already flowing," I said. "Has been since you've been in just your boxers."

He tugged my hair. "I planned to make you brekkie. But I couldn't find the coffee or the cackleberries."

"What?"

"Eggs. For an omelet."

"I like omelets." I licked my lips and leaned into his chest. "But I'd like to eat you more."

"Behave. The cat will rip me to shreds."

I opened the canister with the coffee and turned on the electric kettle. After pouring the boiling water carefully over the expensive ground beans, I handed Hayden a cup.

"Never seen a cuppa made like that."

"How do you do it? Straight up on a drip machine?"

He snorted. "I order out when I'm in Melbourne. Everywhere you go, even the shitty milk bar on the corner will have a fifty-thousand-dollar coffee machine on the counter. We list our coffee in terms of notes and accents and *terroir*. Like Napa does its wine. That would be annoying if the coffee wasn't so amazing. Sydney's not quite as good, but I haven't been spending much time there, even if it is where my mail goes."

"Well, now I'm worried about serving you coffee," I joked.

"I have to say my local coffee is better than the stuff I drank in Italy, and on par with that in Spain."

"Do you like the traveling?" I asked, hesitant.

"Not as much as I thought I would," he said, his eyes broody. "Cheers." He raised his mug in a salute and took a sip. "That's bloody fine," he murmured.

"As good as your Melbourne stuff?"

"Not likely, love. But good for a Yank effort."

"Keep talking to me like that and I won't go to dinner with you." I rolled my eyes.

He slid in close to my back, his hips bracketing mine, my head falling back into the solid wall of his chest. His free arm wrapped tight around my waist while he continued to sip his coffee.

"Hush. This is the best morning I've spent in years. Probably ever." Hayden rubbed his nose against the sensitive spot just behind my ear. I set my mug on the counter seconds before I dropped it. Between his words and his long body clad only in boxer-briefs, I'd never get past my quivering mass of hormones and focus on any task.

"Finish your coffee, love. We're off for a run."

"How'd you know I run?"

"With legs like that, you have to," Hayden said. His eyes heated as he took in my bare legs.

100

"You just want to see me in spandex," I joked, trying to ease the nearly insurmountable sexual tension building between us.

Hayden's grin was wide and naughty. I shivered as heat slid from my chest, down deep into my belly. I picked up my mug again, took another sip of the coffee.

"Fair dinkum. Get dressed. We're off."

I pouted as I set my mug in the sink.

"None of that, Sweet Briar."

"My dad used to call me that," I said.

"I can see why. You're sweet. Now, let's be off. I'm a man on a mission."

"Why?"

He flicked his index finger across my chin. "I've cracked on you. This is more than having a naughty." He shrugged at my silence and quite possibly the confusion on my face. "Sex. It's more than sharing a quick rub off."

"I'm glad we agree on that." Amusement warred with concern. I knew his band was waiting for him, just like I knew many musicians stashed lovers in every city-of-call. Even Doug, Lia's late husband, had treated that part of music as a given, setting up his sexual exploits in tandem with a new gig.

There'd always be someone competing for Hayden's attention, a woman trying to take my place, willing to do something more daring.

I went into the bedroom, subdued. Pulling out my workout clothes, I sighed in frustration. I didn't want to be the Seattle listing in Hayden's phone. I couldn't handle anything less than exclusive. Not with Hayden anyway. As I tied on my running shoes, I considered whether I should back out of dinner. Of seeing him for the rest of the time he was here. That would be the prudent decision.

Hayden was petting Princess's back when I entered the kitchen. He'd set out another plate of salmon, this one even bigger than the first he'd given her, and filled her dish with dry food. Her water dish was full and our mugs were in the dishwasher.

He even managed to make his day-old jeans and tee look sexy. He nodded when he saw my bag; it contained a change of clothes for after our run.

"Maybe dinner isn't a good idea," I blurted.

He crossed to me, his arms coming around my waist. I was stiff, not wanting to let him in further. Already, after less than twenty-four hours in his company, I was within inches of heartbreak. And I wanted him. Badly.

"I was trying to reassure you, and it came out all wrong. You want me to back off because we're in deep." He leaned his forehead against mine. "But I can't. Even with the shit my mum dumped on me, the time with you is the most honest—the most real—I've spent in years. That's what I meant."

"It's okay, Hayden. I've spent enough time around musicians to understand the lay of the land." I forced my eyes to his. "You're touring. That's a crazy schedule. You won't be in the same place for more than a couple days at most. And there's always something new to tempt you. Booze, women, drugs."

He rubbed his thumb from my cheek down to my lip. "I don't want to talk about the tour. I want to tell you how gorgeous you are. How much I enjoy your company. Having a cuppa with you, watching the sunrise, that was beautiful. So if it's just dinner, that'll be enough. Because you're the first real friend I've made in years.

But I'd be lying if I said I didn't want to shag you like crazy."

His arms around my waist kept me upright. His words, they melted every jaded edge I'd ever built. I sucked in a deep breath and forced my eyes to his.

"Whatever we're doing, it's profound," I said in a hushed voice. "I'm not sure I'm ready."

He pressed a kiss to the tip of my reddening nose. "I feel the same. But I'm not letting you out of my sight long enough to focus on all the reasons why this is crazy."

I shouldn't have agreed. But when he grabbed my hand, I let him pull me from the condo. After locking up, we rode the elevator in silence, his thumb continuing to rub the back of my hand. I drove to his hotel and we walked through the lobby, still holding hands. Sure, people gawked, but I chose not to care. I was going to enjoy this as long as I could.

CHAPTER FIFTEEN
Hayden

Briar set a grueling pace for longer than my typical route of five kilometers. She slowed as we approached the Pike Place Market District, her ponytail swishing across the back of her sweat-slicked neck. Thoughts of licking that salty wet spot had kept me going for the past fifteen minutes. She beelined toward the entrance of the market.

"Hey, Dave. How's the family?" she asked as she stopped in front of a long chrome counter. Dave was older, probably in his late forties, early fifties. Balding. Big nose, thin lips. His black T-shirt featured a white logo that read Dave's Coffee. Creative bloke. His arms were thick either from stacking boxes or eating large meals. Maybe both.

A man in the corner of the small space tracked Briar, his eyes devouring her exposed skin. I stepped in close, wrapping an arm around her waist and shooting the dickhead a back-off look. He grinned sheepishly and melted into the growing crowd.

It'd been so long since I'd felt possessive about a woman. I'd spent three years dating Allison Phillips, the last year at uni and then as I began the grueling process of turning my passion for music into a lucrative career. She'd broken our relationship off, telling me she was pregnant with some grad student's bub. Six days later, my dad's heart quit beating. While the events weren't related, I'd backed away from any further entanglements, always remembering those months as some of the toughest in my life.

I'd loved Allison. Or at least I'd been falling in love with her. I wasn't too clear on the difference. Just that my heart hurt when she left me.

I turned back in time to shake Dave's hand. His eyes scanned each of my features.

"G'day," I said.

"You're the Aussie rock star! From Jackaroo. Hot damn, Bri. You know the coolest people. Thanks for coming by."

"No worries. Briar wants a drink."

I glanced behind me, seeing the people beginning to turn toward me, rabid interest lighting their eyes. Crikey. I didn't want to do a meet and greet here, not with Briar.

"I told Hayden you have the best coffee in Seattle. He seems to think we can't compete with the stuff they brew in Melbourne."

Dave beamed, his double chin quivering with pride. A quick glance back from the corner of my eye showed more people's heads turning in our direction. The crowd behind us was growing.

I leaned in. "I'd like to keep the mob forming off Briar's back. Any way we can get those to go double-quick?"

Dave's face slackened with surprise as he saw the people loitering behind us. "Yeah. Course. Coffee's on me. Shoulda kept my big mouth shut." He glanced up again, a sheepish scowl flitting over his face.

"Is it always like this for you?" Briar asked, studying my tensing profile.

I shook my head. "Nah, just since the last EP landed. 'She's So Bad' got loads of airplay, even here. At least that's what the label told us."

She nodded, her eyes clouding with concern as the people pushed in closer. "It did. Though it's a pretty angry song."

"Hayden, can I get your autograph?" A girl's scream lifted over the early-morning hum of the place.

"Bollocks," I muttered. "Business calls." I dropped a kiss on Briar's surprised lips and turned toward the crowd.

"Step away from my girl, folks. I don't take kindly to the idea of her getting hemmed in or crushed."

I walked toward the small alcove that housed a few tables. "I need a pen," I said. A young woman in a suit handed over a pen and manila file folder. I signed her paper and smiled when she told me how much she loved "Arms of the Night."

"Bet Dave would appreciate you buying a cuppa. Best coffee in Seattle," I added with a wink.

Dave let Briar through to the back side of the counter, where she tried to stay out of his way, occasionally plating up a scone or bagging a muffin as Dave ran around the small coffee bar, filling orders. Resigned to my task, I smiled and chatted, giving fans our North American tour schedule and dodging questions about the replacement pianist Jackaroo brought in to cover for me.

"Just taking care of some family business," I said, eyes flicking toward Briar. They would be all buzzy about me showing up here while the rest of my band was headed to Asia.

I'd text my mates, let them know whatever pictures went live didn't show the whole situation.

"Are you dating her?" A college aged girl asked. She was pretty, her dark eyes framed by skin a shade lighter. Her thick, black hair was slicked back from her face, showing off high, elegant cheekbones and red-painted lips. I turned to look at Briar. Were we dating?

"We're serious," I said.

The girl glanced from me to Briar, who was helping Dave with a large to-go order. "Lucky woman."

"Pretty sure I'm the lucky one. G'day."

106

Twenty minutes later, I stood, stretching. I hated the cameras the most. Everyone had a cell phone, of course, and everyone assumed they had the right to invade my morning by taking pictures of me, sweat stained and thirsty. I knew photos were already loaded up across a multitude of social media and aggregator sites. This part of fame I could definitely do without. From the pinched look on Briar's face, I assumed she felt the same way. Bloody hell. I'd miscalculated.

I'd planned to wine and dine her tonight, wooing her until she was so enamored with me, the fame wouldn't bother her when the story about us hit. Media coverage would follow, as it always did, usually in the form of an unrelenting tidal wave, trying to suffocate me before I could paddle to the surface.

Dave motioned me over, his face serious and apologetic. Once I was behind the counter, he handed me a white paper sack.

"Sorry about the crush, man. I made you and Briar coffee. I threw in a bag of my favorite beans and some muffins."

"Appreciate the thought. You okay?" I asked, turning toward her.

Briar nodded, but I could see the worry forming at the corners of her eyes as a television news camera lifted over the crowd.

"I wondered if they'd show," I said. "I don't want to do an interview now."

"Took them nearly half an hour. Must be a busy news cycle," Briar said, some of her humor pushing through her concern.

"You have a back exit?" I asked.

Dave pulled back a thin curtain. The space he revealed was all stainless canisters and racks of baked goods. "Goes to the alley. Never thought I'd need it for more than deliveries." His laugh was nervous. "Good seeing you, Bri. Come back soon. Both of you. I'll do better with my excitement next time."

I clicked open the pen the young professional gave me and scrawled my name on one of Dave's to-go mugs.

"No worries, mate. It's been crazy since the album went live. Thanks for the cuppa."

I shepherded Briar, who held our coffees, out the back door, before leaning back against the ratty brick wall. I shut my eyes, drained. "I hate that part. Too many people."

"Don't all rock stars love their fans?" Briar asked. She took the bag from my hand.

I opened my eyes as she offered me a tall paper cup. "Buying our music, sure. I've never liked performing though. I mean, yes to the piano, no to the ferals."

"You say the oddest things."

"Ferals. Young crazy people."

"Ah." She took a sip of her drink, thinking. "That seems odd. To do something you don't really like."

"How's it different than half the adult population? And I didn't say I didn't like the people. I don't like them pressing on me, the expectation of being on, being interesting, being the rock star they've built up in their heads."

"Must be difficult to balance both ends," Briar said with a frown.

I shrugged as I sipped. "This is good, but still not as good as my stuff. I'll get you to Melbourne and show you how it's done."

Briar's lips flipped up in a reluctant smile. "Sure. I didn't think about you getting mobbed in there. I'm so sorry. The paparazzi are going to be looking for you now. I understand if you want to go back to your place, lie low."

"Why ever would you apologize? I'm the one who ruined our coffee date. It's the invasion of my space whenever I try to go out that I hate so much. I'm just a bloke who happens to play music. I want to take my girl to brekkie, same as the rest of the world."

"I should've been smarter," she fretted. "I really am sorry, Hayden."

"You should quit worrying. Now, time for a shower so we can go up to the hospice." I grabbed her hand, threading my fingers through hers. I pulled down my ball cap and put on my sunnies, pulling Briar back into the crowd.

———

Back at the hotel, I managed to answer a few e-mails from Flip and Ets, letting them know my mum's situation was deteriorating. As I wrote them, I couldn't stop picturing Briar naked under the hot water, soap bubbles dripping across her pale, soft skin as she showered just a few feet away from where I sat.

A ping sounded from my laptop and shook me from my fantasies. He'd responded immediately, in typical Ets fashion.

"See you met a bit of arse. Nice distraction. Hope she's making the death-walk easier."

I frowned at the screen. I wasn't answering that shit. Next message was from Harry. I wasn't sure he ever slept, not with the multiple stupid stunts Ets had pulled in the past year.

He wanted to know if he should send the label's publicist into the fray on the pictures that were popping up—pictures of Briar and me. A few were from lunch yesterday. We appeared calm, a couple enjoying a meal. I liked that.

No one was mentioning my mum yet. I blew out a relieved breath. More were from us today, both during and after our jog. Briar's face was guarded, eyes downcast at everyone in the market. Except in one photo.

I held my breath, her eyes grabbing me even through the thousands of pixels on my laptop. Her desire was so obvious, I found my fingers on the cool screen before I'd realized I'd lifted them.

I was already a hot mess, and I hadn't even slept with her yet.

I typed back to Harry. *Let people know she's important to me, and I'm asking for privacy during this difficult, personal time. Or whatever the hell you send out in a statement.*

He responded almost instantly. *One step ahead of you, mate. Press release is here. Give it a look-see, and I'll send it out in ten. And you owe me for holding Ets back. He said to tell you to stop shagging the sheila and get your arse back on tour.*

That wasn't what Ets said—his language would've been much worse. Well, Ets could just wait.

Reading through, I noted that Briar was a close personal friend. A sardonic smile formed on my lips as I signed off on the release and closed the laptop.

Standing, I stretched, scratching my full belly. Dave's muffin was good—made with those huge marionberries. No wonder Briar liked that place.

She stepped out of the bathroom, a hotel robe wrapped around her lean runner's body. I'd missed her whole shower. Figured.

Even from the distance, I could smell the fresh, floral scent of her shampoo. I grinned as she took a brush out of her bag and began running it through the wet strands of her hair.

"All yours. I didn't want to hog the space. I'll be ready in fifteen minutes."

"I won't." No way in hell I was going to be ready to leave with all her naked glory right here in front of me. Especially considering what awaited me. My lips curved up. This…this was a much, much better way to spend the morning.

She winced as the brush caught in her hair. I plucked the brush from her hand, falling victim to an overwhelming need to squeeze each gram of enjoyment from our time together. Maybe the expiration date on our shared time made each moment special.

I led her toward the big picture windows with great views of the sound. She glanced at me over her shoulder, and I pressed a soft kiss on the corner of her mouth. She inhaled, her body melting back into mine. Liked that, she did.

I grinned as I adjusted my grip on her. Taking my time, I placed more small kisses there.

She hummed deep in her throat, and I cupped her cheek. Pressing my lips to hers, I waited a heartbeat for her to part her lips. She did, and I slid my tongue into her mouth, lapping up her taste and fanning the flames of desire between us in long, lazy swipes of my tongue.

She moaned and struggled to turn fully into my arms. Blood pumping hot and thick through my veins, I stepped back and turned her until she once again faced the window. Lifting the brush, I swept it through her wet hair, letting it pull to the ends. Briar released a breath and relaxed.

"Mmm. You're good at brushing my hair."

I smiled at the slightly ragged quality of her voice.

"I've never done this before." I paused, hesitant to reveal too much of myself. But this was Briar. We were in a space that no one could enter. So I said, "Hair brushing or courting a woman. Never wanted to."

She turned her head a little, and I let the brush hover over her. Her blue eyes were dark. Her lips parted, a little swollen from my kiss. Her cheeks bloomed with soft pink color.

"I like firsts with you, Hayden."

I smiled, surprised by how much I agreed with her. I handed her back the brush. "Me, too. I'm going to grab a shower."

"Now?" she asked, surprised.

"Yeah," I said. "I need to wash off all the sweat."

"So—what? You kiss me like that then plan to leave me waiting?"

I raised an eyebrow, studying her flushed, strained face.

"Did you have a better idea?"

A smile curled across her luscious lips as she walked over to her bag, pulling out a pale pink bra. The sheer cups were edged with bright satin. She dropped the robe to the floor and picked up the matching panties.

I quit breathing. All that luscious, pale skin was on display. The long sweep of her spine flaring into her hips. The high, firm globes of her arse tapering into her trim thighs.

My eyes lifted to her back and I waited, breath bated deep in my chest, for her to turn around. I wanted her breasts in my hands, my tongue rolling her nipple into a tight bud.

She slid her panties up those white thighs. I groaned as the soft fabric cupped her bum. She put on her bra, hooking it quickly. She turned toward me, her long fingers cupping the outer edge of her bra. My mouth went dry.

"I'll just finish getting ready. Why don't you hop in the shower?"

Some sound came out of my mouth, something between a gasp and a groan. Briar smiled, her fingers running toward the top of her breasts, right at the edge of her bra.

CHAPTER SIXTEEN
Briar

I'd never been looked at the way he was staring at me. He made me feel sexy. Needed. Which made me needy in return. I shook my hair back over my shoulders and he gasped. Stepping nearer, I was close enough to see how dilated his pupils were. But he stepped back, hands shoved into the pockets of his sweats.

"What's wrong?"

He'd pulled back at Dave's shop, eyes glazing over and body language requesting space. I'd hoped he'd be better away from the crowd, but something in his attitude was still off.

"I'll grab some clean clothes. Be a second."

I gripped my fingers in his pullover. "Hayden. Are you angry with me? For taking you to the Market?"

I stumbled back when he swung toward me. His jaw was tight, lips compressed. Sighing, scrubbing his hands through his hair. He dropped his fingers to the upper swell of my chest, trailing them down over the cup of my bra where my fingers had been a moment before. Now that he was touching me, I could feel the need pouring off him, feeding mine.

"No, Briar. I'm not angry with you. I'm frustrated with myself. This thing we're starting—like you said, it's deep. I don't want to hurt you. I…" He blew out a breath. "It's just more real now that I'm here. The idea that I could end up like her. When I think about the episodes, the anger…I could pull someone down into that pit with me. I can't do that to you. I just can't."

I stepped in, ignoring his grunt. Wrapping my arms around his waist, I laid my head on his chest. He pulled me tight enough I struggled for a full breath. This demon he was fighting, his mother's illness and the old hurts it had caused, was winning.

"I'm happy to go visit your mom and Rosie. You can stay here or head over to the studio. Bill was serious about you using the key he gave you. Go bang out your aggression on the keys."

A laugh rumbled up his chest before spilling out his mouth.

"Thanks for that, love. There's a much better way to bang out my aggression, but I really want to woo you."

"Why?"

"For the first time in just about forever I've met someone who sees *me*. Who cares about *me*. And I want to make sure you understand it's reciprocated."

"I know you care about me." I sucked in a breath. "You can care about me more. In bed."

"My, you're primed." He leaned down and kissed my hairline, just above my forehead. "I'm getting you all covered in my sweat."

"I like your sweat," I panted.

"And I like you. More than I should. Let me go, Briar."

I obeyed, wondering if I'd just lost him completely.

Something showed on my face. Probably my fear. Hayden cupped my cheeks in both of his hands, pressed his lips against mine hard enough to clank teeth. His tongue was inside my mouth, ravenous. I gripped his hair near his nape and held on. He pulled away his lips on a groan that sounded almost like a sob. His lips trailed down my neck and I arched into him, my body more than ready to comply.

"Bloody hell, Briar. I can't stay away from you. And I should. I know I should. We're meeting at a time that's all about strong emotions. Those same reasons for getting together now will rip us up when these stolen moments unwind."

"I don't want you to stay away," I whispered. "Please don't shut me out."

"I can't seem to, and that's the hell of it." His tongue caressed the skin along my collarbone. "I'm going to hurt you. I realized how much it's going to hurt me to hurt you at the Market and again while brushing your hair. I like spending time with you, Briar. But I have to leave. Soon."

I cupped his cheek, waiting until he met my eyes. His swirled with dangerous emotions—too many to count. They mirrored my own. Which was why I'd tried to back out of dinner earlier. Unfortunately, at the Market I'd realized just how deep I was already in this relationship with Hayden.

Time to make a choice—one I hated making for myself. But we were both old enough to know that our emotions were tangling, and that was enough to give us pause.

Hayden and I shared more of ourselves in a short period of time than I'd ever shared with Ken in all my years with him. I wasn't playing safe; I wasn't pulling back and hiding behind my normal cloak of numbness. Neither was he. The result was electrifying and terrifying.

He waited, breath choppy.

"No." My voice was firm. "You'd hurt me more if you pushed me away now." I couldn't have spoken a truer statement. "Hayden, I've been around the block, I understand this is short-lived. You have a life somewhere else. Mine's here. But this is the time we have together. Leaving is going to be painful no matter what. Regrets will just make me feel worse."

He stared into my eyes, his still dark with anger and disappointment. We stayed like that, me in just my lingerie, his arms wrapped tight around me as I curved into his body.

"You are one smart lady. Or maybe I'm too confused from how much I want you to muster a logical response." He buried his nose in my cleavage.

"Nothing's stopping you." He looked up at me, and I met his gaze, holding mine level and sure.

His mouth settled over mine, softer this time, reverent. He backed me across the room, his kisses light but filled with emotion, his hands sliding from my hips to my waist, up my rib cage, to my breasts. His thumbs flicked across my aching nipples, and I arched forward plastering my body to his.

"Oh, please."

"You want this? Me, inside you?"

"God, yes."

He pushed me back against the mattress, which caught me behind the knees. I sprawled back, clawing at his shoulders as I fell. He smirked, eyes darkening.

"I'm deciding what to take off first."

"Don't tease me."

"Yes, lots of teasing. It's the anticipation that'll make this so much better."

I arched my hips off the bed, my fingers fumbling toward the elastic of his running pants. "Now. I want you now."

"Bossy." He sat back on his heels, nostrils flaring at the high-cut silk-and-lace panties playing peekaboo with my sex. "I like it."

He climbed over me, arms tensed to keep from putting any weight on me. I knew he was going to try to drive me crazy, and I didn't think I could stand a long buildup. I wrapped my legs

116

around his waist. I pushed off my far shoulder, landing on top of Hayden with a smug smirk.

His astonishment quickly turned darker, more sensual. "That was bloody sexy."

"You're sexy."

His hands palmed my bottom, thumbs smoothing in long strokes over the soft material. I leaned down, my smile pressed to his as we kissed again. And again. And again.

"You pinned me. What next? I'm yours for the taking, love."

Oh, that accent.

"Clothes. Off."

"This is your cricket match."

I leaned back to frown in confusion.

"It means do as you will," he said with a chuckle. "Condoms are over there." He waved vaguely. "I should get one."

He walked across the room and I licked my lips. As soon as he was back, I pushed his pullover and the still-damp T-shirt up over his ribs. I kissed my way up, my tongue learning each of his ribs, the dip between the two sides. I trailed my lips over the thick ridges of muscles that led down to his belly button. He hissed out a curse when my tongue delved into the small indention.

I squealed as I whirled, ending up under him again. "Too slow," he mumbled against my lips. Pulling my hands up over my head, his mouth sealed over my left nipple through my bra. "Sweet Briar. You feel better than I imagined. Taste sweeter than I hoped."

"Please."

"Ah, you like me in charge."

"Yes," I whispered.

He dipped his sun-kissed head. "Good." He nipped my shoul-

117

der, teeth scraping over the delicate skin there. I moaned, arching into him. We rolled again and he ran his hands down my sides to grip my hips.

"You're so responsive. That's bloody hot."

I wanted to tell him I'd never flamed this fast before. "Less talk," I panted.

Hayden leaned up, abs flexing—dear heaven—in a drool-worthy crunch to help me pull off his pullover and shirt. I ran my fingers down the inside of his arms and the outside of his ribs. He shivered. My fingers slid in a whisper-soft caress down over his stomach. We both moaned as my fingers slid lower, under the waistband of his sweats.

He fumbled, gripping my fingers as I trailed them lower. I huffed as he slid our hands up our bodies. He pulled his mouth from my neck.

I threaded my fingers through his hair, thrilled, as I kissed him. Long, hard, deep, just like I wanted him inside me. Digging my toes into the back of his sweats, I yanked them down. He pulled back, surprise and pride lighting his eyes.

"Good trick."

He toed off his shoes and shimmied out of his pants, sliding back up my naked limbs. My bra disappeared and I gasped at the sensation of skin touching skin. Hayden was hot. His skin sizzled against mine, and I pressed into him. More. I just needed more.

He went willingly as I rolled, but we'd misjudged the end of the bed. I yelped as we fell. He twisted, taking the brunt of the fall. We landed in a tangle of limbs.

"You okay?"

"Fine," I said. "Don't stop."

"Wasn't planning to."

He pushed my panties down over my hips. He palmed my hip-bone, his fingers finding the smooth flesh low between my legs. I arched upward as he slid his fingers lower, delving between my slick lips.

"Bare. Crikey, you're killing me. I've got to see this."

He pulled back, eyes traversing the length of my flushed body. I writhed as he pressed the pad of his thumb to my clitoris, two fingers sinking in deep, past the knuckle. I bit my lip, twisting into his hand and then away. I needed more of him.

Rotating his fingers, he rubbed against the front wall of my sex. His thumb turned a slow circle and my body bowed. I clawed at his shoulders as the ripples started deep inside, building, my body bucking with the strength of the release.

He ripped open the condom wrapper and slid into me just as the last tremors eased through my body. My muscles tensed immediately, primed and begging for more.

Hayden rose up on his elbows and cupped my cheeks, his fingers buried deep in my hair. "You feel amazing."

"Mmm."

"Did I leave you speechless, love?" he asked, leaning forward to press kisses to the corner of my mouth.

"You left me both relaxed and wound tight. You feel right inside of me."

I gripped his forearms as he pulled out. I lifted my hips up, but I was pinned under him. I waited, breathless, quivering. He slid back into me. Each stroke was strong, sure, and nudged me back toward the pinnacle I'd reached just moments before.

Desire bloomed hotter as he pumped into my body. His eyes

119

narrowed as he leaned down to kiss me. My nipples chafed against his chest hair. I tilted my hips and wrapped my legs high on his back, locking my ankles.

He bit my lip before rearing back to his knees. His hands slid to my hips and he pounded into me again and again, driving me up, up, up. And over.

CHAPTER SEVENTEEN
Hayden

Briar's face as the orgasm took her—I'd never forget her look of raw pleasure. That, more than the tight clench of her body, pushed me into my own release. I gritted my teeth, but the moan still ripped from my throat as I slammed into her as deep as she could take me.

The release quivered through my muscles in long pulls of pleasure. After I caught my breath, I rolled off her, surprised that my arms had collapsed and my full weight must be crushing her.

Her blue eyes were still dazed.

"Good for you then?" I asked, unable to keep the grin from flitting across my lips.

"Never orgasmed like that. Let alone twice. I figured multiples were like unicorns. A myth we tell women so they'll keep striving for that moment."

I kissed her. A soft one full of thanks. Her fingertips caressed my bristly cheeks.

"Maybe it's you," she said, her voice soft. "Maybe it's this way with all women."

I smoothed her damp hair back from her forehead. "No, it's us. Together."

She smiled, her eyes shining through her insecurity. I couldn't decide what she was worried about. Unless her ex told her any sexual dissatisfaction came from her not being enough instead of his not taking the time, slowing his pleasure, to love her properly. From what she'd told me, he was that kind of man.

"You sure?" she asked.

I didn't like her tentative. I kissed that spot I'd quickly become addicted to, just beneath her eye. "About this, yes. Now, time for a shower. Gotta clean you up, dirty girl."

"Someone has ideas. Great ideas."

I laughed, wrapping my arms around her narrow waist, pulling her tight to me as the stirrings of desire ignited once again within my body. I couldn't worry about anything but this moment. Even the dread of visiting my mum was dulled because Briar was going with me. She'd hold my hand and hold me up if I needed the help. Where I should feel fear, I only felt a deep, deep peace.

———

"Don't you listen to music when you drive?" I asked.

"All the time. But I'm nervous about you seeing my prepro-grammed stations. What if I listen to music you hate? Is that a deal breaker?"

Laughing, I leaned forward and pressed the On button. Rachael Yamagata's soulful voice filled the small space, offset by a soft piano melody.

"Nice," I purred, leaning my head back and mentally playing the keys with her.

"She's no Jackaroo," Briar said, lips quirking up. Her shoulders loosened.

"Save the flattery, love. After this morning, I'm plotting how to get you back in my bed." I glanced at her from the corner of my eye, watching that blush sweep up her neck. "Or in the shower as quick as possible."

"Behave," she said, but her voice was breathy, making me want

122

to pleasure her again. Instead, I leaned back into the seat and let the music wash over me.

I'd never much preferred being a passenger, but I didn't mind Briar taking the reins. I shied away from why that was, focusing instead on what I'd say to my mum. Had she talked to my father over the years? Why not contact me later, when I was older, more established? When she couldn't hurt me, at least not physically.

Dad had been circumspect about Mum's leaving and, really, about their relationship in general. I could count on one hand the times he'd mentioned her after we'd moved to Melbourne. He'd said that she needed time to get well.

But if he'd paid for her treatment at the center after her arrest, there'd be documents somewhere to prove her story. I would find them.

I squeezed Briar's fingers as I left her at the door to Rosie's room. She put her hand on the back of my neck and pulled me down for a kiss. It was just what I needed—soft and full of caring.

Buoyed, I walked into my mum's room. She was asleep, so I pulled out some notes on a new song I was working on. Mum stirred after an hour.

"Hayden?" she mumbled.

"Yep."

"Are you real or a dream?"

"Real."

She stared at me hard, her eyes unfocused. "I'm sorry I didn't contact you. I wanted to."

"Then why didn't you?" I asked.

"I was afraid." Her face crumpled and tears trickled from the corners of her eyes. The oxygen pumped in a harsh, steady rhythm, overriding her muted sobs. "You had every right to be angry with me."

I swallowed past the emotion building in my chest. "Thank you."

"I hurt you. I never wanted to hurt you but I did. I did."

I was silent, unsure how to respond.

"I was sure you must hate me after that last time," she said, a quiver filling her voice. "I wasn't a very good mother."

Kelly popped her head in.

"Okay if I take some vitals?" she asked.

It wasn't, but I didn't know how to tell her that. So I leaned back against the window ledge while Kelly talked to Mum, who was less coherent.

"Can you get him the box, Kelly? I want him to have it. I saved it for him."

I followed Kelly to the door. "Why's she so loopy?"

"We increased her pain meds. Arlene—the night nurse—said Miriam had a rough night."

"What does the higher dose of pain medication do? Why up them?"

Kelly touched my shoulder, something she did automatically, not out of comfort. "She's dying, Hayden. We're trying to keep her comfortable. I'll get that box. Be right back."

I grabbed her elbow as she turned away, took a deep breath, and forced myself to ask the real question. "So what's the timetable?"

Kelly shook her head. "Not long."

I went back into the room. Mum's eyes were closed, her breathing shallow. I leaned over her, caught the faint whiff of some scent I didn't like. "You can't do this...tell me you didn't contact me again for my sake and leave it at that."

Nothing. Disappointment slithered through me. I stared at her, willing her for an hour to open those nearly translucent eyelids. Like she had so often in the past, my mum chose to ignore me.

"Sorry it took a while. Emergency with another patient," Kelly puffed. "Here's that box."

It wasn't big. Which was its own disappointment somehow. Not much bigger than a shoebox. I eyed it, once again willing my mum to wake. She didn't.

Much as I wanted Briar here to steady me, this was too personal—something my mum's broken mind wanted me to have. I lifted the lid with an unsteady hand.

Two photo albums. I opened the first and stared at a familiar picture of my mum, her belly large with me. The photo must have been one of my dad's favorites to have made it into both their collections. The rest of the spread showed me at birth and within the first days of life. My life, each milestone, each year, meticulously catalogued. I blinked back the moisture building in my eyes when I got to a photo from my eleventh birthday. That was the first one I celebrated in Melbourne. I flipped by each of my school pictures, the newspaper articles from my concerts.

I set aside the book and opened the next. My high school self stared back. Flipping the page, I found a few candids of me heading off to college, home for a long weekend my sophomore year with my hair dyed blue and a piercing through my eyebrow.

I rubbed the spot absently, shocked at the memory. Dad had hated the piercing so much I'd taken it out just to get him to stop complaining. God, I'd nearly forgotten.

Ten pages in and the pictures stopped. My life—my mum's knowledge of it—ended with a write-up in the Sydney paper. We'd just signed our first record deal. Within two years I'd be here, a rocker at the top of the world stage, trying hard to keep his emotions together as he held his mother's pitiful attempt to stay connected to his life.

I flipped through the rest of the pages in quick succession. Not a note. Nothing to apologize for beating the shit out of me that day or for leaving my dad to raise a child alone. No mention of her bipolar disorder. Not a whiff of concern at the possibility of passing the disease on to me.

I shut the book and leaned my head back against the uncomfortable armchair. Crikey. She'd thrown me with this.

Because within the albums, I sensed her love, her need to connect, just as she'd said yesterday. But she hadn't done the one thing *I* needed—contact me. Let me know she cared.

She didn't wake the rest of the time I stayed there.

I stood, stretched my stiff joints, and walked down the hall. Briar was laughing with her friend. My smile was instantaneous and caused me to pull up short of the door.

Briar had managed to burrow deep inside me so quickly. We probably wouldn't last, because this much emotion would flame out. Wouldn't it?

Probably. I rubbed my eyes. I didn't know what to think about any of this. I stepped forward, needing to get out.

"Hey," Briar said from the chair across the room. My chest compressed with a thick ache at the sight of her. She waved me in. "Rosie, this is Hayden."

"I saw you perform in Melbourne years ago. That's when I still traveled, obviously." Her eyes sparkled, yellow edged into her healthy complexion.

My mum was further along this same path. I swallowed as the realization struck: my mother mightn't wake back up.

"G'day, Rosie. Hope you liked the show, then. Met your cat, Princess. She's prickly as."

I glanced over at Briar, still unprepared for her searching look. I didn't need that now. The ache in my chest was building into a burn. If I didn't do something soon, the pain would consume me.

"Mum's not waking and I need a bite. Can I grab you something?"

"Briar was just coming to find you. It's my nap time," Rosie said, her voice full of sardonic humor. "Dying people have similar schedules to toddlers. We don't always act much better, either."

Her eyes were full of understanding and sympathy as they met mine. I didn't want a person I'd never met before to feel sorry for me.

"Right-o. I'll be out front," I said to Briar. "Come out when you're ready."

Briar nodded, but hurt crept into her big blue eyes. Dammit. I'd already fucked this up.

Briar leaned down to hug her friend, undeterred by the wires and the frailty of Rosie's body. I shuddered.

I strode through the building, needing away from the stale, antiseptic air. Shoving through the doors, I didn't bother to stop when I hit the light mist.

My mum could've figured out a way to make spending time with me happen. People with bipolar disorder developed and maintained strong, healthy relationships with their kids. One of my friends in high school struggled with the disorder until she was properly diagnosed and treated. I'd looked her up on social media during the interminable wait for those bloody photo albums. Now, Julia was a doctor with a six-year-old son. That's what medication did—gave Julia a life. My mum could've chosen that route, too.

But she hadn't, so she couldn't have wanted me. Not if she'd never contacted me. No matter how painstaking her collection of my life's work—she hadn't tried once to contact me.

I was a bad mother.

My fingers tangled in my hair. She ruddy well was. Deathbed confessions and changes of heart were too little too late.

Briar's hand slid up my shoulder to tangle in my hair. I pulled her into my arms, my nose buried in her neck. My shoulders shook.

What. The. Hell?

"They happen," Briar said, voice low, soothing.

"What happen?"

"Bad days. Especially here. Shows you just how unfair life is."

"She drops that shit on me yesterday, and she can't even wake up long enough to explain her reasons. Not that there's one that'll make sense." I stepped back. Grabbing her hand, I pulled her toward her car.

"Maybe it's just as well, Hayden. You're really upset."

"She left me a box. My bloody inheritance to show she'd kept up with my musical career. As if that'd make up for her lack of interest for nearly twenty years. You drive. I'm still trying to remember which side the steering wheel's on."

She shook her head as she clambered into her car. I slammed the door shut, catching the faint glint of a telephoto lens. I turned from the paparazzi, refusing to give them more than they'd already managed to take.

Briar waited until I was buckled into my seat before starting the ignition. "What's your eating pleasure?"

I discarded the idea of telling her about our photo tail. Not much I could do about it.

"You're the Seattle expert. Surprise me."

"I know the perfect place." She pulled out her phone. Her thumbs moved over the screen with surprising speed. A moment later, her phone beeped with the distinct ding of an incoming text. She smiled. "Perfect. The pap won't be able to follow."

"You saw him."

Briar rolled her eyes. "You can call it reporter instinct. Now, let's see if I can lose him." She touched the side of her nose, and for some unknown reason, I smiled.

Briar drove through the city, eyes intent on the traffic around her. After many twists, turns, and last-second u-eys, she pulled into the lot behind a rambling wooden warehouse. No signage. She opened her car door, so I did, too. Getting out, my arms prickled with the faint chill from the light breeze. So different from Sydney's muggy, drugging summer warmth.

"Here we are. The original bottling location for Dogwash Brewery."

"I think you brought me here to kill me. Looks creepy enough."

She edged in closer, and I threw my arm across her shoulders, bringing her in tight to the line of my body. I wanted her closer, me inside her, but she hadn't offered. Plus, we were out of the car, here in this hellhole of a parking lot.

"I know Dan, the owner. I wrote a piece on him years ago, when he'd just started brewing. He has a small kitchen on-site. His club's killer."

"All this talk of death. Let's try something else for a mo', shall we? But eating, I'm good with that. The muffin was great but not filling. I'm close to gnawing off your pretty fingers."

"It's especially good when paired with their Golden Retriever Blonde."

"What is it with you Yanks and pets?"

Briar shrugged. "We like animals in the Pacific Northwest. We also recycle everything that we can—and some things we probably can't just to feel superior—and refuse to fluoridate our water." She led me around some crates and to a back door. She knocked twice, hard. "It's part of our charm. Along with gray skies, cool temperatures, and some of the most vibrant greenery in the country."

We waited. The alley was clean but narrow. Too dark and secluded, especially for a woman alone. Briar slammed her fist against the door again.

"This better be good," growled a voice. The door flung inward, revealing a large man. He must've weighed in at one hundred and fifty kilos, maybe more. I edged in front of Briar when he frowned. She elbowed me back and fell into the man's arms.

"Good, it's you! I haven't seen you in months," the man howled, a grin splitting his wide, jowly face. "So glad you let me know you're back in town. How's your sister? What's Abbi up to? Simon—he and Ella good?"

I cleared my throat, feeling like an arse, standing here while Briar was mauled by a guy with a good fifty kilos on me.

"Dan, this is my boyfriend, Hayden." Briar pulled out of the hoss's arms to beam at me.

Boyfriend. The title settled with surprising ease, especially when I wrapped my arm around her waist.

"Briar's got herself a man." Dan clapped his hands, rubbing them together like villains do in movies. My stiff shoulders tensed more. "Oh, this is too good! Wait. You aren't a doctor, right? No

God complex?"

"No, mate. I'm a musician. Very human. Probably neurotic."

"And you're foreign. You play country music?"

"Some influences, sure, but mostly alt rock."

"Meh. Not my thing. Still, glad you're not a doctor." Dan pulled me into a bear hug that was even tighter than some of my wrestling matches in school. More like the full body plaster I loved to give Briar. He leaned down and I worried the yobbo was going to kiss me. Instead, he whispered, "Hurt her and I'll kill you."

I nodded the little bit I could manage against his massive chest. "Got it, mate. How about a little less manhandling? I prefer the women. Well, one lady, anyway."

Dan released me. I stumbled back. The man was as high as the koalas that nibbled Eucalyptus leaves all day.

His laugh rumbled across the room. I turned wide eyes toward Briar. Why the hell did she bring me to meet this nutcase? She smiled and shook her head.

"Relax." She took my hand, and, damn me, I did. I trusted her. The weight in my chest eased, but my brain fired a million reasons why trust was stupid, making me dizzy.

"Like I said in my text, we could really use one of your sandwiches." Briar batted her long lashes over those big blue eyes, and Dan melted even faster than I did. Good to know I wasn't the only one, but, at the same time, I didn't like the way he reacted to my girlfriend.

"Beer first. I've got a new one you need to try, Bri."

Dan pirouetted—something I never would've believed possible if I hadn't seen the move with my own eyes—and trundled across the room, weaving between about ten battered oak tables. The chairs were sturdy, clean, but the faint smell of spilled beer leached from the floor.

"Dan's part of the Northwest's microbrew movement. I met him about eight years ago just after he'd leased this place," Briar said as we followed Dan, her fingers entwined with mine.

"This girl has one helluva beer nose on her. Hasn't missed one yet."

Dan set us up in the spotless industrial kitchen bristling with stainless steel. At one of those huge, clear-glass fridges, he pulled out a cask. Setting it on the counter, he poured three froth-topped pints and shoved one in Briar's hand before handing me mine. Lifting his glass, he waited.

Briar sipped, smacked her lips. Her brow wrinkled as she sipped again. "Wheat and rye?"

Dan boomed out a laugh, reminding me again of an angry bear. "Nothing gets by you, Bri."

"Lemon?"

"Yeah, the peel." Dan turned to me. "Well? What do you think?"

I took a tentative sip, let the liquid roll across my tongue. "I'm Aussie. We love beer. Practically raised on the stuff. This, though, this is special. Better than a lot of the drub I've tried."

"My summer special now that it has Briar's stamp of approval," Dan paused, eyebrows raised. At Briar's nod, he smiled. "I'll put it on the menu at our place."

"So this isn't your restaurant?" I asked.

"This is my brewery. Where I try some recipes to see if I want to put them on the menu for my restaurant. About that lunch."

Dan busied himself in the kitchen as Briar's phone buzzed. She fumbled to pull the case from her pocket. A quick smile flashed across her face, her eyes all lit up bluer than Sydney Harbour.

"My sister just confirmed she and Asher are coming into town. Asher's set up an acoustic jam at The Vera Project. It's a local music venue. Lots of bands play there. Want to come with?"

"Of course! Well, if I'm still here."

Her face fell, a frown building, but she ducked her head and responded.

"Hey," I said. "I hope to be. I'm really interested in what Asher will do to arrange his big electric pieces to acoustic."

She finished her text. "I told Lia we'd meet up with her some time tomorrow if you're still around. She said she hopes to meet you."

"Is she like you?"

Briar shrugged. Dan slid a couple of plates in front of us and I picked up a crisp to munch.

"Nah. Lia's quieter. More of a watcher even than our Bri. She's got this aura," Dan said, narrowing his eyes as he considered. He set his own plate down, gulped his beer. "Zen-like."

"Just like you, then. An angel of calm." I bit into my sandwich. "This is really good."

Briar's lips lifted up in the semblance of a smile, but she seemed worried.

CHAPTER EIGHTEEN
Briar

Watching Hayden come close to unraveling earlier was hard, but not as hard as when he'd pulled back from me in Rosie's room. He'd been ready to bolt when he met Dan. Thankfully, the food and beer relaxed him enough to enjoy the meal, even crack a couple of jokes.

This wasn't the same man I'd seen last night at Rosie's, or even this morning in his hotel suite, and little shivers of worry crept up my spine.

"Bye, Dan. Thanks for lunch. And the beer."

"Any time, Briar. You know that."

I stood on tiptoe and kissed Dan's cheek, surprised when Hayden shifted closer to me. I bit back a smile. He was staking his claim. On me. Hayden's fingers curled into my waist as he held out his hand.

"Thanks, mate. The beer was fantastic."

Dan beamed. "Maybe I'll make something and name it after you. Even if you don't play good ol' country."

"If you do, I'll send you some autographed stuff."

Dan's smile grew. "Well, then, that's mighty nice. An Aussie rock star in my brewery. What a day."

Hayden walked me to the door, opened it, and waited for me to step out. I sighed at the drizzle. I pulled my sweater tighter at my neck.

"How do you handle this weather?"

"You get used to it." Which was true. *Used to* didn't mean *like*.

"Don't women worry their hair will frizz and their makeup will smear?"

I opened the car door, and Hayden waited for me to climb in before shutting it and sliding himself into the passenger's seat.

"My hair is always frizzy, and I don't wear much makeup, just in case."

Hayden turned to look at me. "I like the way you look, Briar. You're beautiful. The little beads of water in your hair give you a halo. I meant what I said earlier. You're my personal angel." He leaned forward, his large hand cupping my cheek as he brought his lips to mine. It started sweet, but the desire we felt burst across our skin. I leaned closer, needing more, as Hayden plundered my mouth.

I moaned low and deep in my throat, my hands cupping his cheeks.

"I want you," Hayden breathed against my lips.

"Yes."

"I'd take you here, in this car, if I could get away with it."

"Yes."

Hayden shook his head, a smile tugging his lips. I pressed mine to his again, licking across his bottom one before dipping my tongue into his mouth. Once again, he broke the kiss off. I whimpered.

"Much fun as illicit sex would be, I don't want anyone else getting an eyeful of your tits." He slid his hand down over my needy chest, massaging the area with his large palm. I couldn't get enough of this man. "Take us back to the hotel. Now."

"Bossy."

Hayden bent his head to bite the side of my neck. "You like it."

"I do," I breathed.

He leaned back into his seat. "Buckle up, Briar. We have deals to complete."

I sat back and clicked on my seat belt. "I'm just a deal, huh?

Merger, I guess."

Hayden rubbed his finger over his upper lip. "I have a feeling you're too much to be categorized." He glanced out the windshield, his thick blond brows pulling into a tight V over his nose. "I don't do this with women. I'm not much for affairs, and I'm definitely not into relationships. Not with my work schedule."

I gripped the steering wheel, my stomach burning as I stared straight out the front, too. "So you're telling me you want to keep this thing casual." I bit my lip, fighting back the tears building behind my eyes. "I shouldn't have introduced you to Dan as my boyfriend."

Hayden's large hand slid, warm, safe, over my white-knuckled one. "No, love. That's not what I meant. This is special. But it's not how I do things." He blew out a breath and leaned his head forward into his hands. "Crikey, I'm making a blow of this."

I smiled, feeling more settled. "Good. I've never slept with a man until we'd been dating for three months. My own personal rule after Lia got pregnant at eighteen. I didn't want to end up with a child tying me to a man I didn't like."

Hayden leaned back in his seat. "Makes sense. Glad you made the exception for me."

That burn rekindled low in my belly. This time from desire. "Not sure I had a choice."

"Right-o. Let's find that bed."

I started the car and pulled out of the lot. "I have to feed Princess. Clean clothes would be a good idea, too."

"To Rosie's then. Don't you have a place here?"

I shook my head. "I lived with Ken."

Silence.

I braved a glance. Hayden wasn't happy. "So you just broke up." His voice was filled with censure.

"No. I stayed with Lia for a while."

"So how long have you and the wanker been off?"

"A couple of months."

"He was there yesterday. Talking to you."

"Actually, he threatened me and called me names. We didn't talk at all."

He grunted, his scowl fierce. "I want to shove his head up his arse."

After a long tense moment, he turned up the music so Jose Gonzalez's new song filled the space. He leaned back, closed his eyes. I didn't know how to take that, exactly, so I drove us back to Rosie's condo, my mouth shut and my mind spinning too fast.

When I exited the car, I shivered, palms cupping my elbows. Even though we were underground, the rain cooled the air. Hayden slid his arm around my waist, pulling me close and sharing his body heat. We rode the elevator up to Rosic's floor in silence.

Once we were inside the condo, Hayden leaned down to pet Princess, who purred at his feet, while I went to the kitchen and pulled out the salmon. After leaving her a slab big enough to feed Dan, I headed into the bedroom, hoping I'd packed a dress. I hadn't packed much—anything—when I left Ken the first time. I'd stolen some items out of both Lia's and Abbi's closets, but I hadn't done much shopping. At first, I'd moped, then I'd needed to get Lia through her breakup with Asher—a breakup that turned out to be a miscommunication. Now…well, I didn't know what I was doing now.

"I don't like the wanker doctor," Hayden said as he stalked into the room.

"Why are we talking about Ken?"

"The idea of you with him makes me crazy."

I spread my arms. "That was before we met. And I haven't been with him in months."

Hayden stalked closer, his hands tunneling through my hair. He cupped the back of my head, forcing my eyes up to his. He searched them before his lips claimed mine. I gripped his biceps, shuffling in closer. Hayden tilted my head, sliding his tongue deeper into my mouth. I moaned as he sought out all my secrets.

He pulled back and met my eyes. "I'm it. The only one you think about like this."

I shivered, turned on even more now that Hayden was jealous. "You are."

"I'll make sure of that."

"Sweet Briar."

I swatted at the hand brushing my bangs back from my cheek. Hayden chuckled. "You're a feisty one."

I blinked and sat up. "What time is it?"

"About six. We both fell hard into sleep. Seems we've worn each other out," he said, wiggling his eyebrows.

I couldn't think of the last time I'd napped. But between worrying over Rosie and fearing Princess would try to maul me, I wasn't sleeping much.

"Gotta get up now, love. We have a dinner date."

"We do?" I yawned, blinking up at him. He was dressed once again, but his hair was damp. I pouted. "I wanted to shower with you."

"Then I would never have gotten to take you out for a proper meal."

"I like you for dinner better."

He grinned before leaning in to press a kiss to my forehead. I grabbed him, but he slid from my grasp.

"Shower if you want. Might want to take off your boots to do it." He winked.

I laughed. My jeans and panties were bunched at my ankles. "I can't feel my feet."

He pulled off my shoes and then the rest of my clothes, rubbing my toes. I fell back on the bed, luxuriating in the moment.

"I made a rezzy for seven thirty." He stepped back and offered me his hand, which I accepted.

"Where are we going?" I stretched. Hayden ran the tip of his finger across my breast, and I shivered.

"Six Seven. I'd take you somewhere else if you prefer. But the hotel should give us the most privacy."

He rubbed the back of his neck and glanced at me. I smiled to reassure him.

"That sounds great. A quick commute back to your place." I winked.

"Thinking to take advantage of this, are we?"

I bit my index finger as I gave him a very thorough once-over. "Yes."

His nostrils flared. "Good." He cleared his throat and stepped back again. "I'll, uh, I'm going to top up Princess's tucker."

He turned and left before I could ask what that meant. I shrugged, instead focusing on getting clean.

My shower was short but hot. I'd opted to not wash my hair, hoping the steam would make it more manageable.

I grabbed the one dress I found—black with a flirty asymmetrical hem that started about three inches above my knees in the front and fell to midcalf in the back. I dug out my one pair of strappy, heeled sandals and a cream-colored teddy I'd spent way too much money on. I considered it for a moment; the lace was delicate, soft. While the lingerie didn't add any cleavage to my narrow chest, the cloth caressed my skin and made me feel sexy.

I slid into my clothing with quick, efficient movements. After a short internal debate, I added enough clothes for a couple of days into my suitcase.

Hayden was in the living room, typing something on his phone when I came out. His breath passed his teeth so I twirled.

"Will this do?"

"How about room service?" he asked, his voice strained.

"Just because I'm toting a suitcase and you orgasmed me into a two-hour nap does not mean I'm without scruples. You promised me dinner."

"I promised to court you," he said, picking up my hand and kissing the back of each knuckle, pausing long enough to let his tongue drift over them. By the time he finished, I was breathless, more than ready to skip not only the restaurant but the meal altogether.

"You look gorgeous, Sweet Briar."

He winked, and I'm pretty sure I moaned. That look combined with the rich timbre of his voice multiplied by his accent—I didn't stand a chance.

"I want to show you off nearly as much as I want to unwrap you.

Bye, Princess. We'll see you in the morning. Not early." With one last pat to the cat's back, he opened the condo's door, taking the suitcase from me. I locked the door and hiked my purse back up on my shoulder. I hated carrying it, but I had too many items I wanted with me tonight, and no pockets.

"Walk in front of me." He hummed low in his throat. "I like the long skirt, but I can't stare at your legs."

I stopped walking and gaped at him.

"Come here. I want to put my hand on the swell of your hip and see if I can figure out what kind of panties you're wearing."

I strode into his open arm and thrilled when he pulled me into his side. His fingers drifted over the soft silk.

"Mmm, not much of anything back here. No wonder I didn't see any lines when I was ogling your bum."

I laughed, shaking my head. The elevator opened and we stepped in, ignoring the three other people in there. Something about bantering with Hayden narrowed my focus so I forgot the rest of the world existed.

"You're Hayden Crewe," someone behind us gasped.

I glanced at Hayden from the corner of my eye, his face tensing in that look I was beginning to realize was him erecting his emotional wall.

I laughed as I faced the woman who was a couple of years younger than me and very pretty. "You mean Larry?" I pointed at Hayden, keeping a little smile on my face.

"Larry?" the woman asked, frowning as she studied the back of Hayden's head. "He looks just like Hayden Crewe. The singer from Jackaroo. That's an Australian band."

I opened my eyes wider. "Hear that, Larry? Australia has musicians. I was told they only had movie stars," I mused, leaning in closer before winking. "The country's best exports."

Hayden made a choked sound and I could see the smile trying to break across his face. I turned to face the woman. "Have you been to Australia?"

She shook her head, still studying Hayden's back. I didn't like the proprietary way she eyed him, like she could see all the sexy dips and ridges.

"I hear it's all desert and totally barren. There're more kangaroos than people. And the dingoes eat people." I shuddered.

The elevator dinged, opening to the garage level. Hayden pulled me forward quickly, forcing me to run in my heels. I wasn't at my best in heels, period. Definitely not running.

He glanced back, making sure the woman wasn't following us. She was still staring at us, so Hayden pulled me behind one of the big concrete pillars. He pressed his mouth against my bare shoulder, his arms around my waist. He laughed, trying to muffle the sound.

"Crikey, Briar. Dingoes eat people?" He laughed again, harder.

I shrugged. "You didn't have to talk to her."

"Brilliant, love. You gave her a phobia of an entire country."

I picked at the seam of my skirt. "She was looking at you like she wanted to lick you all over."

"I know that feeling. It's what I want to do to you all the time."

I blew out a breath. "I'm not used to jealousy. It's not me."

He leaned down and placed a soft, sweet kiss on my lips. "It's us. Now, about that dinner."

I pouted. "Maybe I should just go back upstairs and hang out with Princess."

"None of that." He flicked his finger over my protruding lower lip, then headed toward my car. "I've made it very clear I'm into you. If you've forgotten, I'll prove how into you I am again after I wine and dine you."

"I do like dining."

"And I like eating with you." A wistful expression crossed his face. "She's lonely," he said as he handed me into the car. "Princess. Handles it like a hellion, but I understand."

"You do? Why?"

He ran his hand through his hair before rubbing the base of his neck. "Having people there to share those moods with—it's the difference between lonely and loved."

I bit the inside of my cheek, taking a deep breath so that I wouldn't shed tears for the boy he'd been, turning into the reticent man he'd become.

Part of my previous job was to pay attention. Hayden interacted with others—his fans, the nursing staff, even his mother—with diffidence. Now, I was sure his mother was the catalyst.

But with me, Hayden was more open. The more he showed me, the more I craved. Keeping Hayden wasn't an option. No matter how much I'd fantasized about it. When he wasn't on tour, he lived in Sydney. I lived in Seattle. Which made each moment, each revelation sweeter. And one tick of the clock closer to my imminent heartbreak.

CHAPTER NINETEEN
Hayden

I'd always loved the quote about music filling the cup of silence. For me, music filled my lonely moments after my mum left, and filled the gaping hole when my dad died. It was my constant companion, the one thing I could truly count on, whether it came through speakers, my own fingers, or just played in my head.

But for the first time in my life, I wasn't concentrating on music. There was someone—Briar—filling the holes in me. Her mannerisms fascinated me, like the way she tilted her head and her hair spilled across her pale, rounded shoulder. Sure, it all came back to wanting her. I did, more with each time we made love. But I liked her. I liked how I could focus on what she said and just listen. And that scared the shit out of me.

Music was my buffer. My escape. And with Briar, I didn't feel the compulsion to seek it out. To use it—to keep away whatever was there on the other side of the music.

I glanced over at her as she pulled up to the valet stand. I picked up her hand where it rested in her lap and kissed her middle knuckle. She smiled at me, a real one that lit up her eyes and made them bluer than the ocean just beyond Brighton.

"I'm looking forward to eating here," she said.

"Ah, but there's more to the evening than just dining."

She raised one of those thin brown brows and waited. I clamped my lips together and shook my head.

"Nope. I'm not going to let you do your quince."

She rolled her eyes and giggled. "I have no idea what you just said."

"It's like we *almost* speak the same language."

Her eyes flared, and that blush I'd come to love bloomed across her cheeks. "We seem to understand each other pretty well."

I leaned toward her, using my far hand to cup her jaw. "Keep that up and you won't get out of the car."

"That's a possibility?" Her voice was breathy.

A young man in uniform walked toward the car. The valet.

"Not with a valet standing there. And, anyway, I have plans," I said. "Courting plans."

I opened my door and stepped out. The valet opened Briar's door and helped her out of the car. We met near the boot, and the distinct click of a camera filled the air. I tried to keep my body relaxed, but Briar glanced up into my face. After searching, her eyes lit on the paparazzi off to our left, near the entrance.

"Come on," I said on a sigh. I opened the boot and pulled out her luggage, trying not to care that our moment was being photographed. Times like these, I wished I'd chosen another career—anything without the glare of fame. My jaw tightened as I walked Briar into the hotel, my hand riding low on her back.

With a mental *fuck off*, I stepped into the lobby.

"You still have your key card?" I asked.

Briar nodded.

"I'm going to stop at the desk for a moment. You go on up." I offered her the handle of her suitcase and smiled.

She took the handle, glanced back at the entrance, and nodded. Best thing about Briar was how quick her mind was. Her eyes held hesitation but she leaned up and kissed me. I liked that. A lot. Too much for a crowded lobby.

I squeezed her waist gently.

"I'll meet you upstairs."

Her bum swayed in the flirty skirt as she walked toward the bank of elevators. A lovely arse. I really wanted to touch it. But first...I approached the concierge and let him know about the problem with the photographer. After repeated assurances the staff would take care of it, I slid my hands into my jeans pockets and headed upstairs, anticipation and lust mixing to form a lovely cocktail in my stomach.

———◆———

After changing into nicer jeans—it's all I wore, really, besides my workout clothes—and a button-down, Briar and I headed down to the restaurant. I'd suggested she leave everything but her wrap in our room. We'd return upstairs after our meal. No sense in dragging a pack she wouldn't need.

Our table was next to the floor-to-ceiling windows, offering an unobstructed view of the sound. The sun hung low in the sky, a fiery ball of crimson that splashed a soft light on Briar's skin, making it glow.

She was lovely, and I was hopeful we could figure out a way to continue to see each other. I didn't throw around the *girlfriend* title lightly. I hadn't had one in years. More important than what I called her, I was going to miss Briar heaps. Too much to leave her behind permanently.

But my mates were waiting on me, and I wasn't sure how much longer I could hold off. I'd missed one show, which the band canceled, eating the cost. Tomorrow they would have Pete sitting at my piano. My fingers itched. I hated the idea of someone else touching my piano keys. I'd found the perfect instrument, the one with just the right weight and balance. I didn't want Pete fouling up my instrument.

I dropped my napkin in my lap as I realized this was the first time I'd thought about my tour and band mates in hours. I stared out at the placid blue water, needing a moment to analyze what that could mean.

More than I wanted it to, I was sure. This thing with Briar caught me on my heels. She pried my stiff fingers from the menu. The warmth from her hand and the soft "hey" were enough to draw me back in. I turned and focused on her beautiful blue eyes. Brighter than the water outside, for certain.

"I'm assuming the seafood's good here."

"Of course. You don't want to tell me where you went?" She rubbed her thumb over the back of my hand.

I shook my head. This was our moment—maybe our last one—and I wanted a fair go at romance. Briar deserved that much. More.

"Tell me about growing up here. Did you live near the water?"

Briar leaned back, and I bit my tongue, refusing to let her know how much I missed the feel of her skin against mine.

Ah, bollocks. Our clock was ticking. I picked up her hand again, smiling when her fingers curled over mine.

"Not too close, no. My mother married a man from the area. They'd purchased a Craftsman-style home in one of the city neighborhoods." She picked up her water and sipped. "The house is over one hundred years old, with lots of little rooms. We ate in the dining room because the kitchen was way too small for all of us."

"So more than just your sister and you?"

She glanced out the window and the light hit her cheek, illuminating her porcelain skin and shadowing her slightly tilted eyes.

"With my dad, no." Her lashes came down, hiding the hurt I knew lingered in her eyes. "I have three half siblings—a sister and twins, boys. We're not close in age or emotionally. Lia was nearly fifteen, I was ten when we moved in. The house wasn't really big enough for us all, but we managed. Especially when Lia moved out a couple of years later." She smiled but it was grim. I'd hit a sore spot with this one. "Then I shared a room with just my half sister, Preslee. She's six years younger than me and Noah and Nate are two years younger than Preslee."

"You liked the beach? I remember you telling me you spent time there."

Briar nodded. "Especially after Lia left. I never felt comfortable at my mom's house, so, yeah, the beach was my refuge."

Like music was mine. "She didn't hurt you? Your mum."

Briar shook her head. "Except for the month between my dad's death and her coming to get us, she was always available. She never planned to be a mom to five kids, and Lia was angry about pretty much everything from their divorce to Dad's death."

I glanced up at the waiter whose name, Jim, was stitched into his starched white dress shirt. He was young with a mop of hair that proclaimed he was either an artist or a hipster. He grinned at me, but his smile amped up when his eyes swept Briar. I cleared my throat and Jim, cub that he was, was smart enough to turn his attention back to me.

Crikey, I wasn't used to this spike of possessiveness. At the same time, pride slithered through me. He could soak up Briar's beauty, but she was going home with *me*.

"Would you like anything else to drink? A bottle of wine, perhaps?" he asked, trying to smooth over his obvious gawking.

"I've developed a taste for the local microbrews." I winked at Briar. "Golden Retriever if you have it." I raised my brow at Briar who smiled back. "Make it two. Thanks, mate."

"My pleasure, Mr. Crewe."

Briar waited until he left before leaning forward. "He wants your autograph, but I bet he's worried he'll lose his job if he asks."

I leaned in, mimicking her arms folded on the table. "I agree. That's why I'm going to sign one of the old concert tickets I keep in my wallet and leave it in on the table."

She laughed, sitting up. "Always a step ahead."

"We learn things, us famous blokes."

"And the rest of us appreciate that."

Our drinks came as we segued into talking music. Briar said she wasn't much of an aficionado but she'd been educated. By her sister, I'd guess.

"Have you decided on your meal?" Jim asked, his voice cracking a little. Poor bugger. Much as I wanted to tell him I was just a regular bloke, I didn't think he'd agree. And Briar's blue eyes were clearly more than the kid could handle.

I raised an eyebrow. "Know what you want, love?"

She smiled, and it was so sultry my pants got tight. "Yes."

Jim cleared his throat. She turned those big blues back toward the waiter, and the little wanker puffed up like a thorny devil. Bloody idiot. She was *mine*.

"I'd like the special."

Jim might as well have had his tongue falling out he was so hot for my date. "Make that two." No idea what the special was, and I didn't care. I wanted our wanker waiter to go away. I scowled at

149

him the whole way across the room.

"He wants you," I growled.

"I want *you*." She raised her glass and sipped, her eyes meeting mine over the rim.

I unclenched my fists and leaned forward so far I could see the faint blue veins in the skin under her eyes. "I'm going to make you scream my name again."

Her pupils dilated and her mouth dropped open for a moment before she licked her lips. "I'm looking forward to that," she said, her voice doing that Marilyn Monroe breathiness that nearly killed me.

"At least twice," I decided.

This time she laughed, the sound smooth and warm, enveloping me in emotion.

"I love your confidence, Hayden."

I paused, her words swirling through my head. But I discarded them, not yet ready to delve that deep, and asked her instead about her most interesting interview.

We talked through the meal, the relaxed convo of two people who knew each other well.

"How can you hate your name?" I asked, setting my fork and knife on my plate. The skate was delectable, and I'd finished it all. Briar was about halfway through her plate, but she set her silverware to the side as well.

"My mother named us. How much do you have to dislike your kids to name them after dahlias and briars?"

"I'm right partial to my Sweet Briar," I said with a wink. "All soft and pink."

"With just the right amount of prick," she replied with a wink of her own.

I threw my napkin on the table. "We're done here."

Jim was at my elbow. I declined dessert while Briar lifted her eyebrow, her eyes laughing at me. I signed the bill, adding a hefty tip. Yank servers didn't make decent quid.

After Jim walked away, I pulled the concert ticket stub from my wallet, signed it, and dropped it on the table. Rising, I took Briar's thin, warm hand. Lacing my fingers through hers, I led her between the tables, nodding to a group of staring patrons.

When a few women detached themselves from the bar, Briar glanced around and pulled me through a shadowy door. We were in a dark, concrete stairwell. She yanked me up the steps. A door opened behind us as we plowed up another flight.

"Probably wasn't even him. He's supposed to be on tour." The voice was high, out of breath.

"It was! He was at Pike Place this morning. I've *got* to meet him."

"Why do you think he ducked out so fast?"

"That woman pulled him. Like she can handle him. Come on. Let's find him."

Briar threw open the door on the next level and led me down the hallway. Her breathing was choppy from running up the stairs.

"Where are we going?" I asked, as out of breath as she was.

"We're running away," she said.

"Got that."

She slid around the next corner and we were at the elevator banks.

"Have you been here before?"

"Yep. For work. Covered a few charity events."

"And you just happened to know that the stairwell was there?"

The elevator dinged open and I dropped her hand, ushering her in the car. Her cheeks were flushed with exertion, her breasts rising and falling against the fabric of her dress.

"I have a freakishly good memory." She shrugged as she leaned back against the wall of the elevator.

"Reckon."

I stood next to her, hands on the brass bar that circled the elevator. Maybe trusting Briar was stupid. She was a journo. Her type always went for the jugular.

She hadn't, though. She'd never made any attempt to use our relationship for personal gain. If anything, she was as protective of me as I was of her.

I ran my fingers through my hair, down the back of my neck. Too many pieces of my life were rubbing up against each other.

The elevator dinged, and the doors slid open. Briar stepped away from me, walking toward my suite. My eyes went back to her bum, the way it swayed in that dress. Perfection.

I hurried forward until we were side by side. I cupped her hip. My thumb rubbed up and down, loving the warmth emanating through the silk.

Stupid though I might be, I trusted her.

CHAPTER TWENTY
Briar

Once we were back in his room, Hayden turned on some music. It was soft, sensual.

"Want some bubbly?" he asked.

"Sure."

He poured me a glass from the chilled bottle that sat next to the gleaming table. Leaning forward, he pressed a kiss to the corner of my mouth. I turned my head so our lips could fully meet, but he'd stepped back. Handing me the champagne flute, Hayden poured himself a glass.

"Want to go out onto the terrace?" he asked.

I nodded. He opened the door and motioned me through. I sipped my drink as I looked out over the sound just feet below.

He ran his hand up my back, stopping at the base of my neck. Tilting my chin up, he kissed me again. I deepened the kiss, loving the way his tongue slid across and over mine.

"I like this date," I murmured.

"You'll like it more before it's over."

"Promises, promises."

Hayden chuckled. He took my glass and set it with his on a small metal table. Pulling me into his arms, he spun me before dipping me over his arm. His lips slid down my neck and over my collarbone. I shivered with need.

"I intend to deliver," he said, his voice as luscious as the champagne, but darker, more sensual. He pulled me upright, his body fitting to mine. His far hand came to my waist and squeezed lightly.

I bit his earlobe as I pressed closer. He made a noise in the back

153

of his throat before he dipped his head, capturing my lips, my mouth. For a man who'd never seduced a woman, he was damn good at it.

"Dance with me?"

I nodded again. Sure, he fed into many of my fantasies, but Hayden wanted this night as much as I did. Maybe more. In my short time with him, I quickly realized he didn't get to be himself with many people, didn't get to show this tender side that was so integral to his personality.

I pressed my lips together, tamping down the need to tell him how much he meant to me. In this moment, as he twirled me around the terrace, singing into my ear, my heart didn't just melt. Hayden owned me.

His happiness had become mine. His needs, my needs. While I'd never considered myself a selfish person, my time here, with him, showed me again how little I let people into my life.

But Hayden wasn't just in my life. He was in my soul. I loved him. Deeply, irreparably. I pressed closer, needing his warmth as I shivered from my revelations. He wasn't ready. Not for my love, not for the responsibility of caring for my feelings.

I kissed him, let him drug me with his lips and teeth and tongue, desperate to feel his warm skin against mine. Desperate, once again, for our connection. This we shared. I couldn't ask him for more. Not yet. Maybe not ever.

After our third dance, after many long, drugging kisses, Hayden pulled me back into the suite. He turned me so that I faced outward, our reflections clear in the glass. He stood behind me, his hand sliding slowly from my waist, up over my rib cage, my breast, my neck, cupping my chin and turning my head to meet his lips.

This kiss was softer, deeper, filled with more than simple passion. We'd met there and it was delicious. This...this was more.

I didn't want the moment to end. I reached my arm up to hold his head closer to mine and moaned when the skin of my back touched his dress shirt.

"I need you, Hayden."

"You have me, love."

"I want you."

"You'll get me."

"Now."

This time he pulled back and chuckled. "Soon."

I unzipped my dress and let it fall to my feet in a pool. His nostrils flared as his eyes traveled up from my heels, over my hips to my chest. "Now," I demanded again.

He ran a finger across the top of my breast, up my neck, along my jaw. I quivered under him.

"Glad you had your nap, Sweet Briar. This need I feel, it's going to take some time to satisfy."

I stepped out of my dress, moved forward and unbuttoned his shirt. Spreading it wide, I peeled his undershirt up his belly, across those trim ribs. Dropping to my knees I pressed a kiss to his navel, my tongue darting out to taste him.

He hissed out a curse, and I glanced up at him from under my lashes. "I can help with that."

He tossed his button-down on the couch and his T-shirt followed. I popped the button on his jeans, kissed him there on the tattoo that snaked along his hip. He cupped the back of my head, pressing my cheek against his stomach. I wrapped my arms around the back of his thighs, cradling his body as close as I could get it to mine.

"When I leave…"

I turned my cheek, forcing his hand from my head. "I don't want to talk about that now."

"You should visit me. In Europe. I'll take you to a castle."

I unzipped his pants, my eyes greedy. "I'd rather you took me *in* a castle." With a tug, I pulled his boxer-briefs down and wrapped my lips around the crown of his erection.

"We'll figure out a way to make that happen," he gritted.

I laved him, root to tip. He moaned, rocking his hips forward, his hands buried in my hair.

I made another pass, then another before finally drawing him into my mouth. He shuddered, throwing his head back. He matched my pace, his control unraveling. I sucked harder, faster, and he lost control.

His hands fisted in my hair, holding me where he wanted me as he thrust into my mouth. My hand rested on his thigh, the other moving to cup his sac. He groaned, his balls tightening. And he came in thick, long spurts that wracked his body.

His hands eased in my hair, and I swallowed, drawing back, kissing his tip. He caught me under my arms and pulled me tight against his body, his hand at the base of my spine. I liked the feel of him there, spanning my back, pulling me even closer to him as if he was just as greedy for more.

He kissed my temple, then my cheekbone. His lips trailing down to take my mouth. I clasped his biceps. Much as I wanted to smile, I was too busy returning his kiss.

Pulling back, he shucked his jeans in barely a blink. I squealed as he picked me up, cradling me to his chest.

"Your turn," he said as he carried me to the bedroom.

"How about *our* turn?"

"The night's long. We'll get there."

———

I glanced over at the clock. Just after six. After my third—fourth?—orgasm, I slid into another sated sleep, Hayden's warm body cradling mine. But now, awake, I couldn't hold back my fears any longer. *If I'm still here.*

Why did I have to fall for the one man who couldn't stick around?

Hayden slid his arm over my waist, cupping my stomach and pulling my naked back tight against his front. He pressed a kiss to the back of my neck.

"You're thinking so loud you woke me. What's wrong?"

I wiggled a little, sighing when he groaned in pleasure.

"Stop that," he admonished. "We'll both be sore."

I turned over and looped my arms around his neck. "I was thinking I shouldn't waste any second of our time together."

I leaned forward and kissed his jaw, making sure my breasts pressed against his chest. His hands slid down my back, a soft caress that caused me to arch, purring.

"Oh! Princess. She's going to be so mad." I shuddered, remembering the cat's angry swipes at my face.

"She can wait another hour," Hayden said as he cupped my ass and pulled me tight into his groin. His erection throbbed between us. "I'm not into wasting opportunities."

"You're right." I smiled as I kissed him.

This was the way I wanted to wake up every day.

A pang of sadness tried to build, but I pushed it aside. I couldn't try to change the rules now. That wasn't fair to either of us. Instead I clasped him closer, reveled in his touch as we made love. Again.

We peaked together, lay replete on the rumpled sheets. He trailed his fingers down my spine. I rested my cheek on his chest and closed my eyes, trying not to let my worries crash over me.

"Shower time. We can feed Princess on the way to the hospice center." Hayden slid out from under me and padded toward the bathroom.

I cupped my cheek and smiled at him. He was one good-looking man. Tall, broad shouldered. His waist tapered into slim hips and heavy thighs. The blond hair on his chest and legs glistened in the morning sun.

"Coming?"

"In a minute."

He turned back to face me. The full frontal view was even better. I licked my lips as my gaze caressed his hard pecs and washboard stomach.

"You misunderstood. I plan to have you coming in less than ten minutes."

I scrambled out of the sheets and followed him into the bathroom.

———•———

Hayden was uncharacteristically quiet, even for him, through breakfast. Something weighed on his mind, something important.

"That first day, at hospice, you told me you listened to part of my convo with my mum. What exactly did you hear her say?" he asked as we drove to the facility a couple of hours later, once again tensing up. His eyes regained that lost-puppy look.

Ah. So much for the romantic ideal of him asking me to join him for the rest of his tour. Probably for the best, but the ache in my chest still blossomed.

"That she had bipolar disorder. That she was a bad mother because of it."

"I don't know what to believe," he said. "I mean for me, my health. My future. The past. All of it."

"You think she'd lie to you. Now?" For some reason, the idea shocked me.

"I went through all my father's papers when he died because I was hoping for more than my mum's name on my birth cert. I know he sold our house here in Seattle, and that he gave my mum the money. But I can't ascertain if it was for her care at the facilities or to get her to leave me alone. A payoff."

"They didn't divorce?"

Hayden shook his head. "Dad kept power of attorney and all the other legal terms for spouses. I don't remember them all. I was surprised when I didn't find a divorce decree. I just assumed he filed when we left."

I nibbled the corner of my lip, hesitating. No, this was all we had. I wasn't going to regret not delving in all the way. "What do you want from your mom, Hayden?"

He continued to look out the window as though he was worried about how far into him I'd see. "Closure, I reckon. I mean, I know some of her medical history, thanks to talking with Kelly and the hospice director. I know the list of meds she's been on, and most of them are for bipolar—and not pain—but I don't know why she never contacted me. I can't wrap my head around that bit." He paused, clearly wanting to say something further.

I caught his grimace in the window's reflection.

"I have to find out how the illness impacted her life. Knowing she had bipolar disorder doesn't tell me if she could've continued playing the piano or had another relationship or...Crikey, I don't know. Lived any kind of life at all. I can't even get a straight list of her previous doctors, let alone the facilities she's been in over the years."

"Would you like me to make some calls?" I asked, my voice hesitant. "I know my way around the system here. I have some contacts who might be able to point you toward the right people."

"You could dig that up?"

"I think so. Some of it, anyway."

"But you'd keep the details you find private?" he asked. "Only tell me?"

"Of course."

He ran his index finger over his lower lip. "I would like your help. You'll be much faster at the research than I will. I don't want my label involved. My mum's health issues aren't something I want out there for general consumption."

I nodded, already considering the best sources as I pulled into the parking lot of the hospice.

"Okay, I'll start with some e-mails and calls this afternoon."

Hayden picked up my hand, pressing a kiss into my palm.

"Meeting you, here, during this...You're a godsend, Sweet Briar."

I wrinkled my nose. "I'd rather be your girlfriend or simply your lover, if it's all the same to you."

"It's not. But I like calling you both of those, too."

I wanted to ask if I could keep calling him my boyfriend, even after he left. If we could keep seeing each other, difficult though a relationship would be. But I didn't. For some reason, I needed Hayden to make that move.

We entered the building, holding hands. I smiled, kissing him at Rosie's door. "I'll see you for lunch?"

He squeezed my waist. "As if I'd miss that hot date."

Horrible didn't begin to describe my morning with Rosie. She was crabby, snappy, disoriented.

After an hour, I walked to Hayden's mother's room. He was looking out the window, hands in his pockets.

"Her vital signs are worse," he said, not bothering to look at me. "She hasn't awakened in over twenty-four hours. It's like she'd held on to say what she needed to me and now she can check out. I talked to the director and her doctor. Not much I can do but wait it out. Hope she wakes again so she can give me some more information."

I stopped, unsure if he wanted comfort. He turned toward me, his face haggard. So different from the man I'd parted from not so long ago. He strode over to me and wrapped me in his arms.

"I'm trying not to be angry that she's left me so twisted up."

"Rosie's not having a good day either. She won't let me read to her."

"I know it's not quite noon, but can we go? The tension in here, wanting her to wake and give me details, it's ripping at me."

I held him tighter. "I hoped you'd agree to that," I sighed, closing my eyes. "Anywhere you want to go?"

"As long as it isn't here, I'll take it."

We were quiet as we left. Hayden's arm was slung over my shoulder. I caught the flash of a telephoto lens from the corner of my eye. Annoyance spiked in my gut. "Can we drive your rental?"

"Sure," Hayden pulled out the key. "You drive, though. I'm buggered."

He opened the door for me, as he always did. That unconscious kindness I appreciated more for it being so ingrained.

"I'm going to Rosie's, I guess. Since the paparazzi are all out in full force." Anger clawed at my chest and gut. As if helplessly watching while someone died wasn't enough. No, people were making money off of those pictures that showed our misery and confusion.

"Right-o," he sighed, leaning back into his seat. "You been to Europe?" he asked as I pulled up to a light. Hope bubbled in my chest. Last night, he'd mentioned taking me to Europe, but this morning, when he didn't mention anything further, I'd assumed his suggestion then was nothing more than the passion talking.

"Parts. I did spend a semester at Oxford. Got over to France and saw a bit of Germany. But I ran out of money and flew home."

"Do you like Europe?"

"The parts I saw, yes."

He cleared his throat. I glanced at him from the corner of my eye, but he wasn't looking at me. He was staring straight out the windshield.

"So if I told you I'd ordered tickets for you to meet me in, say, Prague, you might consider joining me there?"

I opened my mouth, shut it. I pulled into the parking lot at Rosie's condominium. Turning off the ignition, I turned to face him. His eyes were full of fear, but behind that swirled hope.

"I know you want to be here for Rosie. You've been better to her than her actual family." The words cut deep, though he hadn't noticed, because he was back to staring through the windshield, rubbing the back of his neck.

"I should be catching a flight now. I'm about to miss a second show and my mum hasn't woken up since my second visit. Ets's e-mails and voice messages are progressively angrier. He said I need to stop finding myself and return to my responsibilities."

I nodded, my throat closing. I gathered my keys and purse, planning to get out of the car. He didn't understand the relationship I'd built with Rosie; he couldn't because I hadn't explained it to him. In this moment, on such a difficult day, when I was raw with grief, I didn't want to explain. I just wanted to *be*. I wanted Hayden to hold me as I would him. I wanted to know he'd be here, with me, when Rosie passed.

My hand was on the door handle when he touched my cheek. I closed my eyes, absorbing his touch.

"I would have gone back already, but I wanted the time with you. I don't want this to end, Briar. Not the hell with my mum. But the bright part. You."

"Thank you for that," I choked out.

I turned back toward him and he raised my knuckles to his lips, kissed each one. Then he turned my hand over and pressed a lingering kiss to the pounding pulse in my wrist. When his tongue touched the sensitive skin there, I threw myself into his arms, needing our connection, even if it was only physical.

When he pulled back a few minutes later, we were both disheveled. He chuckled.

"You look good mussed."

I rolled my eyes, but I smiled back.

He took in each of my features. His face falling into serious lines as he cupped my cheek. "I was serious. I don't want this to end," he said.

"What do you mean?" I asked. My chest was tight with need for him but also to tell him how much I cared.

"Us. This. We're good together. Damn near perfect in bed."

And my building elation crashed. Sure, the sex was phenomenal. Best I'd ever had. But I'd thought that was due to our emotional connection. "Let's go upstairs," I murmured.

"Say you'll think about it."

"I'll think about it."

———◆———

After eating a quick lunch, I curled up next to Hayden with my laptop. He slid his arm around my hip while I shot off a few messages to the sources I'd cultivated. I stressed the need for complete discretion, not that doing so was necessary. I reached out to these people specifically because I could count on their ability to keep quiet.

Hayden's relief was palpable. "I needed this. To start the process to find out more about my mum's life," he said.

I was thankful I'd been able to do something useful for him. And once Lia confirmed the time at The Vera Project, Hayden bounced around the small space. The closer the clock ticked to 8:30 p.m., the more my nerves fluttered through my stomach.

I was about to see the public side of Hayden, and for some reason, that burst the carefully cultivated bubble I'd crafted around us for the last few days. I knew our pictures were plastered on every gossip rag and aggregator site, but I'd managed to avoid most of them. I didn't want my relationship with Hayden polluted by others' opinions.

Lia met us just inside the door of the venue as we'd planned. She hugged me, long and hard, before turning to Hayden, who was standing just behind me. I glanced up in time to see him blink in surprise at Lia's bright gray eyes. They were arresting, especially now that they once again bubbled with life.

"Hi, there. Asher's looking forward to seeing you. I'm Lia, Briar's sister." She held out a small hand. Everything about Lia was more petite than me, and for the first time in years, I felt lanky, gawky.

"Nice to meet you. Briar's told me a lot about you," he said, his normal reserved self. He shook her hand as he nodded at her shirt. "I really like The Peach Kings, too. Is Asher backstage?"

Lia smiled—the bright one I was still getting used to again. She nodded—all that was possible over the now-screaming fans. Thankfully, they were all facing the stage where a band segued into a new song strong with rolling riffs and frenetic drumming. The music was good. But this wasn't my scene.

Much as I wanted to run outside, Hayden wanted to be here. I sucked in a big gulp of stale air and squared my shoulders. I liked the guys in Asher's band. They were smart and down-to-earth. Tonight would be fun. Going on tour with Hayden would be fun, too, if I could shake the niggling feeling crawling up the back of my neck.

We followed Lia back around the speakers, and I sighed in relief. For having bypassed both another round of mobbing fans as well as the assault on my eardrums. I'd never been that interested in live music—maybe because I'd seen Lia's life disintegrate as Doug delved further into that world.

Lia had had her own concerns about plunging back into the music scene before she and Asher officially became a couple. I'd have to ask her if her worries vaporized or if she was just willing to push them aside.

The hallway was cleaner than I expected, the walls painted a dark color. Lia knocked on a door, which opened to a long, tanned arm reaching out to snake around her waist. She giggled as she disappeared into the room. Hayden's lip flipped up as he waved me in.

"Hayden! Good to see you, man. Been a while."

Asher stepped away from Lia long enough to shake Hayden's hand.

"Thanks for the invite, mate."

"I told you to look me up whenever you're in town. You've been killing it all over the ANZAC charts. Heard you did all the piano layovers yourself. It's smoking, how you mixed the chords." Asher stepped back toward Lia and pulled her into his side.

I yearned for Hayden to mimic Asher's actions. He didn't. My stomach twisted again, more painfully than before. Why was he being so distant?

"Thanks. It's rough in a couple places, but Ets refused to record again."

I shoved my hands into the rear pockets of my jeans, hoping it would cover how badly my fingers shook.

"Lia said you're in town because your mom's sick," Asher said. "Sorry to hear that."

Hayden cleared his throat. "My mum's in hospice here. She's from the area. I met Briar at the facility a few days ago. Best thing to happen to me during this ordeal."

I stepped forward, hearing the tremor in his voice. He reached out, hand fumbling for mine. Once he held it, he squeezed, silently asking for comfort. I squeezed back as I moved closer, letting him know I was there.

"My mom had breast cancer," Asher sighed.

"Had?"

Asher nodded, his eyes darkening. "She died a few years back. I miss her." Lia laid a hand on his chest. I rubbed my thumb over Hayden's palm, wishing for the same freedom to express my feelings.

"Rough, mate." Hayden's voice was raspier than usual. I pressed in close enough for my breast to rub against his biceps. He threw me that look I was coming to know so well. The one I wanted to keep just for myself.

"So fucking true," Asher sighed, bringing Lia closer to kiss her forehead. He glanced at Hayden over Lia's auburn hair. "You up for some jams?"

"Acoustic?" Hayden asked.

"Our gig is. I've been reworking 'Sweet Solace' and 'Moonshine Eyes.'" Asher tucked Lia's hair behind her ear.

They didn't touch anywhere else, but I could feel the love and lust swirling between them, potent and beautiful.

I wanted that. Always had. Now I knew whom I wanted to share my love—my life—with. I glanced up at Hayden to see him looking down at me, that look of desire mixed with concern. I wondered if my face held the same look—but for different reasons.

CHAPTER TWENTY-ONE
Hayden

A triumph of rock, the night wasn't. It was more like a laid-back jam session in a best mate's really big garage than a gig. Seattleites didn't have a clue how lucky they were. Three of the biggest names in rock were up on a small stage in the middle of their city having fun riffing off each other. That didn't happen often. Not like this.

Learning music on the fly didn't worry me anymore, but I was nervous about messing up the Supernaturals' standards. The chord progression wasn't too tough, but it took us a few songs to hit the timing with confidence.

The fans were more gracious than I deserved, but Asher, Bill, and I enjoyed pushing the melody and tempo. My fingers flew over the keys and sweat pooled at my lower back, just under the waistband of my jeans.

I grinned at Asher as I hit a long, complicated series of trills. He laughed as he and Bill let me go, bobbing their heads as I worked through the melody. This was what music was supposed to be. This was the high I missed when I didn't touch the keys. I finished and Bill segued into a frenetic progression down the fret board. Asher and I caught on and I slid back into a more percussive role.

Briar stood next to her sister offstage. Lia Dorsey wasn't what I expected, but, then, neither was Briar. The sisters were deeper, more sensitive than most women I'd met. They also held this well of patience I didn't understand. At least Briar did. She'd put up with my broodiness. Lia seemed to do the same for Asher, keeping him calm and focused. He was more grounded and happier than the last time I'd seen him.

Maybe if Briar toured with me, she'd give me the balance I hadn't known I needed. I met her gaze, mine heating with thoughts of what it'd be like to look at her like this all across the world. We'd sneak out for a few hours, kiss at the top of the Eiffel Tower. I'd dance her along the edge of the Thames.

We hit the place I could really show my staccato finger work. I leaned into the keys, letting the beat and energy carry me. But I kept my eyes on Briar. Her pale skin flushed, I hoped from the memories of our morning together. I smirked...or last night. My grin widened. Really, any of the times we'd been together.

She wasn't timid in bed. Or out. I appreciated that. I wanted a woman who knew her body and her mind. Briar knew both, and I'd already learned how to strum her desire, building to a crescendo before backing off for the featherlight touch of *pianissmo*. My fingers followed my thoughts. Her lips parted as she held my gaze.

My phone buzzed, but I ignored it. Keeping my focus on the music and Briar.

She knew what I was thinking, the way I'd play her up, up, up and over into a rich orgasm that ripped a scream from her throat and left her spent and warm. Just right to slide deep inside her. I finished the song with a flourish, smirking at Briar's shallow breathing.

My phone buzzed again. I pulled it from my pocket and the smile slid from my face. Local area code. Both missed calls were from the same line. I raised my phone to show Asher I needed to step off the stage. I caught Briar's eyes, concern replacing the desire that heated them just moments before.

I didn't really need to hear the voice mails, but as soon as I was offstage, I forced myself to start with the first. My feet were much

169

surer than my heart as I walked to the dressing room in time to listen to the second message.

Briar ran into the room, her hair fluttering around her face and shoulders.

"My mum died. In her sleep."

Briar's fingers touched her lips. "Hayden," she whispered.

I tensed when her hand reached out to grab mine. I didn't want her to touch me, not now. Her eyes filled with hurt when I stepped back. I understood, but I didn't need her emotion, not with all mine churning in my gut, a terrible cyclone building more and more until it spewed its wrath.

My mum made her choices. I'd live with them, best I could. Later.

"I need to get to the center. Sign some documents."

"You don't want to wait until the morning? I think that's normal procedure."

My stomach lurched. "No. I don't want to wait."

"Then I'll take you."

"No," I said. "You stay here, enjoy the time with your sister."

"I'd rather go with you," she said, voice soft. Not quite pleading.

I struggled against my need to touch her, wrap myself around her, let her help me through my grief. She wrapped her arms around my waist, and I couldn't fight it. Not my attraction to her nor the anger and sadness my mum caused.

"Fuck all." My voice cracked. Briar burrowed deeper into my body, and I pressed my face against her neck. "I'm not ready."

"I know, Hayden. I get it. I'll be with you the whole way through."

My arms slid down her back, gripping her tight. I tipped my head back and blinked, many times, hard. What I was doing to Briar wasn't fair. I knew it and I couldn't force myself to let go.

CHAPTER TWENTY-TWO
Briar

"Let me tell Lia the plan. I'll be back in a sec."

He swallowed hard, his jaw tense. His tight rein on his emotions was more frightening than his first attempt to push me away. I'd have to be strong enough not to let him force me out again. Like I knew he wanted to.

Lia was waiting halfway down the hall for me. She must have followed me back from the stage. "His mom," I murmured.

Lia nodded, eyes dimming. "Figured it must be. Is she worse?"

"Gone," I said.

Lia gripped my hand. We stared at each other in that brightly lit hall, the sound of laughter and applause drifting toward us. "How's Hayden taking it? What can I do for you, sweetie?"

I shook my head. I wasn't sure there was anything anyone could do, especially if he succeeded in shutting me out. I pulled Lia into a hug, needing her warmth and support. She stroked my hair, and I let the tears fill my eyes. We'd been here a few times, she and I. She understood how hard it was for me to watch Hayden struggle with his mom's death. She waited until I was once again in control of my breath.

"Okay. I'm ready."

She brushed the last of my tears from my cheeks. "I'm proud of you, Bri. Not just for what you're doing for him. Though that's big."

I squeezed her fingers and went to find Hayden. He was staring at the far wall of the backstage room, his eyes unfocused. My fingers brushed his arm and he jumped.

"Whenever you want to leave."

He cocked his head, his gaze cataloguing each of my features. "Thanks for coming with."

He'd made no effort to grab my hand, so I reached for his. I wasn't surprised to find his fingers cold, his palm clammy. "I told you. You don't have to do this alone."

His next words were so low I nearly missed them, as if he didn't mean for me to hear what he said. "It's all I know."

I bit my cheek from the inside, hard. I didn't want him to see what those words did to me.

Hayden opened my door, the good manners too ingrained for him not to, even at a time like this. I wanted to kiss him, touch him, anything to thaw the painful barrier he was building around himself.

Our ride was silent, so like the ride to The Vera Project hours earlier, but heavier. He sat in the passenger's seat, somewhere between stunned and fuming.

I tapped the steering wheel. Twenty minutes ago, we'd both been high on desire. Now, I swallowed hard and glanced at Hayden from the corner of my eye. He was leaving me emotionally, and I was powerless to stop it.

I parked in the lot and turned to him.

"Thank you for being here. With me." His voice returned to having that formality he used when dealing with people he didn't know. Exiting the car, he waited for me to join him, his hand trembling a little on my lower back as we headed into the building.

One of the night-shift nurses let us in, obviously expecting us. "The mortician is on his way," she said. "If you want to go see Miriam, now's the time."

Outside the door to her room, Hayden dropped my hand; his body tensed. Opening the door would be like opening Pandora's box. Only worse. There was no hope for reconciliation left inside. In fact, there was nothing.

As the door shut behind us, I shivered. Hayden gripped my hand as though I was all that was keeping him afloat, pulling me in even closer.

For the first time, Miriam wasn't attached to any machines. Her pallid skin was slack, her eyes closed.

"I didn't realize the tension there. Around her mouth." Hayden's eyes rose to find mine. He held my gaze, his eyes drowning in a sea of uncertainty and pain. A place I couldn't reach. "I just thought they were wrinkles."

My heart twisted at his shattered look. She'd pushed him away, left him alone for years. He shouldn't feel bad he hadn't seen all of her pain—she hadn't bothered to see his. "You came for her. You were here when she needed you." Even as I said the words, I knew they were platitudes. He dropped his gaze, our connection. I wrapped my arm around my elbow.

"Mr. Crewe. I'm sorry for your loss."

More platitudes, but Hayden nodded at the staffer. I took in the dark, comfortable clothes, hangdog features, dark hair pulled back in a tight bun.

"She was peaceful. We made sure she didn't feel any discomfort these last few days."

"Be sure to tell Kelly I appreciate her assistance," Hayden said.

"Of course. We have the release paperwork for you, when you're ready," she said. "I'll be outside."

"Got it. I'll be there in a minute."

I stood there, near the door, unsure how to help him. With Hayden, up until this moment, we'd been in synch. Now, he was a beat off my pace, and I stood, frozen, unsure what he needed from me.

"Give us a moment, Briar. I need…this is private."

I nodded, though he didn't see me. I walked out the door, nodding to the staffer who stood across the hall. Even her shoes were sensible. I was inappropriately dressed in my sequined tank, skinny jeans, and heeled boots. I leaned against the wall and tilted my head back.

I couldn't be angry with Miriam for dying. She'd been so sick. And she was the reason I'd met Hayden in the first place. I peeked in on Rosie, whose chest rose and fell in the sharp, even movement of the oxygen machine.

I stepped away from Rosie's door and waited. The staffer and I studied each other, neither of us speaking. There was nothing to say, after all.

Hayden met me outside the door within minutes, his face set, eyes empty. I swallowed down my tears. Those were for me, for my loss of him. Now wasn't the time to let them fall. He took my hand, but his grip was loose. My heart stuttered.

Dammit, he wasn't allowed to pull back. I clasped his fingers tighter but he walked on, not acknowledging my attempt.

"You don't have to stay," he said, his voice quiet.

I flinched. I waited until he met my gaze.

"I told you I'd be with you the whole way through."

The blank look cracked, and I saw the lost little boy behind the thick mask Hayden wore. His chin trembled before he mashed his lips together. I cupped his cheeks.

"I'm here, right here. Don't forget that."

The mask slipped further, his throat working to stave off the building sob as he tried to clamp the emotions back under his control.

After an interminable minute, he pulled me close and buried his face into the curve of my neck. His breath slid across my skin in abrupt puffs. His arms plastered me to his front, but I was fine with that. I swayed a little, hoping the movement would be as soothing for him as it'd been for my niece when she'd been so over-wrought after her father's death.

"Why does her death hurt so much?" he asked.

"Because you loved her. Even though she hurt you, you loved her and wanted her in your life."

His breath puffed across my cheeks and his fingers dug into my sides as he gripped me tighter. "I need to do the paperwork," he said. "I need this done."

The staffer led us to a small, clean office. Hayden shook hands with the mortician, a neat, balding man in a rumpled dark suit.

"Thanks for coming tonight. I know this isn't exactly typical." Hayden's voice was thick, his words clipped. I hugged his arm to my chest, trying to stave off the shivers building there.

"Not a problem, Mr. Crewe. Sadly, this isn't my only pickup here tonight."

The staffer handed over page after page, all designed to let go of Miriam's earthly rights. Hayden was meticulous, reading each document before signing anything.

"We'll take the body to the funeral home now that we have your approval. Come by when you're ready tomorrow. We'll discuss the funeral procedure then."

The mortician flipped a page, his eyes moving with quick efficiency behind his bifocals. Did people choose this job on purpose, like some people wanted to be a chef or a firefighter?

Some must, and I was thankful they did. The service was essential, helpful. This was a time when people made a real difference. Helping families in the grieving process was noble.

"I have written here she wanted to be cremated. Do you have a copy of her will?"

Hayden shook his head, jaw tensed so tight it looked like it might shatter.

"I have copies of the file that the hospice director sent over yesterday. It's all in here."

After a long moment where Hayden made no move to take the papers, the mortician set them on the table and rose. Slipping his bifocals into his rumpled shirt pocket, he made a show of stacking the papers.

I couldn't take Hayden's stillness any longer. I slid my fingers along the back of his hand where it lay on the table, threading my fingers through his tensed ones.

"Do you need anything else from us?" I asked.

He shook his head. "No. Condolences," he said in a tired way that made me think it was his salutation, like anyone else's goodbye.

I rose, my chair scraping across the cheap pile of the institutional carpet. "Let's go." I tugged at Hayden's hand. Urgency built in my chest. I needed him away from here, away from the memories of his mother.

Hayden stood, his long body wooden with exhaustion. "Thank you for your help with my mum."

Hayden shook the mortician's hand, and collected the papers he'd been given, his left hand still gripping mine. With each heartbeat, his grip firmed. Soon, I couldn't feel my fingers anymore, but I didn't ask him to let go. I hoped he considered me his anchor tonight. I needed to be that for him.

Walking out of the building, Hayden turned back.

"I hate that building." His voice held an edge I didn't like. In that moment, I stood before a man I didn't know. How could I know him, when we'd only met days before? Then his eyes dropped to mine and they were so filled with sadness and longing, I couldn't help but edge in closer.

Some things—some people—the hours, days, weeks didn't matter. I knew the fundamentals of Hayden's character, same as he knew mine. That's what mattered.

I leaned my head against his shoulder. I had no words.

"Let's go."

He pulled me to my car, opening the door for me to slide in. "It's quite late. You okay to drive?"

"Sure. Where to?"

He blinked, surprised. "My hotel."

I started the engine, hoping to quickly dispel the chill from the midnight fog. I drove to the hotel, trying to ignore the wet tendrils licking over my windshield. Water droplets formed and spilled across the glass, reminding me of tears.

I pulled up to the valet stand and turned to Hayden. He was staring down at his hands clasped in his lap. The lighting was poor, casting most of Hayden's face into shadow.

"You're coming up. Right?" he asked.

"If you want me to, yes. I'd like to."

He raised his right hand to my face, cupping my cheek. "I don't want to be alone." His voice was soft, more of a plea.

I nuzzled closer, turning to press my lips against his cool skin. "You're not. You never were."

He climbed out of the car, came around, and helped me out. Tossing the keys to the lone valet, he began to walk fast, his long legs eating up the distance to the elevators.

With each breath, his emotions untethered further. By the time the elevator dinged for his floor, I expected him to howl out his anger. He pulled me down the hall toward his room, slamming the door open in his haste. I managed to close it with more care.

"Hayden, it's after midnight. People are sleeping."

He spun me around so my back was against the door. His breathing was erratic as his body pressed me into the unforgiving wood. The door handle dug into my hip. His fingers splayed through my hair as his mouth slammed against mine.

The kiss was all demand. I braced my hands against his forearms and let him take. He plundered my mouth, each swipe of his tongue deeper and harsher. His need burned into me. I answered his as best I could, trying to keep up. He broke the kiss long enough to yank my top over my head. Fabric caught, ripped, but Hayden just kept pulling.

"I need you," he groaned against my throat. "Right now. I need to be with you. In you."

"You have me."

"I *need* you, Briar."

I speared my fingers through his hair, letting my body give its answer.

CHAPTER TWENTY-THREE
Hayden

The driving rush to lose myself in her body was unlike anything I'd ever experienced. I was rough, but I couldn't stop. More, I didn't want to. Briar made that sexy noise where her breath caught in her throat, and my brain flashed to a maelstrom. I tore her pants down her legs with a quick jerk, then popped open the button of my jeans as my teeth found her nipple through her lacy bra. The noise she made was between a grunt and a scream, and I wanted more. Wanted to bury myself in her softness. Briar would help me forget. Briar would ease me, love me, keep me from shattering.

I yanked down my zipper, quickly freeing myself from my clothes. I shredded the delicate silk and lace of her panties. Her eyes were large, her teeth gripping her swollen bottom lip as she stared up at me.

We met there, the two of us. We met in lust and it was beautiful. *She* was beautiful.

"Briar, I need. You." I knew she didn't understand what I was telling her. I'd do better later. Right now, I didn't want to be alone. She wouldn't let me be alone. She'd promised and she'd meant it.

She wrapped her arms around my neck and tugged at the short hairs on my nape until I kissed her again. I couldn't wait. I slammed into her body, shuddering with thanks that she was ready for me. I pumped out, the pace frantic. Too hard, too fast but I couldn't stop, couldn't slow down.

Now that I was in her, the need to fall into oblivion built. I gripped her bum, pulling her thighs up to my hips as I pounded into her, desperately reaching for the pleasure and peace she'd offered me in the past.

She clenched around me, spurring me on. Her mouth and body were my only tether. Nothing else mattered as long as Briar's soft warmth surrounded me.

Her fingers tensed against my neck. I liked that. Too much. I lifted her higher, taking all her weight onto my arms. I used her hips as a counterbalance to my frantic thrusts. My fingers gripped her harder, needing to set the pace as she writhed, twisting her mouth free to gasp for air.

"Hayden. God. Please."

I held her tighter, molding our cores together, as I carried her to the bed. Even though everything in me screamed against it, I let her slide off my body. She made a sound of distress. I reached around her and pulled the covers back. I unclasped her bra, shoving the straps down her arms. My mouth surrounded her nipple, laving, sucking, biting. Her fingers sifted through my hair as she took a shuddering breath.

She didn't understand the drive to own her was still strong. Stronger now that she was naked, just like she was supposed to be. I pushed her backward, ready to finish what I'd started. Her nipple popped from my mouth as she fell, an inarticulate sound ripping from her throat.

I kicked off my shoes and pulled off my jeans and underwear. I yanked my shirt off my head. She leaned up to kiss my navel. I wanted to hold her there. But no. I didn't want to be gentled.

In a quick move I flipped her over so her front was on the bed. Yanking her hips up, I slammed back into her. Her fingers scrambled for purchase in the sheets as I regained my momentum, her hips held high and tight against my thighs.

Sweat formed and dripped from my temples, my chest. My arms screamed with the effort of holding her up in such a position. But I was focused on her tight, hot channel. Shock sliced through me when she tightened further, her chin tipping to the side. She shoved her fist into her mouth as her body tensed past the point of bearable. She screamed and sobbed as she unwound around my pounding.

When she cried out my name, I went over the edge, too. The release was so deep and hard, I had to brace my arm on the bed. This woman was my salvation.

I leaned my forehead into her back and let the release take me in long shudders as my arm kept her hips tight against mine.

My vision tunneled to just Briar, the softness of her mink-brown hair and the delicate ivory of her skin.

She sprawled across the bed, her breathing returning to its normal rate. My muscles quivered as the last shudder eased from my body.

I groaned and fell to the bed, managing to land beside her. Her eyes were closed, her lashes a black sweep against her cheeks. I pulled the sheet and blankets over us before I tucked her tight against my chest. Where she belonged.

Briar placed her hand on my chest as her trim thigh slid between my legs. I settled my head on top of hers, smoothing my fingers down the fine silk of her back.

"I love you." She whispered the words.

Letting out a breath, the last of my tension ebbed from my body even as something hard and heavy built low in my gut. Before I could think too much about it, the oblivion I'd been chasing for the last hour—that much-needed sleep—slammed its fist into my skull. But my dreams were shattered fragments I couldn't quite catch.

———◆———

Light was just creeping over the horizon when I woke, feeling more drained than I had when I'd started the night. Briar was curled on the other side of the bed, the sheet low.

Her hips were covered in bruises in the shape of my fingers. All over her beautiful skin.

I levered upward and leaned over Briar's soft, prone body. Multiple contusions marred the soft skin on her hips and waist. Fainter markings from my teeth covered her breasts. I winced, horror building in my chest, as I counted each one.

No. I wouldn't hurt Briar. I *wasn't* like my mum. Since she told me of her bipolar disorder, I'd studied the list of symptoms, knew each by heart, knew I had less than a ten percent chance of being diagnosed myself.

But the proof of my delusions lay before me.

CHAPTER TWENTY-FOUR
Briar

The suite was quiet when I woke. Sunlight streamed through the window. I stretched, winced, and stretched some more. I bit my lip, my body achy but my heart full. I loved that Hayden turned to me in his grief. He was so walled off with everyone else, but the need on his face, the grief and desire in his eyes as he leaned in to kiss me last night brought it all into focus.

For whatever reason, he needed me just as much as I needed him. We could figure this out. I loved him enough to try. And he'd already asked me to meet him in Europe.

I sat up. Hayden must be in the shower. I dropped the sheet and walked toward the bathroom. The door was open, the room empty. He must be in the living room then.

Brushing my teeth, I decided to shower before I found him. I needed to head over to Rosie's and feed Princess before I took him to the airport. There was no way that cat could survive much longer without another meal.

I knew Hayden had to leave. And that hurt, deeply, but we'd talk about how soon I could meet him. With a plan in place, we'd both feel better.

I wrapped myself in the hotel robe, combed my hair, and walked into the living room. The table was set with a large coffee, a fruit salad, and a croissant. He'd already learned my favorite morning meal. My smile was quick, warm.

The note next to the breakfast spread gave me pause. *Went to the funeral home to hammer out the details. I need this done. ~ H*

He'd pulled back again. Uncertainty crept across my skin. Something in his note—no, I wouldn't worry yet. I ate my breakfast slowly. I dressed and filled a to-go cup with more coffee, checking to make sure I had the room key card, my purse, and my car keys before heading down the elevator.

As the elevator doors opened to the lobby, I hit a wall of cameras. The reporters' voices rang out, questions thrown so quickly I couldn't process what they were asking. They pressed in closer, trying to get another picture of my face, then another.

"How long have you and Hayden Crewe been seeing each other?"

"Do you plan to join him on tour?"

"Did you know of his mother's illness?"

"Are you attending his mother's funeral?"

"Why didn't you leave with him this morning?"

This was the part of journalism I'd always detested, mainly because it was such an invasion of another person's privacy. I lifted my arm up and pushed through the sea of bodies. As one, the group turned with me, pressing close enough for me to feel the hard plastic edge of one of the camera lenses. Panic rolled up from my now-queasy stomach.

Another flash, then another. I was the fox being run to ground. I quivered, an instinctive need to hide taking over.

Where the hell was Hayden?

I was tall, but most of the men outweighed me by a good fifty, even a hundred, pounds. They didn't budge.

"Step back. Please," I said, raising my voice to a near shout to be heard over the questions. A security guard was wading into the sea of bodies. About time. If I could just get to him, he could lead me out of the group.

"If you'll step back I'll answer a question," I said. My fingers clutched my bag, holding it tight in front of me like a shield. I was in an old pair of jeans, my hair damp. The vain part of me shuddered to consider how unflattering these pictures were going to be. But the rational part of my brain was much more frightened of being mobbed and trampled.

The group grumbled but backed up a little. I caught the guard's eyes, mine wide, begging. He dipped his head in acknowledgment and continued to push through the bodies. At least thirty people. This was insane. I shook my head, trying to push through the daze that so many people were interested in my life.

No, not mine. Hayden's. Worry swelled my chest. Did he know how bad the frenzy was?

I edged toward the front exit, my footsteps small, subconscious. The sea of reporters flowed in front of me, wanting to capture the emotions on my face.

The guard settled at my side. "Thanks," I murmured.

He nodded, face grim, arms set in a no-nonsense stance that showed off his tall, bulky physique. "Your car will be here in a minute, Ms. Moore."

I could do this. "Okay, what was your question," I asked one of the closest reporters. I continued to edge backward. Only ten feet to the door.

The woman was small, her eyes hungry. She reminded me of a terrier, nuzzling deep into a tunnel to yank out its quarry. I managed another couple of shuffle steps as she preened.

"Why weren't you on the flight with Hayden this morning?"

My poker face didn't hold. I cracked as the words sank in. My mouth dropped open. Dammit, I was a reporter myself. I could handle this. I forced myself to smile. My face felt wooden, fake.

"Hayden's going through a difficult time. Losing a parent is traumatic under the best of circumstances. I'd appreciate it if you'd all give him some space as he works through his grief."

I nodded toward the security guard, who stepped forward in front of me as I bolted out the door. I dashed around the valet and practically dove into the driver's seat. My chest was tight, my lungs aching.

He wouldn't have left. Not without a goodbye.

I drove to Rosie's, needing distance from the flash mob.

Hayden was hurting. The reporter was trying to throw me. Unfortunately, I couldn't check with Hayden, find out the truth for myself. I'd left my phone in my purse last night and it ran out of battery at some point.

My pep talk to myself wasn't very good because my fingers still shook, and it took me multiple tries to open Rosie's door.

Princess's *mrow* of greeting was followed by a purr. At least someone was happy this morning. Such a change in her since we'd met Hayden.

I closed the door softly and bent to pick her up for the first time. I needed the comfort of another warm body. I plugged in my phone and set about making a fresh cup of coffee. I'd lost my other cup in the mad dash to my car. I took a deep breath as the text app chirped, followed by the voice mail one. While my fingers itched to pick up the device, I opened the fridge instead. I pulled out a packet of lunchmeat I'd bought earlier in the week. Before I'd met Hayden. I closed my eyes, trying not to let the panic crash over me.

"It's not salmon, but you'll cut me some slack, right, Princess?" My voice cracked. I filled her bowl, made sure her water dish was full, and washed my hands so I could doctor my coffee. Out of ways to procrastinate, I grabbed my phone.

Seventeen texts. Twenty-three voice mails. My stomach churned. Either one would offer painful news if there were this many.

I took a sip of my coffee, proud I got the mug to my mouth without spilling a drop. I opened the text app. The first one was from Lia, from late last night, making sure we were okay. The next was from Hayden.

Arranged details with the funeral home. Heading straight to the airport. Thanks for the last few days.

I blinked at the message a couple of times. It didn't change. He'd told me *thanks*? In a text message? What the—who did that?

The hurt was there, I could feel it building. But right now I was wallowing in righteous anger.

I took another sip of my coffee and checked the rest of the messages. All from colleagues looking for the scoop about my relationship with Hayden, his relationship with his mother, his abrupt departure. This was going to be one hell of a story.

My mind buzzed with thoughts of the last few days. The last few hours. The only thought I could focus on was that he'd left me. He hadn't finalized any plans for me to meet him. He didn't *want* me to join him. Just like he'd never planned to tell me goodbye. I was such a fool.

Princess meowed and arched her back, winding her body through my legs. I picked her up again and buried my face in her fur. I'd started this. I'd finish it. I set the cat down, pressed my ear to my phone, and listened to my voice mails. Same thing as the texts. Many from people I barely knew. All wanting a piece of me. Anything I had to give.

Too bad I'd given it all to Hayden last night.

The final few messages were from Lia, all making sure I was okay.

I managed to collapse onto the couch. *Was* I okay?

Princess settled into my lap, her wide eyes reflecting my confusion.

I pressed the Call Back button, needing something to stop the rush of emotion building in my chest.

"Briar! I've been frantic. What's going on?"

I opened my mouth. For a moment, I was struck mute. But then a sob rose up and burst forth.

CHAPTER TWENTY-FIVE
Hayden

Nothing felt right. I couldn't get comfortable.

"Need another pillow, Mr. Crewe?"

The flight attendant's eyes were blue but too pale. They weren't the stunning color of Briar's. Crikey, I needed to stop thinking about her. I refused to think about her smile when I'd asked her to meet me on tour.

She'd have realized that was a mistake just as I had. And there was no way she'd want me now that I'd hurt her.

I closed my eyes, my guilty conscience tracing each of the bruises I'd left on her skin. Like my mum had marked me. Bile rose, hard and fast. I managed to swallow it down, barely.

"I'm fine. Thanks."

"Not a problem. Be sure to let me know if I can do anything to make you more comfortable."

The words were professional, but the tone and look were seductive. I glanced out the window, trying to ignore the woman's obvious interest. Once she walked down the narrow aisle, I pulled out my notebook, planning to go over the difficult chord progression I'd developed for the new song I'd started when Briar took me to play piano.

Ten minutes later, I gave up. All I could think about was Briar. About the marks I'd left on her. About her soft words of love last night.

Leaning my head back against the hard seat, I closed my eyes and saw Briar, waiting for me. Instead of meeting my gaze, she faced Puget Sound. Her eyes were sad, her gaze downcast.

That was silly. Even if she was upset now, we'd met in lust. Shared a few days. She'd be glad to get back to her life, and…. well, I'd survive. It's what I did.

I opened my eyes and pushed up the plastic screen covering the airplane window. I shouldn't have left her. Not the way I did. I should have apologized for using her body. I should have told her, if not in person, then in the note, how much she meant to me.

But those bruises I'd left on her beautiful skin…How did I apologize for that? How did I tell her I feared it would happen again and again with me losing more of my control each time? Just as my mother had.

Until the day Briar ended up in the ER, battered and scared out of her mind, because of me.

"Drink, Mr. Crewe?"

The flight attendant was back.

"Coffee. Black. Thanks."

She poured it, handed me the Styrofoam cup I knew Briar wouldn't approve of. Must be something about spending time in the Northwest. In just those few days, I'd managed to absorb some of their earth-friendly initiative.

"I was sorry to hear about your mother, Mr. Crewe."

My eyes snapped up to hers. She wasn't going to leave. If I asked her to, I'd seem rude. But I didn't want to deal with a fan right now.

"Appreciate it."

"Your friend looked upset. Was she close with your mom?"

What the hell was she talking about? "My mum was in hospice. She had cancer."

"Yes, I read that. It's all over the news."

I leaned back and closed my eyes. My friend. Upset. The pieces fell together. "You mean Briar?"

"Tall brunette."

The coffee sat heavy in my stomach. I'd left early…there was no way the media could have found out already. "Can I see the picture you're talking about?"

"They're all over the Net. Just pick a site."

I pulled out my phone. "Okay for me to use now?"

She shrugged. "Sure. Let me know if I can get you anything else."

I nodded, scrolling through the menus to get access to the Internet. My heart tripped at the number of times the piece had been shared. *Fucking hell.* I clicked on the first one, trying to brace myself for the worst.

And there she was. Briar. Hair damp, eyes wide, surrounded by reporters.

Why hadn't I considered that? She was scared. Alone. Fragile. But so beautiful.

The picture was taken in the lobby of The Edgewater. And there were so many other photos—all of Briar with that same scared look in her eyes. Where was security? The paparazzi obviously surprised her, but the hotel was supposed to be prepared for these types of events.

The coffee churned in my stomach again and I barely swallowed it down. Security was there for celebrities. *I* was the celebrity, and I'd checked out hours ago, leaving instructions for all of Briar's bills and needs to be put on my card. I didn't think the media would turn their focus on her in my absence.

After going through the photos, I read the story, my heart rate escalating with each word. She'd been so brave, facing the reporters. I'd left her alone to clean up my mess. And she'd defended me. Offered

191

up an explanation for the inexplicable. For the way I'd left her.

I didn't even have the decency to look her in the eyes and say goodbye. I'd sent her a text message, cowardly arse that I was, and run away from my deepest fear.

I checked another site, then another, mouth hanging open as I realized just how big this was. First, that I'd been photographed with a woman at all. Second, that I'd left her without even a Dear John ending. But no one pounced on that part. Because Briar kept her mouth shut.

She'd promised me the day we met that she wouldn't share any details of my life. She'd kept her word even though she had to have read my message by now. Even though she must hate me.

Then one picture caught my attention. In it, her eyes were wider, her mouth hanging open a little as the hurt settled over her face. Definitely pain bleeding into her eyes.

The realization hit me like a hard punch to my gut. She'd learned from a journo that I'd come to the airport. I lacked the balls to tell her myself, and she'd learned from one of the vultures after I walked away. And now I knew, I didn't leave *just* her body bruised.

My break from Briar was as big—if not bigger—than the story of my mum's death. No articles of my mum's mental illness yet. And they might not learn of it. Not as long as they were focused on Briar. Site after site ripped her apart, saying I never would've stuck by her because she wasn't pretty enough for me. Because she was too old. As if her year and a half on me was equivalent to the thirty-five-year gap between my parents' ages.

I glared at that comment, wishing I could give the writer a piece of my mind. Briar was gorgeous, and if she read that, I knew she would be crushed.

Another commentator said I'd only marry an Aussie. A famous British gossipmonger said Briar couldn't be everything I wanted in a woman, not if I dropped her so quickly. That I was just looking for an easy lay, so Briar must be nothing more than a groupie with low morals. The next two said the same: Briar was only a fling, a nobody. Someone to simply while away my mum's last days with.

They'd gotten it so wrong.

I wanted to wrap my arms around Briar, keep her safe from this. Laugh with her over how wrong the journos were—like always. Kiss my favorite spot under her eye, brush her bangs back from her forehead. Rub my thumb across her plump, wide lower lip.

I dropped my head against my fists. This—the mess I'd made— all stemmed from my mum's death. I'd let the situation spin out of control.

And the realization hit me, a cricket ball straight to the head. I was uncomfortable because Briar wasn't with me. I missed the weight of her head against my neck, the scent of her soft hair. I missed the warmth from her body, the curve of her breast and hip snuggled into my side.

But we'd been honest with each other. She knew I wouldn't stay. Couldn't stay. It's just…I shouldn't have left. At least not the way I did.

And I sure as hell shouldn't have sent her a text message. A lame-arsed one at that.

I was an adult. Time to man up.

I grabbed my phone from the seat and opened my e-mail. I started typing. Not to Briar, not yet. I'd do my best to limit the damage. I owed her that.

No, I owed her much more. I owed the world an explanation

for how much she meant to me. I'd give it to her, to the rest of the world. Let them know she'd be joining me. Soon. Like I'd planned since the moment she introduced me to Dan as her boyfriend.

I paused, considering. I should call her. No. I wasn't ready to hear the hurt in her voice. I'd text her.

"The captain has turned on the Fasten Seat Belt Sign." A tinny voice came through the speaker above me. "Please turn off all electrical devices as we begin our descent into Hong Kong."

Heat seared my gut, moving up into my chest. I typed faster. Harry needed to get this now. I needed to fix as much of this as I could.

"Mr. Crewe, you need to turn that off, please."

"I'm almost finished."

"Now, Mr. Crewe."

I sighed, and shut down my phone. Going ballistic wasn't going to solve Briar's current paparazzi issues. Staring out the window, the tension built in my shoulders. I wanted Briar there, gripping my hand. Letting me know I wasn't alone.

But I feared I was. I'd been afraid of loving her. I'd been afraid she'd reject me once she saw the bruises. But most of all, I'd been afraid I'd hurt her again. So I'd left. I'd made the choice for both of us. Without asking her what she wanted. What she needed from me. She'd given me so much.

I swallowed the thick ball of emotion building in my chest.

I'd really fucked up.

CHAPTER TWENTY-SIX
Briar

"Ah, honey. Where are you?" Lia asked, her voice gentle, like it had been after our mother skipped town for another man, leaving us confused and adrift. She hadn't needed that voice, with me at least, in years. I cried harder, wishing I hadn't let Hayden past my normal barrier.

But he'd struggled with his relationship with his mother, too. I'd seen the anger and confusion there, in his lovely brown eyes, unable to resist the urge to comfort him. I'd shared with him, thinking he was a good man.

I curled my legs up to my chest. Because now, I wasn't sure about anything except that I hurt.

"Bri, breathe, honey."

Wow. I was upset.

"Briar! I need you to tell me where you are."

"At Rosie's." The words were garbled, but I guess Lia understood enough.

"What's her address?"

I rattled it off between sniffles.

"Pack a bag. I'll come get you. You're staying with me."

"I have Princess. Rosie's cat. I can't leave her. The cat or Rosie. She's still in hospice."

"The cat can come, too," Lia said. "Rosie will understand."

"You're allergic to cats. So is Abbi. I can't leave either of them alone, Lia. Rosie's family hasn't come to see her. Well, Ken did. But not because he actually cared. She's dying, all alone."

"*You're* not staying alone, Briar. I read some of the stories before

I got too angry to continue. The media isn't going to let up, not until someone else screws up their life. We'll figure the cat situation out together. Asher called his PR team for help. It'll be faster and easier if we have someone else be the face. Where's Hayden?" Hesitation laced through her voice. I knew she knew.

"He left." I took a deep breath. "He was on a flight by the time I woke up." I said the words, but they didn't sound like they came from me.

My mind detached, and I returned to the state I'd lived in the entire time I'd dated Ken. How I'd felt since my dad died. Maybe since my mom left us, letting us know we weren't important enough for her. I didn't like this place, but it was safe.

The tears stopped like I'd clicked a switch. Maybe I had. I planned to stay here in this bubble.

"Bri, honey, being alone now is a bad idea. Remember how you came to Rathdrum for me? I want to do that for you. We'll figure out what happened. Maybe there was an emergency…"

Doubt filled her voice. I'd told her, he left me. Discarded like a piece of trash. I closed my swollen eyes.

"I need some time. Bye, Lia." I ended the call, turned off my phone, and tossed it on the table. Then I sat, dazed, waiting.

Nothing came. Not a thought. Better, no emotion.

Eventually, Princess's claws kneaded my legs. I didn't flinch, not even when she hit the bruises on my inner thigh. *Mrroow?* Princess nuzzled her head against my chin. So I laid it there, on her back, listening to the cat purr.

Somehow, morning came again. Standing was painful, in part because of the bruises but also because I'd sat for so long, my limbs stiff. A long, hot shower wasn't an indulgence, it was a necessity.

I dressed with more care today, knowing I'd see reporters again. After blow-drying my hair, I realized I didn't have my makeup kit. It was still at The Edgewater. I couldn't even go out of the building like this.

No way I'd let anyone see how devastated I was. That would lead to more rounds of questions, more pictures. My best defense was looking as good as possible, putting up the carefree façade that bored paparazzi and gossip readers.

I dug through Rosie's drawers until I found some concealer, her blush, eyeshadow and makeup brushes. Lipstick. I spent nearly an hour trying to pull off the look I wanted.

Finishing my cup of coffee, I set the mug in the sink and picked up my phone. I dreaded turning it on, but I couldn't ignore it. Guilt swirled through me. What if something had happened to Rosie?

I clicked on my phone and fed Princess again. The cat purred, winding through my legs. I made a show of petting her while I waited for my heartbeat to even out.

I wouldn't be any more ready. Picking up my phone, I glanced at the 1000+ sign on my e-mail.

Later. Voice mail first. Lia left multiple messages that I ignored. After ensuring none of the messages were from the hospice center, I opened my text app. Three hundred messages. I shook my head. I needed a new number.

My finger hovered over the one from Hayden. He'd texted me again? Probably to say he was sorry about the vampiric journo arses. Well, that didn't fix the actual problem.

I'd spent an hour on my makeup. I wouldn't cry and let him ruin that, too. I opened the text, careful not to read his words as I typed my message to him. *You made your choice when you walked out on me. You don't get to contact me again. Ever.*

Simple. Direct. See? I could handle myself. Princess stared up at me, her wide eyes delving into me.

"Don't. I don't want to go there."

She pressed against my leg, rubbing her jaw up and down. God, I was taking comfort from a cat. I didn't even like cats.

Calling my service provider, I asked for an unlisted number.

Twenty minutes later, I owned a new number and only Lia, Abbi, and a handful of others knew it.

I pulled my purse over my shoulder and fluffed my hair.

"See you later, Princess. Don't do anything drastic today. The couch can't take another round of your claws."

I opened the door as I settled my sunglasses on top of my head. The reporters were waiting in the lobby, just as I'd anticipated. I walked out, chin high, ignoring their impertinent questions and camera flashes. They wanted a picture of me—they could have it.

I turned at the last moment and gave them a cheeky grin. *Deal with that, assholes.*

I slid my sunglasses down over my teary eyes once I was out in the thick mist that had settled over the city. Because those vampiric *arses*, especially Hayden, wouldn't get to my heart. It no longer existed.

CHAPTER TWENTY-SEVEN
Hayden

"Hey, mate. Head in the game."

I offered Ets a rueful smile. "Sorry."

"After the show, Hayden, you can distract yourself with whatever vice you want. Seven of them at the same time for all I care. Now, though, we've got fans waiting to see that pretty face." He tapped my cheek like he used to. I shoved his hand away. He bloody well irritated me. They all did.

The past two days, all I wanted was to curl up with Briar, tell her what I was feeling.

Not even my keyboard helped. All the notes sounded stiff, my timing off just enough to wind me up further.

"Give me a sec." I shook out my arms, rolled my head around on my shoulders.

"Right-o. Look," Ets said. "We get you're torn up about your mum's death. But we need you here. Focused. Last night was a disaster. If you don't pull your head out of your arse, we're calling Pete back in to play for you."

I nodded, both in acknowledgment and agreement, though resentment built in my chest. My mates had rescued me from multiple missed cues at last night's show. I couldn't keep performing like this. I knew that. But Ets was being a dickhead.

No, Ets was being Ets. I'd always considered him no-nonsense, and he was a good mate because of it. He always got his point across, no bullshit. But I'd been wrong about him. That coldness in his eyes ran deeper since Mila disappeared. His temper spiked quicker. I'd sympathize with the end of his youthful dreams if I didn't want to punch him right now.

"Got it, mate. Thanks for the sympathy on my mum."

"You're getting plenty from the rest of the world. And it's not like you actually knew her."

True. Though I wouldn't tell him why. He might've been my band member and the person closest to me, but I didn't want him to know about my mum's disease—and the fact I might very well be a ticking time bomb waiting to blow my lid into crazyville. Those bruises on Briar's skin…I'd worked myself up into a frenzy, certain I must have bipolar disorder if I'd willingly hurt Briar.

Thanks to the e-mails Briar sent the afternoon before I left and her blind copying me on all her messages, I'd gotten the names of a few of the psychiatrists at two of the facilities my mum frequented in the years between my return to Melbourne and her sojourn into hospice. Instead of hitting the after-party last night, I'd spoken with the doctor who'd spent the longest period treating my mum—nearly a decade both before and after my dad and I left. He'd gone over some of her basic diagnosis, but with HIPPA—whatever the hell that was—he couldn't go into any real detail. He'd been winding down the call when I finally built up the courage to ask him my real question.

"I know bipolar disorder runs in families."

"True," he said.

"What's the timeline like for onset?" I asked.

"Hayden, are you asking me if I think you're bipolar?"

I cleared my throat. "Yeah."

"I'm assuming you know the list of symptoms."

"I do. Well. Had a friend in high school with it. I studied up again once my mum told me she suffered from it."

"I see. So, are you manic? Super into whatever you're doing?"

"For a while. Music, specifically the piano, that was my escape."

"I'm talking about barely sleeping, impulsively quitting your job. Maybe going on a shopping spree you can't afford."

"No, never," I admitted.

"Do you have trouble sleeping? Have you been so depressed, so empty you've wanted to end your life?"

"Sad and lonely, sure." Especially now that Briar wasn't lying next to me.

"But not to the point you quit what you love and thought about suicide?" he asked.

"No." I sighed in relief.

"Then I think you're probably okay. Granted, it'd be smart to get a full psychiatric evaluation. But just because your mom struggled with bipolar disorder doesn't mean you will. And, for the record, she talked about you constantly. You were the reason she was here, the reason she wanted to get well." He was quiet for a moment, considering his next words. "For some of my patients, wanting to get well isn't enough to release the illness's hold over their mind. Unlike other diseases or even a broken arm, we can't see the problem so sometimes people go weeks, months, years even without a diagnosis or proper care. That makes recovery harder. Not impossible, but much more strenuous."

"So my mum wanted to get well but couldn't actually kick the disease? Like a cancer patient who can't get rid of the entire tumor?"

"Something like that," he said.

With a quick thank-you, I hung up the phone. I closed my eyes, tension easing from my neck and shoulders. I might have hurt Briar, and that was wrong—something to apologize for—but I had control over myself, my mind.

"Earth to Hayden. That's the third time I've called you," Ets snapped. "You're all over the place, mate. We've got important business here. Focus now, then you can flake out all you want later."

"You're a dickhead," I said.

Hurt flashed in his eyes before he flipped me off. He slammed the door. Ets and I had been mates since uni, but this tour opened up many of our insecurities—especially once the story made rounds that I was the creative driver of our band—and we'd grown apart because of it.

For the first time in years, I wished I'd developed a deeper relationship with someone else. I liked my band mates, but I couldn't talk to them, not like I'd talked to Briar. I ran my fingers through my hair. She dominated my thoughts. She'd replied to the groveling text I'd finally gotten the balls to send.

She hadn't read it, I'd bet, and her response was terse.

I couldn't muster the courage to call her, because hearing her voice would slay me, leaving me whimpering like a bub in nappies. And when I'd tried to text her again, my stomach had twisted.

She'd disconnected her number.

I leaned my head back against the wall. I'd hurt her, physically marked her. Of course she didn't want to talk to me.

I opened my text message app and texted Bill, Asher's band mate. We'd exchanged numbers at his studio my first night in Seattle, and now he was one of my only connections to Briar. A starting point.

Left 2 fast to finish up my biz in Seattle. Can u put me in touch with Asher?

Now I'd have to wait. Again. The time change kicked my arse. I was exhausted.

I couldn't sleep. Not that I wanted to. I didn't. My dreams were a mixture of fading pleasure and remorse. Each time, I dreamt Briar was covered in more bruises. The worst dream focused on her black eyes morphing into my young face.

I checked the American news and gossip sites again, for the millionth time today. Reporters still followed Briar. She'd been photographed with her sister, Asher, and their kids. I couldn't begin to imagine what Asher thought of me. While that bothered me, the blankness in Briar's eyes kept me up last night and distracted me at practice today.

I was headlining a huge worldwide tour—my biggest dream come true. And I couldn't enjoy any of it.

I clicked on a link that led to a new picture. She'd been photographed at the hospice center, visiting Rosie. Her jaw was set and her eyes were flat, lifeless. Briar, my Briar, no longer existed. Sure, her beautiful face still filled the screen—those soft, wide lips, her high cheekbones. The full lashes. But the light in her eyes was dimmed; they were vacant, even.

I hated the tour that kept me from her nearly as much as I hated being the reason for the stillness in her eyes.

———◆———

"Better show tonight, mate."

"Glad to have Hayden Crewe back in Jackaroo."

My mates clapped me on the back as we exited the stage after our second encore. We walked through the back area. I scowled at Harry, who'd opened one of the rooms to reporters. They nearly fell over themselves to get to me.

"Hayden, tell us about your relationship with Briar Moore."

"Were you and your mother estranged?"

"Why weren't you at her cremation?"

"What do you plan to do with her ashes?"

"Why did you really break up with Briar?"

The last question stopped me. "Who asked that question?"

"Which question?"

"Is Briar meeting you on tour?"

"The question about Briar," I said.

A hand shot up from the back of the crowd. Crikey, the reporters were four-deep at least. Never seen this many before.

"One, my relationship with Briar Moore isn't any of your business. I'd appreciate very much if you'd quit writing about her. You haven't got it right yet. Two, Briar is the most amazing woman I've ever met. That's it."

I turned, ignoring the escalating shouts, and walked into the green room.

"Not a good idea to answer the wanker," Flip said.

"Oh? I was supposed to just let him print his speculative tripe about her?"

Ets shrugged. "It'd die down faster if you didn't feed them a trickle. You know that." He used the bottom of his T-shirt to wipe his forehead. "Let's go see who Harry stocked in the dressing room."

I ran my hands through my hair, scrubbing at the shorter bits in the back. Answering reporters wouldn't get Briar talking to me again. With the time difference, it was dead of night in Seattle. Bill needed to answer me because I needed to hear Briar's voice, to tell her the whole truth about my mum.

What I really wanted was to tell her everything in person, but I didn't have a spare second during the next month.

"Just let it go. That Yank was fun, I'm sure, but there are tons of women around who'd be more than happy to get you off," Ets said, his face serious. "Time will help with the heartache, mate. Trust me." His dark hair hung in thick, sweaty ropes around his face, his thin black eyebrow ring stark against his pale skin. He was nearly as tall as me, and I knew women considered him a good-looking bloke. Until he opened his mouth. He led me into the room bursting with young, beautiful women. Long hair, perky tits. Gorgeous curves, mostly uncovered.

A leggy blonde disengaged herself from the other women in her group and walked toward me, her hips rolling. A model, then.

Ets groaned. "She's a beaut."

She was. "Hi. I'm Mara." Her hands slid up my arm, pale fingers locking around my neck. I let her tilt my head down, willing my body to do more than remain unresponsive, but my brain screamed I was cheating on Briar.

"G'day, love," I said. "Enjoy the show?"

She nodded, biting her lip as she peeked up at me from under her lashes. "You were amazing."

"Glad you had a good time."

She kissed my jaw before standing on her tiptoes and pressing her large breasts into my chest. "*We* can have a better time now."

Ets clapped his hand on my shoulder. "Knew you wouldn't let that Yank keep you down long. Have fun, tiger."

The slap was light but it might as well have been a knockout punch to the jaw. Mara rubbed against me with sinuous grace. Ets grinned at me like a loon. I staggered back.

"What's wrong?" Mara asked, concern pulling at her brows.

"Nothing. Just a little woozy."

Ets raised his eyebrow, the ring there gleaming dully. "Get on with it, mate. Once you purge the Yank from your system, you'll be 'right."

Briar's eyes, so filled with tenderness as she held me when I told her my mum was dead, flashed before me. The way she tilted her head back when she laughed, spilling that rich mink cascade over her gleaming shoulders. The way she'd told me she loved me, just before she drifted off to sleep.

"I don't want another woman." I enunciated each word carefully, like I would for someone who didn't speak much English.

Mara teetered back, eyes wide and filling with hurt. "Look, you're beautiful," I said to her. "But I can't. I'm involved—"

"Are you fucking kidding me?" Ets growled.

"I'll catch you later. Enjoy your party." I nodded to Mara, tipped my head toward Ets. And turned, only to realize there was a camera pointed at me, documenting the entire tableau.

Bloody hell. There'd be pictures tomorrow. Ones I couldn't explain away easily. Ets or Harry, one of them, set this up. I was sure of it. I spun on my heel and stalked toward the door.

In the hall, Ets grabbed me by my T-shirt, his pale eyes sharp under his dark brows. "You are acting like a complete wanker."

I brushed his hand off. "Thanks for the opinion I didn't ask for."

"Either screw some other chick or suck up your fake heartbreak, Crewe. We both know you don't actually care about the sheila."

"That's where you're wrong." I slammed the flat of my hand into the wall next to his head. Ets's jaw tensed but his eyes never left mine. "I do care. And she does matter."

"Since when do you care about anyone?"

That one hurt. Right between my ribs, straight in the heart. For years, my success was my sole focus. But I'd changed. Correction. Briar changed something fundamental in me.

"Since now."

Ets scoffed.

"Just because you've turned into a massive dickhead since Mila left—"

"Don't mention her name," Ets snapped. His eyes darkened and his eyebrows tugged low. We glared at each other. "We've got another few months to go on this tour," Ets said. "I don't know what you're messing around at—what your mum's death did to your head—but you can't go back to playing like shit."

"Are we done?" I asked. My cheeks were stiff, my fists balled tight. I stepped back, unwilling to punch Ets, no matter how much he deserved it.

"Yeah, we are." He spun on his heel, throwing his arms out to the gaggle of groupies standing in the doorway of the dressing room. I shook my head, disgusted by his shitty attitude toward women in general. I'd never thought about it, but Ets used and discarded women like most people would a tissue.

"He's been in a mood since you left. He knows you carry the band, which upsets him."

I dipped my head in acknowledgment of Flip's words.

I opened my phone and forced myself to look up the websites, finding the picture where Briar looked straight into the camera. Her cheekbones were more pronounced and her eyes were dazed, empty.

Whether I wanted to admit it or not, my feelings for Briar weren't going to go away. If anything, they were stronger now than

207

they'd been even three days ago. Hell if I knew what to do with that. How to fix her empty eyes or my empty heart.

Ets was right about one thing. I'd never cared before. But I cared about Briar. She'd told me she loved me.

"Staring at the picture isn't going to change anything," Flip said, hand on my shoulder.

He might get it. "I miss her."

"Right-o, mate. Got that one. Question is, can you do what you need to do to make everyone happy?"

"Is that what you do?"

Flip chuckled. "Hell to the no. If that were the case, I'd be at home, rubbing Cynthia's belly, talking to my bub."

"So you're saying it's not possible?"

Flip rubbed his chin, considering.

"I think you have obligations. Same as I do. Those come first right now. Stardom and families don't mix great."

"You miss Cynthia?"

"Course, mate. Wish she was here now."

"But?" I asked.

"Life's a bitch. I get to see her in sixty-one days."

"When's the bub due?"

Flip raised his eyebrows. "Twenty days."

"Gonna miss the birth, then."

He shook his head. "Not by my choice. Harry set all the dates before we found out. But I'm not happy with the situ any more than you are. Just making the most of this moment."

"And enough money to live off of?" I asked, pocketing my phone.

"Too right, Hayden. We've got that now." He leveled me a look. "Most people are going to expect us to go right back into the studio to record another album. You'd need to be writing for that to happen."

"I haven't written a song this whole tour. Not feeling it. My mum dropped some shit on me. I didn't handle that well. I didn't handle leaving Briar well either."

"We all know about that," Flip said, his voice dry. "So now you have to figure out what's more important—the past you can't change, or the woman you clearly care about. What you want looking forward."

CHAPTER TWENTY-EIGHT
Briar

The pictures of Hayden with another woman shouldn't have hurt so much. But they did. His arm was curled around her waist, her lips on his jawline. I sat in Rosie's room, holding her hand long after she fell asleep. Then, only then, the tears rolled down my raw cheeks. When she woke, she asked the night nurse to bring me water.

"Me dying isn't worth these tears, Briar Anne."

"You're worth a lot more than tears, and you know it." I managed to smile.

"Oh, I'm going to miss you, lovely girl," she said, her voice cracking. The oxygen machine hissed as it blasted another breath into her failing lungs.

"I'll miss you more, Rosie."

"You think your life's all over. Being young is so stark. He's a fool, but at least he isn't also an ass like Kenneth."

I finished the water and sighed, closing my tired eyes.

"Wash up and go home. Get some sleep, Briar."

"I'm not sleeping well."

"Then go home and lie down on something comfortable. I'll be here tomorrow."

"What if you aren't?" I asked, my voice breaking.

"Then it's finally my time," she said. "And I'll say a huge thank-you to the angels for giving me as many years with you as I got."

———— • ————

The next morning, and four days into living with constant paparazzi attention, I was too frazzled to even consider walking out-side. Even in full makeup, dressed for a job interview or cocktail party, the comments on my body and fashion were brutal. There were so many ways I wasn't good enough to date an internation-al rock star, though clearly that was no longer happening, thanks to Hayden's latest photos with the girl after his concert. She was young, blond, gorgeous. Everything I wasn't, and if I hadn't already been aware of that, the comments under the photos and each news story pointed out my lack.

The worst were comments about things I couldn't—and wouldn't—change. My boobs were too small, my hips too wide. My eyes weren't symmetrical, my hair was a boring, plain brown. My jeans were pedestrian and made my butt look flat.

I'd finally turned off my Wi-Fi connection, the only way to break the cycle of scrolling through the comments and then feeling hor-rified by the cruelty people dished out.

Why anyone would want celebrity status was beyond me.

After the one day I went out to eat with Lia, Asher, and the kids, I'd spent the rest of my time holed up with Rosie at hospice, leaving only long enough to sleep and feed Princess. Yesterday, the doctor confirmed the tumors had spread into Rosie's lungs. She was down to hours.

Lia tried to talk me into moving in with her again, but I couldn't. And not just because of Rosie's failing health. Lia and Asher were so damn happy—each time they touched or even shared a look in my presence was like salt being rubbed in my bleeding heart. Not that I could tell Lia that. Instead, I used their impending move back to the Seattle area to my advantage.

"I'll see just as much of you if you're here."

"Not for the next couple of weeks, Bri, and the story's hot now. By then, the media will have moved on to something else. You know how it goes."

I did. And now that I'd been on the other side, I knew for certain I'd never work in the industry again.

I'd never felt so adrift. I'd always known where I was going and how to get there, because financial security was so important to me. All those years ago, after my dad died, there'd been days when my stomach was so empty, I was sure my belly would cave in.

Lia and I never talked about that month—ever—and now that I was older, I was sure that time was scarier and harder for her than it was for me. One night, she'd made me a sandwich and then went to the window to stare out while I ate it. Now I realized why she hadn't sat with me, looked at me while I ate. It had been the last of the food we'd had in the house, the last we'd get until our mom finally picked us up three days later. I'd never felt hunger the way I'd felt it then.

Now, money in my bank account meant I never had to worry about where my next meal came from. While I'd saved enough to live on for the next few months—thanks to my hoarding skills and my current rent-free living arrangement—I'd have to figure something out. Soon. I swallowed the stitch of panic that built in my throat.

"You holding up okay?" Lia asked. Lost in my thoughts, I'd nearly forgotten she was still on the phone. I shifted so I could stare at the ceiling.

"I don't know. Visiting Rosie's keeping me going."

Lia remained quiet, which probably meant she had something to tell me but wasn't sure how I'd react. Princess jumped into my lap and I ran my hand over her sleek flank. She turned twice and settled against my belly, her favorite spot.

The cat and I had come to an understanding, for which I was grateful. After I'd explained her mommy wasn't coming back, Princess accepted me…in a temporary surrogate role. Last night, she curled onto the bed, her warm body a lifeline during the dark hours when I couldn't sleep. Wide awake in bed, I relived my short affair with Hayden, wondering how I'd managed to so quickly fall in love with a man who'd told me he wasn't looking for love.

"Hayden called Asher today."

"Okay."

"He wants to talk to you."

"Asher?" I asked.

"C'mon, Bri, don't do that."

I smoothed Princess's soft fur, letting my fingers burrow in close enough to feel the heat from her skin. She turned those big eyes toward me, as though sensing my falling mood.

"I don't want to talk to Hayden."

"I see where you're coming from."

I sighed. "But?"

"No *but*, Bri. He hurt you. The way he handled the situation was pretty terrible. And then there are the pictures of him with that girl."

"But." Dammit. The tears stung as they hit my nose. "I still love him."

"I know." I pictured Lia pulling on her hair—a nervous habit she'd done for years. "He told Asher he's sorry he hurt you. That he never meant to. And he didn't sleep with the girl."

"Well"—I sniffled—"he did hurt me. Because he left and because of the blonde. Whether he had sex with her or not."

"Before you jump down my throat, I know what I'm asking. I also know that one day you'll regret not getting the closure."

I huffed. "I hate when I can't argue with your logic."

"It's the curse of being the younger sister. I'm always going to be wiser."

"I'm not sure four and a half years matter that much," I said, my tone dry.

"They matter enough to make me smarter than you. Just think, if I hadn't listened to Asher when he came here to explain his reasons for staying away during his divorce proceedings, I might still be depressed and wearing the same pajamas."

"You do like to wallow."

"Everyone deserves a good wallow, Bri. You've just never been patient enough with yourself to grieve."

Princess's big, wide eyes remained trained on me. She licked her thin kitty lips. "This hurts. So bad. And...and...Rosie's almost gone. I can't stop and let the rest hit me." The lump in my chest expanded. "I can't talk to him. No way."

The silence dragged out. I pulled the phone away to make sure we were still connected. She started talking again just as I put the phone to my ear. "You can't hide from your feelings, Briar. They'll come out, eventually. And it's worse if you try to suppress them. I wish I was there with you."

"No you don't. I'm depressed and bitchy."

"If it makes you feel any better, Hayden's desperate."

"I think he just wants to apologize. For the continued press maybe."

Lia hummed. "He texted Bill. He's called Asher twice. That's too much effort for just an apology."

I scratched Princess under her chin, wincing when her claws dug into my bruised hip. "The girl then. That was bad form. Even for a rock star."

"They aren't rock stars for their good behavior, Bri."

I digested that. "Doesn't matter. He was wrong."

"True."

"Then why do you want me to talk to him?"

Lia sighed. "For you. I want you to tell him he's an asshole. He shouldn't have left the way he did. He knows you're dealing with Rosie's death. And he sure as shit shouldn't have messed around with the girl."

"I hate her." I sniffled, wiping my nose on one of the crumpled tissues I kept in my pocket. "I'd hate him, too, if I could."

"I'll do enough hating for both of us."

I tore apart the tissue, ripping it into smaller and smaller bits, thinking.

"You said he was sorry he hurt me?"

"He told Asher that multiple times. Why?"

"I don't know," I said slowly. I wasn't going to spill Hayden's secrets, not even to my sister. Stupid though it was, I needed to protect him. "What, exactly, did he say?"

"Um, Asher said his words were, *I'd never hurt her on purpose.* But he had to know leaving you would be hard on you emotionally."

"But that's not what he meant," I murmured. Why hadn't I connected the bruises to what I knew about Hayden and his mother earlier?

Lia sucked in a breath. "What else could he mean?"

"I woke up the morning he left with some bruises. On my hips. From his hands."

"What?" Lia's voice was low, dangerous. I'd only heard her like this once before, when a classmate intentionally hurt Abbi's feelings. "He *bruised* you?"

"No. God, no. He was crawling back in his shell. Like I do. You know. I didn't want him to, so I pushed for intimacy, and things got…rough. In a good way. It helped him back from the edge, but between the text he sent me that morning and what he said to Asher…I think that's what he meant."

Princess blinked at me with her large, sapphire eyes before licking her lips again. Yeah, it was a pretty reasonable guess.

"You sure?"

"About it being unintentional? Yes."

Lia exhaled hard into the phone. "Good. Because if he did mean to hurt you, I'd have to fly to Asia to destroy him."

"Lia!"

"How do you feel?" Lia asked.

"The bruises? You know how easily I bruise. Touch me wrong and poof! If I'm right though…" I sighed. "I'm going to have to talk to him."

"You owe him *nothing*. Especially now that he took pictures with another woman. Telling him he's an asshole is one thing. Forgiving him is another. And you shouldn't feel obligated to do so. Asher agrees with me."

"I think there's more to it that I'm just beginning to understand. And that's going to eat at me."

Lia grunted, her annoyance wafting through the phone like an invisible vapor. "I want you to be happy, Bri. And *safe*."

I thanked her then clicked off my phone. Princess still watched me.

"Should I give Hayden my new number?"

Mrroowww.

"That's all you have to say?"

She lifted her paw and began to lick it.

"Talking to you isn't helping."

CHAPTER TWENTY-NINE
Hayden

Flip and I clinked beers. Jake and Ets were across the room, chatting up some of the fans.

"To Mumbai," I murmured.

"Best show in a while," Flip said. "Good to be out of Asia, I think."

I sat my half-empty beer on the table. "Felt good. The show. Leaving for Europe tomorrow will be excellent."

Flip tugged on his soul patch. "Any ideas what you want to do after this tour?"

Everything inside me stilled, even my heart. Next second it pounded, harder and louder than normal.

No way he could know what I'd been thinking.

"Not sure. Probably grab some holidays. You?"

"You're in love with her—the Yank."

I picked up my beer. Not seeing Briar this week made me antsy. I was an addict in full-blown withdrawal.

"It was like that for me, with Cynthia."

"She good?" I asked.

She'd miscarried last year so had been extra careful about this pregnancy, spending most of it on bed rest.

Flip's face split in a wide grin. "Talked to her before I came backstage. She's great. The baby's moving heaps, keeping her up a lot of the night. Wish I was there to feel him tussle about."

Lack of sleep wasn't something to be excited about—I'd give anything to put together five straight hours right now—but I was happy for Cynthia and Flip.

"Good news then, mate."

"So do you love your Yank?" he asked.

"It's all jumbled. I mean, I met her whilst my mum was dying. All the feelings, they were intense. But…" I said slowly, "when I think about Briar, separate from my mum, it's all positive. It's like my mum's death soured it all somehow."

"That'll color any scenario."

"So it's a right bloody mess."

"You're going to have to talk to her. Tell her you're not happy here without her. Soon."

I shot him an angry look. "I've been trying. She changed her number."

Flip smirked as he lifted his beer to his mouth. "Women were always too easy for you. Especially when you were giving off that I-don't-give-a-shit vibe. I like seeing you all tied up over a girl. She's gorgeous, by the way."

"Yeah. She is. But she's also sensitive. And funny. And she's a better runner than me."

Flip laughed. "Definitely love." He slapped me on the back. "Thanks for asking about my plans. Me, I want to get home for some family time. Just thought you should know."

"Right-o. Appreciate that, Flip."

He sauntered off, waving to a gaggle of lovesick girls before heading out to the tour bus. A couple of months ago, I'd thought Flip was an idiot, leaving the company of pretty girls to go play video games or read, whatever a man did when his lover wasn't with him. But I got it now. I wanted nothing more than to do the same.

I stood, planning to call Asher again. The timing worked. Good thing about being up so late here in Mumbai meant it was afternoon in Seattle.

219

"Come here, Crewe. Meet Indira."

Fucking Ets. I wasn't interested in making small talk with a girl ten years younger than me. I scowled, causing his smirk to slide into a full-blown grin. Yeah, he was angry with me for my comment about Mila. I should have kept my mouth shut.

"She's your biggest fan," he needled.

"Good to meet you, Indira," I said, holding out my hand to shake hers. She stood, giggling. If she was twenty, I'd be shocked. "Hope you enjoyed the show."

"I did. Very much." She batted long lashes at me. I stepped back, wary. I refused to have my picture taken with another sheila. No way. Last time I called Asher, he'd reamed me for ten minutes about the photos with that blonde before he even let me state my business.

"Right-o. I have some calls to make. Enjoy your evening."

Ets glared. Extricating himself from another girl who was latched on to his arm, he followed me from the room.

"What the hell's your problem?" he growled.

"Right now? You. I didn't want to meet that girl, and I sure as hell don't want to invite her back to my bed on the bus."

"Since meeting that Yank you're a complete bore."

I bit my tongue. Fighting with Ets wouldn't help. I shoved my hands into my pockets and rolled back on my heels. "Anything else?"

"Just that meeting that woman was the worst thing that ever happened to you."

"You're wrong, Ets. Briar got me through one of the hardest experiences of my life. What if it was your mum? Wouldn't you be thankful for someone holding you up?"

Before he could answer, I turned on my heel and left the room. Clearing the rest of the roadies and the last few girls trying to get past security, I dialed Asher's number.

"Hayden, I can't help you out, man. You gotta quit calling me. You dicked over Lia's sister. Not once but twice."

Heat crept up my neck. "I never meant to leave her like that. It just kind of happened. I told you. The blonde—nothing happened."

"Doesn't matter what I think. You look like you're enjoying her attention in that photo. And that makes you an asshole. Dahlia's words."

"Asher, I *need* to talk to Briar. If I didn't have back-to-back gigs, I'd fly out there. Hell, I'd already be on a plane."

I'd thought of it more than once. But leaving wasn't fair to my band. We'd worked our arses off for this, and I couldn't put my personal life in front of their careers no matter how much I wanted to.

"Look, I remember what being twenty-nine's like. Stupid comes naturally. But you hurt Briar, which means you hurt Dahlia, and that pisses me off."

"I've been working my end of the PR," I snapped. "I can't make them leave her alone. I would if I could. I miss her." I sighed. "I'm worried about her."

"Then you should've stayed long enough to talk to her. And you shouldn't have let those pictures get out." Asher's tone bordered on murderous.

"I fucked up." Way more than Asher knew.

"She's in a media shitstorm you created, and her friend's dying. Dahlia's begged her to come here and she won't. So she's alone. What the fuck, man."

"We've gone this round, Asher. I'm sorry. My mum dying...I still don't know what to do with that." Hell, I was already in deep, what did it matter if he knew my most personal secret? "My mum

221

had bipolar disorder," I said, my voice quiet. "She said that's why she left when I was a kid and didn't contact me again after a particularly bad depression." I sighed. "I'd spent time in the hospital after that episode of hers."

After a long pause, I heard Asher let out a sigh. "That's even worse than the shit my dad pulled," he muttered. "I hate my old man."

"Thing is, until I met with my mum, I hated her for leaving. So seeing her, hearing why she'd left, messed with my head. Especially finding out she kept up with my life but just never bothered to actually reach out to me, let me know she cared."

"How old were you?"

The heaviness of that truth ripped at me. Along with questions like whether I should forgive my mum for being a victim of her illness.

"Ten."

"Much as that sucks, doesn't make what you did to Briar okay."

"I should've thought more about how Briar would feel. I'm trying to fix it."

Asher sighed. "Look, Dahlia's been talking to Briar. Usually a couple times a day. Dahlia's suggested Briar talk to you. It's her decision. Let her make it."

"I can't. I *need* to talk to her, Asher. This is—" I blew out a breath and leaned back against our tour bus. "I love her." My voice grew stronger, the tension lessening in my shoulders. "She deserves to know that."

He sighed, long and hard. "Fuck. If there are any other pictures with another woman, I'll fly out there and break your hands so you can't play the piano. Are we clear?"

"As water."

Asher groaned. "I can't believe I'm doing this."

"Why *are* you helping me?" I'd been curious.

"I lost Lia when I was young." His voice was gravelly. "It fucked me up for years. *Years.*"

"So you get it? I'm not trying to be a wanker."

"Doesn't matter if you're trying. You're being one."

That tone brooked no argument. So I waited.

"Fine." Asher dragged out the word. "Look her up on Facebook. She's one of my friends on my personal page. You can message her that way. But I didn't suggest it."

As much of an olive branch as I'd get. I'd take that, at least for now.

"Tell me about performing in Mumbai. We've never been there," Asher said.

We talked for another few minutes, and I relaxed into the convo, glad to have someone with so much industry knowledge to talk shop with.

"Dahlia's calling me. She's probably found some new house she wants to look at," Asher said. His smile bled through the phone connection, and I murmured goodbye. Jealousy ripped through me. I wanted that life, that ease, Asher had with Lia.

I turned to see Flip standing on the top step of the tour bus. His eyes were filled with humor and even some sympathy. "It's a bitch, falling fast and hard. But Cynthia and the baby are worth all that emotion I don't know where to put or how to handle." He patted my shoulder. "Trust me."

"It's getting Briar to trust me that's the issue."

Flip shook his head. "Can't help you there, mate. Just know women's hearts are fragile. Thankfully, not as fragile as ours. We're weak bastards."

"Care to do something?" I asked.

"Like what?"

"I haven't got a clue."

"You not wanting to play music all the time is still weird."

I shrugged. "Perspective, mate. I'm finally seeing there's more to life than pounding some keys."

Flip laughed again. "Pounding a woman you love is better, I agree. Come on," he said, nodding toward the tour bus. "Let's play that car-hijacking game. Give yourself a badass persona and the confidence you need to make the next move."

CHAPTER THIRTY
Briar

I'd woken up just before 5:00 a.m., wide-awake. Lia's words from yesterday came back to me. *You can't hide from your feelings, Briar. They'll come out, eventually.*

So I picked up my phone and pulled up Hayden's contact information. Seeing his tiny picture—his fingers poised over a piano—made me ache. Not just my heart, but my middle. That was the problem with really good sex. There was no substitute.

For hours, I lay in bed staring at my phone. I wrote, deleted, and rewrote a message. Before I could change my mind, I closed the messaging app. Just because I missed him didn't mean I should contact him even if he had reached out through Facebook. I deserved a man who trusted me enough to talk through whatever was going on in his head.

Setting the phone down, I headed to the bathroom. I needed to shower before I went to the hospice center. Late mornings were Rosie's best time. I wanted to be there for the few hours she was awake.

I let the hot spray pound at the tension in my lower back as I catalogued all the reasons why Hayden wasn't worth my time. The list was long, and with each new item, my resolve firmed. I even took my time shaving, deciding I'd wear a knee-length black skirt and a keyhole lavender blouse I knew Rosie liked.

I stepped out of the bathroom, steam billowing around me. Wow, I'd been in there a long time. My phone rang. I pulled my robe tight around my neck as I rushed to answer the call.

My stomach heaved then settled with icy unhappiness as I read the caller ID.

"This is Briar."

"Briar, it's Kelly from hospice. I'm calling about Rosie."

"Is she okay?"

"Her vitals took a major dive."

I'd been expecting the news, but the reality still cut deep. Really deep. Worse, I wanted Hayden's arms around me, holding me tight until I was strong enough to help Rosie finish the job of dying.

"We wanted you to know. She asked for you when she woke up this morning." She would. Rosie knew I'd be there for her. I'd promised. I pressed my thumb against my eye. Like I'd been there for Hayden. Stupid of me to think of him so much now.

"I'll be there as soon as I can." Hanging up the phone, I tossed it onto the bed and scrambled toward the closet, pulling out the first item I saw.

I hurried through my routine. After shoving my feet into my gray slouch boots, I hurried back into the bathroom and flipped on the hair dryer. Not the outfit I'd planned, but it'd work. My long burgundy tunic hit midthigh on my gray skinny jeans. Dark colors to match my darkened mood. I ruffled my hair, wishing it would dry faster. With quick, efficient strokes, I added a little mascara and lip gloss, bypassing my new, annoyingly long makeup routine. I clicked off the dryer and raced through the bedroom, grabbing my phone before heading down the hall. I tossed it into my purse as I hurried into the kitchen.

"No time to hear about your morning, Princess. I've got to get to hospice. I'll tell Rosie you miss her."

After plating a large piece of fresh fish for Princess, I made my coffee and put it in a to-go mug. I was out the door in ten minutes, racing through the last of the commuter traffic. I ran into the building and hurried down the hall.

"Briar!" I turned at the sound of Kelly's voice.

"Oh, God. She's already gone."

"No. Oh, I'm so sorry, honey. No. I just wanted to let you know we've gotten a couple of calls for you here. From Hayden. He's worried because you didn't respond to his messages earlier."

Kelly raised her eyebrows, obviously hoping for some good gossip.

"I'm going in to see Rosie. If Hayden calls again, tell him Rosie's running out of time."

"Already did. He said he wishes he was here with you. As you were for him."

Not enough to do anything about it, like come help me. While I understood lots of people counted on him, I wanted to be the most important person in his life. I tilted my head back. In anyone's life. I hadn't been.

My mom left at the first opportunity. Ken never cared about me as much as he did his job, his image. Hayden was just one in a long line of people who took what I offered, giving nothing back. And I just couldn't do it anymore, couldn't keep giving myself to people. I'd rather be numb than feel like this.

"Thanks, Kelly. I appreciate the message."

I opened Rosie's door, shutting out Kelly, Hayden, and the rest of the world. This time in here, this was for Rosie.

Rosie turned her head and met my gaze.

"Hey, there," I said, trying to smile.

"You're having one hell of a month, sweetie," Rosie said. She shook her head, her thinning, white hair shifting on the pillow.

"What are you talking about? I'm great." I sniffled. Rosie's skin was yellow, sagging. Besides Lia, this woman was the most important person in my life. I cleared my throat and tried to smile. Rosie deserved my best, just like she'd always given me. "How are you feeling?"

"I don't want to talk about this damn cancer anymore. How are you holding up?"

"Rosie—"

"Talk to me."

I settled into my chair, placing my purse at my feet with inordinate care. I didn't want to meet her eyes. "I don't know what you mean."

"Will you stop with all the bullshit?" Rosie coughed. "I saw the pictures on my iPad."

"I didn't know you could have one of those in here."

"Probably can't. Stop looking at me like I'm crazy. I want to talk about your Piano McHottie."

A giggle burst from my lips. "You did not just say that."

"I didn't say it right? Darn. I practiced it for a while."

"Why?"

"That's what one of the blogger people called Hayden."

"Oh. Well, you said it right then. I hate the paparazzi."

"Who doesn't?"

"I've been thinking about what you said that first day I came to see you," I said. "When you asked me what I wanted to do now that I'd lost my job. I decided to go back to school to get a degree in grief counseling. I want to help families deal with this." I spread my arm to encompass the room.

Rosie's eyes softened. "You have the best heart. I'm so glad Ken didn't talk you into marrying him. He would've made you bitter and resentful. Like him. Except we can add entitled to his list."

Today really couldn't get any weirder. "Ken isn't that bad." He was, but he was also her nephew.

"That boy has always been a pompous ass. I blame his parents and even me, trying to give him some happiness in the form of material possessions."

"He's just…such a doctor." Which I'd wanted. Until I met Hayden.

"He was born into it. His father was, too. I'm so glad I looked beyond that high society mindset and married my late husband. Best decision ever." She smiled. "I can't wait to see him again. He was the love of my life."

I gripped her cold fingers. "I want you to be happy." My chin trembled.

"I would be if I knew you were settled. So let's talk about Hayden. He's a much better person for you than Ken could ever be. Better looking, too. But he hurt you."

I twisted my fingers into the material of my tunic. "I love him. Hayden, I mean."

Rosie's frail fingers gripped mine with an amazing amount of strength. "I know you do, lovely girl."

Her eyelids were sinking, her face slackening into sleep.

"Was there something you wanted to tell me?"

"Left the money to you. For the grief center. Love that idea. Don't let Ken bully you."

"I don't see Ken anymore. Which is good. How could he bully me? And what money?"

Rosie struggled to open her eyes, failed. A frown settled between her brows even as her breath slowed, the cannula's hissing loud in the quiet room. "Counseling," she mumbled. "Do it. For me. And for you."

I raised the back of her dry hand to my cheek. "I will, Rosie. I'd do just about anything for you."

I sat with her, watching my friend fade.

———◆———

Sometime in the afternoon, Kelly came in and checked Rosie's vitals, making notes in the chart. "She wake up again?"

I shook my head.

"Get some air, Briar. You've been in here for hours."

"I want to be here. In case she needs me."

Kelly pulled out her phone. "I've got this and I've got legs. Walk around a bit. It'll do you good."

I stood, wincing as my hips popped.

"I'll just do a couple laps of the parking lot."

Kelly squeezed my shoulder. "We got this. You take care of yourself."

Problem was, I didn't know how to anymore.

CHAPTER THIRTY-ONE
Hayden

Still nothing. I'd sent Briar a private message hours ago. Desperate, I'd called the hospice center. Frustration clawed up my shoulders when Kelly finally came to the line. I'd asked the receptionist—the one Briar put in her place that first day I met her at hospice—for Kelly, pretending I needed to thank her for her care of my mum. I didn't want to give that receptionist anything she'd consider gossip, knowing she would sell Briar out faster than I could play *glissandos* on my piano.

"Briar isn't here yet," Kelly said when I asked for her.

"But it's after ten. She's always there by now," I'd said, my frustration leaking into my words.

"I'm sorry, Hayden." But Kelly's voice had said she wasn't. "Rosie's dying. She won't make it through the day. So you'll just have to wait until Briar's ready to talk to you. Which she shouldn't after you decided to kiss that other woman." The connection clicked off. Great. I'd been hung up on by the hospice nurse.

Dammit, I needed to be there for Briar today. Like she'd been there for me. Instead, I was playing the piano in some venue in Prague. Should be one of the biggest thrills of my life, seated near where some of the greatest masters had played.

Such a hollow victory.

From the look Ets threw me, he was seriously angry about my last stumble during one of our most popular songs. I bent over the keyboard, trying to push everything but the feel of the keys from my mind. Didn't work. I was worried about Briar. When we walked off the stage before our encore, I pulled my phone out

231

of my pocket again.

Nothing.

Gnashing my teeth, I flipped through the aggregator sites. My heart nearly stopped.

She stood outside the hospice center in the dusky light of late afternoon, in the spot where I'd first seen her. Her right hand wound around her left biceps like she did when she was trying to hold emotion in. Some of her hair caught in a faint breeze, lifting from her shoulders to fly around her in a halo of mink brown. Her soft lips were parted, as if she was about to speak.

Even through the lens of the camera, the sadness pouring off her was crushing.

"What the fuck, Crewe?" Ets slammed his hand into mine, knocking my phone to the ground.

"If you broke that, you're buying me another," I said. He'd picked a bad time to mess with me. All the emotions swirling through me were now focused on this dickhead who thought he owned my life.

I bent to pick it up.

"Get your head in the game, Hayden. This is the real deal. What we've worked *years* for. Some piece of ass isn't going to take that from me."

I'd just bent to pick up my phone, but with his words, I stood as I slammed my fist into his jaw.

"I told you not to talk about her," I snarled into his face, gripping his shirt.

"Oi!" Jake stepped between us. Jake was way bulkier than either Ets or me, and I stumbled back, but I continued to glare into Ets's reddening face.

"We have to go back out there. You know, to the concert that twenty thousand people paid good money to see us perform," Jake said.

I pointed my finger at Ets. "Keep him away from me."

Ets growled back as Jake pushed him toward the stage. "Get out there, mate. Go do your ladies' man thing."

Jake and Flip turned toward me. I shook my hand, balling it into a fist and wincing at the sting. "You need to play," Jake said. "Don't muck this up for us, Hayden." He stalked onto the stage. I inhaled a sharp breath.

Flip squeezed the back of my neck, his fingers helping to relieve the worst of the tension there. "It's hard, being so far away. I get that. So does Jake. But Ets has a point. You gotta keep your head in the game. We need this tour, Hayden."

I nodded. Bending, I picked up my phone. The case was dented but the screen remained intact. I read the headline below Briar's picture: Broken Hope Hasn't Stopped Angel of Mercy.

I clicked the phone off, trying to work through the frustration and anger churning through my gut. Stepping back onto the stage among the screams and shouts, I walked straight to my piano. I sat, my eyes on the keys. I waited, expecting Ets to start with that catchy guitar riff. He struggled with his cable.

Flip tipped his head toward me. I placed my fingers on the keys and let them drift, picking up the melody I'd started in Seattle. My stomach settled, but my thoughts stayed focused on Briar's eyes in that picture. When I'd needed her, she'd been there, standing close, sharing her warmth and her love.

My fingers danced over the keys, the yearning pouring out. I was aware, in a vague way, that I'd hit my zone. The crowd was silent, but I kept playing, letting the emotions flow out through my fingertips.

233

I blinked, feeling better than I had in days. Coming back into the present, I glanced up, my lips twitching up in a grin.

"I just got some bad news backstage," I said into my mic. The crowd waited, silent. "In case you haven't heard, I'm dating a lovely woman. She's the perfect age and height for me." The crowd laughed, as I'd intended. "Briar's strong, really strong, but her friend's dying of cancer. Like my mum did last week." The crowd's *ahh* was soft. They were listening, hard.

"I can't be there for her like she was for me. This here, this is what I want to say to her. I miss you, Sweet Briar." I paused a beat, considering. What the hell, I was in neck deep, might as well let the wave take me right under. "I love you."

The gasps and sighs from our fans lifted around us, almost a living entity all its own. I glanced over at Flip, who shook his head, but I caught the flicker of amusement before he slid into the deep, smooth beat of our next song. I followed, waiting for Jake and Ets to join in. Another round and I leaned in and sang the lyrics, wishing I were singing to Briar. We played four more songs, the longest encore we'd ever done. When the last song ended, we took a bow to the loudest applause I'd ever heard.

I moved to center stage and bowed along with the rest of the band. I dipped my head a little and the sound of females screaming reached a hysterical pitch.

"Good move there, mate," Jake said out of the corner of his mouth. "You saved the show and then some."

After bowing one last time, I walked off the stage, catching the towel one of the roadies tossed at me.

"You're still a wanker," Ets said, his shoulders stiff, a bruise forming on his jaw. "You've done nothing but screw us up all week. So don't think your sensitive little stunt out there today made up for it."

"Wouldn't want to think I'd get an ounce of forgiveness from you, Ets," I replied, scrubbing the towel over my damp hair. "I'm off to the bus. Gotta get ready for the trip to Berlin."

Ets growled but he was smart enough to stalk off. He'd dick over a couple of women tonight and be back to his bright, shiny arsehole self in the morning.

"Beautiful melody," Flip said.

I nodded.

"One of the best things you've ever played."

"Thanks."

"Got a name?"

I considered for a moment. The tangled mess that punctuated my relationship with my mum, the time I'd had with Briar before—the life I wanted with her forever. "Between Breaths."

"Gonna have lyrics?"

I nodded. Flip smiled as he tugged at his tribal earplug. Took me a few months to get used to those. He'd gotten relatively small ones, but I kept hearing my dad's voice in my head: *Short-term body manipulation is a long-term body sentence.*

I hadn't understood that at sixteen, probably because my dad was over seventy by then, and he wasn't just old, he was doddery. My body manipulations were a tat and that eyebrow piercing my dad had hated. Removing the bar so soon after getting the piercing hurt but at least the holes had healed.

"Took some balls to say that out there. I don't think I've told the world I love Cynthia."

I shrugged. "Rosie means a lot to Briar. She deserves to know she's got people around who care right back."

"Maybe, but you know the media's going to lick this shit up. I'll walk you to the bus. You're going to be inundated as soon as they find you."

"Not why I did it, mate."

"I get that, but as part of the band, I'll say thanks anyway. We'll ride this news-wave high." Flip raised his triple-pierced brow. "As long as you keep playing like you did that last set."

I entered our bus. Grabbing some clothes, I headed toward the tiny shower stall. I'd get cleaned up before I tried to call Briar again. Maybe this time, I could actually comfort her. Maybe...Crikey, I sounded like a lovesick teen girl.

I *needed* to be there, in the same place as Briar so we could talk through all the shit I'd messed up.

CHAPTER THIRTY-TWO
Briar

I don't know how long I'd been standing outside before Kelly ran through the hospice doors and toward me. She didn't have to say a word—I knew the look on her face. I sprinted inside, wishing my heart would be fast enough, hard enough for both Rosie and I.

By the time I reached her room, Rosie was dead. Kelly held me while I cried. But I didn't cry so much for Rosie. She'd been tired and so ill; deep down I was glad she'd never suffer again. I cried for me and how much I'd miss her. I cried because I wanted Hayden there to hold me the way I'd held him when his mom died.

It wasn't until after midnight that I finally shuffled into Rosie's apartment. I was exhausted, but Princess explained her need for food in no uncertain terms. I fed her and then waited on the couch—the next part of our recently developed ritual. She rubbed her head into my chest as I stroked her soft, luscious fur. Princess's purr relaxed me, and I stretched out on the couch, pulling the throw over my shoulder.

"I'm sorry your mom's gone," I told the cat. She blinked up at me before rubbing her cheek into my chin. "Yeah. We'll be okay."

***

Lia showed up at ten thirty the next morning with the Seattle paper. Her knocking woke me from the longest sleep I'd had all week. My exhaustion had moved past the physical into the emotional when I'd finally fallen asleep in the early hours just before dawn.

"You're supposed to be headed back to Rathdrum."

Lia shook her head. "We stayed at Simon's so Asher could do some mixing. And I figured you'd need my shoulder, especially after I saw the most recent picture."

"I do," I yawned. "But maybe coffee first." I rubbed my eyes.

"I'll make some," Lia said. She pointed at the paper. "Read that. There's more, but that article's a good place to start pre-caffeine."

I stared, openmouthed, at my face in the photo and the headline, Broken Hope Hasn't Stopped Angel of Mercy. I skimmed the story, which went into detail—too much detail—about my relationship with Hayden, his mother and her battle with both mental illness and cancer, and finally Rosie.

There was so much in there, I didn't know what to address first.

"Hayden has to be upset about his mother's condition being in the paper."

"He's already responded to the reports. And Asher said Hayden mentioned it to him."

I absorbed the information, still skeptical. I picked up the paper again. "Rosie left me her condo?"

Lia shrugged. "That's what the paper's reporting. The wording is the *bulk of her estate*. That sounds significant." She moved into the kitchen while I continued to read. "Did you know?"

"I figured she was well-to-do. Ken's whole family is. She said I'd need to fight Ken off." I shrugged.

Lia came back with two mugs of coffee made from the beans Dave had given Hayden. I'd been saving them…but I hadn't been to the store, choosing to order takeout and share the fish I'd found in the freezer with Princess, and they were the only ones left in the place. I sipped and sighed, melancholy dancing with the acid in my stomach.

"How are you holding up? And remember, I, like the rest of the world, saw the picture. Shoulder," Lia said, patting the spot.

I leaned my head against her, remembering how I used to do this when I was little. "I miss Rosie. But I'm in worse shape emotionally because I fell in love with Hayden."

Lia wrapped her arm around my shoulder. "I know."

"Because of that intrusive picture? I can't think of when they could've snapped that. I was outside for all of ten, maybe fifteen minutes."

"No. The way you acted at The Vera Project. I've never seen you so in tune with anyone before. Don't get me wrong, Bri, I love you, but you've always taken care of yourself—built a wall that's hard for most of us to break through to get to the soft core you keep so guarded."

"You know why," I said.

"I do, and I get it. But I'm worried. He didn't just hurt you." She stroked my hair. "It's like he broke a piece of your soul."

The tears gathered in my eyes, but I blinked them back. "I'm pretty sure he shattered it. Dammit, I didn't want you to see this part."

Lia stopped petting me, her hand curving around my shoulder, hugging me close like she did after Dad died. "That's what I was afraid of."

"I didn't expect him, the feelings. I mean, I felt a connection... we both struggled with our relationships with our mothers. But somehow he wormed his way inside my heart before I knew I needed to keep him out."

"And you can't pry him back out without losing part of you," Lia said, her voice soft.

"Exactly."

"Mom called me this morning. She's worried about you."

"She's called me, too. Last night. I ignored her. Like I always do."

Lia sighed. "Maybe it's time to mend that bridge."

"Why? Are you saying you're going to forgive her for how she treated us? For kicking you out at seventeen?"

"I'm saying I don't want to be angry anymore. Just like I don't want to see you this hurt. With The Asshole, you were a little gloomy but more disappointed with yourself than anything. This time it's so much more."

I closed my eyes, trying to ignore the sting in my nose. "He's never called me. Text, sure. A private message. That's not enough."

"He wants to talk."

I shook my head. "But he *left* me. I knew he would. But I lost sight of reality when he asked me to come join him on tour. I'd planned it all out. I just assumed he'd miss me as much as I missed him."

"That's the hardest," Lia murmured. "I never understood how Doug could do the things he did to me and Abbi. There are days I'm still angry with him."

Princess jumped up, purring. She nuzzled into my lap, large eyes glaring at Lia.

We sat quietly. "I'm going to have to leave soon. I can feel my eyes beginning to burn," Lia said, apologetic.

"No worries. I'll be fine."

"You can come stay with Asher and me any time. Well, actually at Simon and Ella's, but you know it's an open invitation. I've got three open houses to go to tomorrow. Want to come? We'll lunch somewhere outside the city. Getting out might do you some good."

"I have to plan Rosie's funeral."

Lia stilled. "Don't be mad at me."

I sighed. "You took the list she left and already started going through it?"

"I did but only after I got the okay from Ken. He didn't want to be involved because, you know, he's an asshole. His mother is apparently too busy."

"I really know how to pick men who care about me. Or people in general." I pulled at my lower lip.

Thankfully, Lia didn't touch that one. "So...I need to tell you when Mom called, she asked what she could do. Actually, she offered to do most of the funeral planning. Said she owed it to you." Lia pulled on her hair. "Are you angry?"

I sat up, set Princess on the floor. "No, I'm relieved. How sad is that? I'll call Mom and tell her thank you. But I'm sure there are details Ken or his mother are going to have to handle." I shuddered. "It's even better Mom's handling the arrangements. The less time I spend talking to Ken the better."

Lia patted my shoulder. "I agree. So will you come out with me tomorrow?"

I blew out a thick breath. I hated feeling so alone. "Yes. I need to do something unrelated to moping and worrying about my future. I'm not going back into journalism."

I'd said the words. Lia waited. She'd always been a good listener.

"I want to go back to school, get a degree in some kind of counseling. I want to help people work through terminal illness. When I was at hospice with Hayden, watching him deal with the paperwork, I realized so many people do that alone."

"And?"

I stood. "Rosie and I talked about my options some. I like the idea. It feels right."

Lia stood and cupped my cheeks. She tilted my head down as

241

she rose on her tiptoes, pressing our foreheads together. "I'm so proud of you, Bri. Even through your heartache you're thinking about others. You're a really good person."

"When's Rosie's funeral?" I asked.

Lia went into the kitchen and got a towel. After dampening it and laying the cloth on her eyes, she said, "Friday."

"That doesn't give me much time to figure out what's next."

Lia's phone beeped.

"Get that, will you? I'm fighting cat dander."

I set my mug on the coffee table and fumbled through Lia's purse for her phone. It beeped again, flashing the beginnings of a message on the screen. "Asher says to call him ASAP."

She took the phone from me, blinking a reddened eye at the screen.

"You don't have to stay."

She pursed her lips and pressed the phone to her cheek. "Hi. The kids are okay?" There was only a faint tremor in her voice when she asked. A few months ago, Lia would have been in full-blown panic mode, but Asher kept her calmer than she'd ever been. I liked seeing this centered version of my sister.

I settled my hip against the counter, trying to guess why Asher needed to talk to Lia. Most of her face was obscured by the towel, the rest by the phone. Her mouth dropped open as she lost her grip on the towel and fumbled with the phone.

"You're serious?" she whispered, glancing at me. "No, I don't think so. Absolutely. Do you think you can do that? Probably best. No, I'll call Preslee or maybe Nate or Noah to feed the cat. They're all over on this side of the city. It'll be easier."

My confusion grew. Why would Lia want to talk to our siblings about feeding a cat? She couldn't mean Princess. She didn't need any other company, she had me.

"Text me when you're close. She has to get dressed and pack some clothes. I'll have to call you with our planned route."

Definitely about me. I went to peer out the window, taking in the crowd eight stories below. A few paparazzi were hanging around, trying to get pictures of me, but that was my new reality. A news van pulled up, a reporter exploding from the side like something out of those chase movies I'd never liked.

Lia came to stand next to me. "Got one network here already. He really said that? Wow. Yes. We'll look at the link. I'd rather not get caught right now. I have hives from the cat." She giggled. "You *would* find that funny. No, my eyes look like I've been on a week-long bender. Huh. You would know. Love you, too," she said, her voice soft. I liked Lia soft. She deserved Asher, having someone to protect her squishy center.

I folded my arm across my middle, gripping my left biceps. I'd thought I'd found that with Hayden.

Lia fiddled with her phone. "Do you have any antihistamine? I've got to help you pack and the cat is killing my sinuses."

"Sure. But…pack? For where?" I pulled out the bottle and shook out a couple of pills. At Lia's silence, I continued to prod. "Something's going on with me. In the media?"

Lia took the pills and swallowed them in a quick motion. "Didn't go down smoothly. Where's my coffee?" Gulping down most of the cup, she settled me at the bar and stood next to me.

"Asher sent me this. The video just went up on YouTube, I guess."

My stomach hit the floor when I saw the name *Jackaroo* in the title of the video. "I don't want to see it." My voice was raw. My emotions more so.

"I think you do. I'll stay right here with you." Lia pressed Play before I could argue again. Her ruthlessness knew no bounds.

"Lia, I can't. I can't see him."

The music filled the frame. Haunting, soft, yearning. Gorgeous. It was the same melody Hayden had played in Bill's studio, but better, filled with a deeper passion.

"Oh," Lia gasped. Music did that to her, burrowed into her emotions more than anything else. Even I knew the melody was beautiful. The longer I listened, the more I yearned to hear more. The video shook slightly as the back of someone's head filled the screen. The videographer shifted, and once again, Hayden filled the screen, sitting at a black grand piano. The video must have been shot last night while they were in Prague. I'd memorized his schedule in one of those sick moments of weakness.

The camera zoomed in on Hayden. His fingers drifted over the keys, his eyes distant, his face drawn. He wasn't paying any attention to the huge crowd, all of whom were raptly listening as his fingers flowed over the keys.

He started talking into the mic, and I stiffened. "He's talking about me? Am I just a way to get more news coverage?" Bile rose into my throat. "That asshole!"

I turned away, but Lia gripped my arm, her fingers locked tight on my biceps. "Listen to what he's saying."

"I don't want to hear him make light of my feelings. What we did, what we shared was *real* for me."

Lia turned up the volume. Nothing. Then Hayden's voice rang clear and steady when he said, "I miss you, Sweet Briar." He heaved out a breath. "I love you."

My knees gave out.

"What?" I wheezed.

"Let's get you packed up. You can meet him in Berlin."

I shook my head. "No. I'm staying here. Where I belong."

"Bri, now isn't the time for stubbornness. The man told the *entire world* he loves you."

I crossed my arms over my chest, trying to hug in the emotions colliding through my system. "He hasn't told *me* yet."

"Briar—" Lia's eyes held a quiet determination that usually got her her way. Not this time.

"No, Lia. Just no. You should go home. I'll go with you to house shop tomorrow."

"I don't want to leave you like this," she sighed.

"You're not. I'm asking for some space." My phone rang. Local number. *Henderson, John, Esq.*

"Briar speaking," I said.

"Ms. Moore. This is John Henderson. Rosie Douglas's lawyer."

"Oh. Hello."

"You're a hard lady to reach. Took me some time to get your number. I'd like to set up a meeting with you to go over Rosie's will. Would tomorrow work for you?"

"Um." I gripped Lia's hand. "Yes, that's fine."

"Say nine thirty?"

"Sure. What's the address?"

I scribbled it onto a pad I'd left on the raised kitchen counter.

Hanging up after exchanging goodbyes, I faced my sister, who clenched her jaw and eyed me with barely concealed annoyance.

"Don't start with me. I'm meeting Rosie's lawyer tomorrow at nine thirty."

ALEXA PADGETT

Lia sighed, running her hand over her hair. "Fine. I'll come with you."

"You have houses to look at."

Lia gripped my shoulders. "They'll wait. Since you won't accept Hayden's grand gesture, I'll come to the lawyer's office."

"I'm not ready to deal with Hayden," I whispered. I moved back to the window, counting the ever-growing media crowd on the street outside.

"Bri, love doesn't have to be so crazy."

The tears were once again in my eyes; I couldn't force them back under my calm façade.

"But...Mom just disappeared." I twisted my fingers of my left hand. "Dad died." I twisted harder and faster. "Ken betrayed me."

Lia gripped my hands. "And Hayden left."

I nodded. I sucked in a breath and forced the words from my clogged throat. "I'm not sure I can survive if he changes his mind."

CHAPTER THIRTY-THREE
Hayden

"Oi!" Flip yelled through the door. "You awake? We're in Berlin."

I pressed the heels of my hands to my eyes and moaned.

"I'm up!" I yelled as the banging commenced again.

"Good. You've got reporters screaming for information," Flip said when I opened the door. He leaned against the frame, hands in his pockets.

"You're a dickhead. I was really out." I shook my head trying to clear the remnants of sleep.

"Figured you'd want a few minutes to wake up before we go down into the crowd."

"Thanks. I think." I glanced around. "Where are Ets and Jake?"

"Already went up to the hotel." Flip rotated his jaw. "Be careful around Ets. He's angry no one in the media wanted to talk to him."

"He's being such a wanker," I grunted. "World doesn't revolve around any of us."

"Does around you, right now, after that show in Prague."

"Yeah, I guess so." I ran my fingers through my hair. "I didn't get in touch with her before I fell asleep. Slammed into me."

"This tour's not made for quality pillow time. And I haven't actually seen you get any shut-eye. Not surprised the need caught up with you, mate." Flip clapped me on the shoulder. "Got this for you." He handed me a slip of notebook paper. A Seattle number. He winked. "I have faith in your abilities."

———◆———

My security team formed a wedge around me, and we waded through the journos and paparazzi snapping pictures. They yelled questions I didn't know how to answer. Getting to the privacy of my room was top priority.

"Thanks, mates," I said to our security team. They dipped their heads down once. Ben, the lead of our security, stood facing the crowd, his height nearly as intimidating as his scowl.

"No problem, Hayden." Ben snarled at the closest journo. "Stay back."

I sighed as the elevator doors slid shut, thankful for the silence. My father's voice filled my head. *It's all about priorities, Hayden. Once you have that figured out, you've got the secret to life. Sure, decisions are still hard, but you know why you're making them. For me, you were tops. Everything else swung around that.*

I missed him. Times like these more than any other. He might've been emotionally distant, but he was wise.

He'd been my only parent, the one to whom I'd brought my troubles, my report card, my confusion after Amanda Nix kissed me in sixth grade and I'd liked her soft lips pressed to mine.

When I'd met Briar, the emptiness of my life snapped into focus. By keeping people well outside the essential parts of me—the id, my dad called it—I'd ensured no one could hurt me. But I'd also ensured no one was there to share my emotions.

Until Briar.

Neither of us expected what happened in Seattle. I'd seen the vulnerability there in her eyes the morning we woke up together the first time. Just as I'm sure my eyes reflected the fear back. We'd circled around our relationship, trying to be careful, but we didn't change the outcome. She was inevitable. And I didn't want to miss any more time with her.

Entering my suite, I pulled out my phone and dialed the number Flip handed me. I almost dropped the phone twice before I fumbled it to the crook between my shoulder and ear, rubbing my damp palms on my shirt. I hooked the door shut with my foot.

One ring. Two. I sucked in a breath, unsure what to say if I was forced to leave a message.

"Hello?"

Crikey. The time change. Great job, Hayden.

"Briar," I said. The weight lifted, my heart settled back into place. I could breathe again.

"Are you hurt?" She sounded panicked.

"I'm fine. How are you holding up? You'll be grieving Rosie…" I trailed off. Not the best start.

"I'm fine." Long pause. "Asher sent Lia the YouTube video. She and I watched it."

I bit my tongue considering my response. "I'm not. Fine, I mean. I want to be there, with you."

"Where are you?"

"Berlin. We've got a show here tonight. I've got sound check soon."

"Break a leg."

My heart slammed into my chest, and I yelled, "Don't hang up." I cringed. This feeling business was harder—messier—than I expected.

"Seriously?" she said, her voice dry. "I think you just blew out my eardrum."

"Sorry. Bad form. But…I was serious about wanting you to join me here, in Europe. I know you can't yet. You're dealing with Rosie's death and all."

"I have to get through her funeral."

"And I can't leave again, Briar. I want to be there with you. For you. But that's not what I wanted to talk about yet."

"Okay." Her voice remained hesitant.

"No, nothing too bad. I mean…How's Princess?"

"She's her normal royal self. She's moved on from salmon to tuna."

"I miss the bugger."

"Well, now that you've cleared that up, I'm going to go."

"Please, Briar, please. I fucked up. Bad. I'm just worried…I hurt you, Briar. The guilt's tearing me apart."

"You're calling me because of guilt?" She sounded confused and annoyed. My heart fluttered.

"I attacked you." My voice lowered, like I was in confessional. Except I wasn't Catholic and had never been willing to admit my sins before. "There's no way you'll forgive me for that, and I understand why. That's why I left. I couldn't see your face when you realized I'd—" Air. I needed air in my lungs. My eyes burned. "I'm so, so sorry."

"I'm not."

Flummoxed, my mouth opened and shut a couple of times with nothing come out.

"If you'll remember, I screamed your name," she said. "Twice."

I swallowed, unsure what else to do. The silence built. "So you did." My heart, which had been residing in the back of my throat, slid back into my chest. It knocked around there, leaving me light-headed.

"I had to apologize for being rough…" Sweat sluiced down my back and my throat ached, but I pushed on. "I want you to know I've never been like that."

"Good."

I'd told Asher out of desperation, but telling Briar now was to build intimacy, the trust I'd destroyed when I left. "My mum had bipolar disorder. You heard that. What I didn't tell you was that she damn near beat me to death when I was ten."

"Oh, Hayden," Briar whispered. Her voice held sympathy for the child I'd been. Not revulsion like I'd expected.

"I'd interrupted her piano practice when I came home from school. I wanted something to eat. She hit me, many times, then grabbed me 'round the neck and flung me into a window. The glass shattered."

"I don't know what to say," she whispered, voice thick with tears. "I'm so sorry."

"That's why I left," I mumbled. "I worried I'd become like her. That I'd hurt you like she hurt me." The sweat returned, covering my back, slicking down my sides. "I didn't want anyone to know. I didn't want to see the revulsion in your eyes. But I'm not. Or I won't. . ." I groaned. "I'm making a muck of this."

"Were you serious? Is that why you left without talking to me?" Her voice was hesitant. I'd bet my bank account her eyes were wide, scared.

I ran my fingers through my hair as I sat on the edge of the bed. "Part of the reason. The big reason, yeah. I was scared."

"Of me?"

I stared at the ceiling. Now or never—she was the priority. "Of what I feel for you. Of how much I wanted us. Of how much being with you felt, well, like home."

Fists pounded on my door.

I stood. "Don't hang up. I'm just answering my door."

251

"I need to go. I'm going to Rosie's lawyer's office first thing in the morning."

"I wish I was there with you. Can I call you later?" My voice rose over the pounding on my door, but the fists kept hammering away.

"You should focus on your tour, Hayden."

"I'll call you. I want to hear about your meeting."

"Bye," Briar said.

I yanked the door open. "What?" I snapped.

"We have a problem," Ets snarled as he, Jake, and Flip entered my suite.

"Oh good. Something new."

They sprawled across the couches in the living area.

"That melody you played when you were dicking around last night?" Jake said. He leaned forward, elbows on his knees.

"At *our* sold-out venue," Ets muttered. "For *our* world tour. For *our* band."

I jerked a nod, confused.

"It's gotten over a hundred million views," Flip said, his eyes warming with a smile. "Cynthia said your declaration was romantic, by the way."

My mouth dropped open, much like a fish yanked from its cool pond.

"So now we've got to figure out where to put that song into the repertoire," Ets said. He looked like he'd sucked a lime without the tequila.

"That pisses you off?" I asked, facing him.

"It's not a *Jackaroo* song."

I crossed my arms over my chest. I agreed. It wasn't something Ets would've wanted on the album. I got that. My gaze flicked to

Flip, who rolled his eyes. I met Jake's stare, and he was stoic. Never one to pick sides, Jake idolized his older brother and wasn't taking Ets's bad humor in stride. I got that, too.

"Okay," I said. "So we add it to the set list."

"Some woman blogger dubbed it Briar's song," Jake offered.

"Catchy," Flip said with a wink.

"Original," I said, straight-faced. "But the song's called 'Between Breaths.'"

"We've got to put it either first or at the end," Ets said with a scowl. "The fans will demand it."

"Did you want to add some guitar to it?" I asked. Keeping Ets happy made my life simpler.

Ignoring my question, with a bitter tone he said, "They love it."

Ah, there it was, the jealousy.

"I intended for the melody to have guitar and lyrics. But I'll play the tune whenever we agree to it."

"Play it first. Then it's done," Ets said, standing. He didn't meet my gaze.

Jake shrugged at my raised brow, refusing to answer my silent request for his opinion. "Dunno, mate. Seems like you run a risk either way. That's what comes from improvising in front of twenty thousand people."

I faced Flip, my stomach churning. His eyes were narrowed and he rubbed a finger up and down his nose, a sure sign he was deep in thought. He nodded. "First is good. With the rest of us, of course. We'll add a bit at each performance. Tell the fans we're building the tune based on their feedback."

I nodded though my stomach had just resettled somewhere near my knees. "Good idea. Keep the focus on the music. Where

ALEXA PADGETT

it should be."

Ets scowled.

"You can go out and play the song, and then we can come on and segue into one of our ballads," Flip said. "That'll be a nice transition. Build the tempo and the crowd."

Ets walked to the door and pulled it open. "We'll practice the first verse at sound check. Don't pull shit like this again."

Jake followed his brother out the door, the good little puppy always at heel.

"Was that as bad as I think it was?" I asked Flip.

"Ets is heaps jealous." He sauntered to the door. Patting his palm against it a few times, he frowned. "You're in a tight spot, mate."

I shut the door. Damned if I knew what to think of my convo with Briar or just now with my mates.

CHAPTER THIRTY-FOUR
Briar

"You didn't have to come with me," I said again.

Asher tugged a piece of my hair just behind my ear. I smiled. He was so playful sometimes. The big brother I'd never had.

"Sure we did," he said. "No way you were getting out of there without me blazing a trail through the ever-growing media presence. Who knew you'd be the 'it' girl of the year."

"But you have better things to do than babysit me."

"Just buying a house," Lia said, waving her hand. "We can do that tomorrow just as easily." The smile slid off her lips. "Why is *he* here?"

I glanced up, my throat tight. I hadn't talked to Ken in nearly two weeks—and that had been just fine. "He's Rosie's nephew. I should probably go say hello."

Lia shook her head, "You are not talking to The Asshole."

"Lovely to see you, too, Lia."

She turned to face Ken, her face devoid of any emotion. I wished I'd mastered that skill. It unnerved him, and he always tripped over himself to be nicer than he would otherwise.

"Ken," she said. "I can't say the same."

Asher chuckled as he slipped his arm around Lia's waist. He leaned down and whispered something in her ear. She smiled, shook her head.

"We'll be over there, keeping an eye on you," Lia said, tipping her head toward the other side of the seating area.

"You brought the entire army this time. For me?" Ken asked, his voice filled with irony.

"Large egos are not attractive," I said, eyes darting around the room. "They usually hide small other things."

He smiled, all enigmatic. "In this case, you'd know that's not true. That's not the reason I'm here—fun as it is to spar with you. According to the paper, she seems to have left you the bulk of her estate." He narrowed those icy gray eyes. "I told you not to go gold digger, Briar."

I crossed my arms over my chest. "Is this why you proposed? Tried to get me pregnant so I'd be trapped into marrying you? To keep the money in the family?"

"How much?"

"I take that as a yes. So Aunt Rosie held the purse strings. You assumed you'd get her fortune either directly or through me. *If* she left it to me." I held up my hand to keep him quiet. "I don't know that she did. That's why I'm here. Because her lawyer wants to talk to me about the details of her will."

Ken's Nordic Sea eyes caught mine. I used to find that seductive, having his whole attention. Now I realized he catalogued my features, doing his best to gauge my reaction so he could recalibrate his attack. And that's what it would be—a full-on emotional assault.

Hayden hadn't played games with me. Yes, he'd hurt me, worse than Ken ever could, but at least he'd always been honest.

He'd sounded contrite, worried even, on the phone yesterday. I was still reeling from his YouTube confession and Rosie's death. I wasn't sure how much more I could handle this week.

"She cared about you," Ken said, moving in closer.

Out of the corner of my eye, I saw Lia tense, half out of her chair. Asher put his hand on her knee.

"Just like I did," he continued. "You leaving me like that hastened her decline."

Ken was *such* an asshole. "You don't get to say that," I said, turning my head away. "Or anything else like it to me. Ever."

"Having a hard time with your conscience there, Briar?" His words were soft, his tone meant to convey sympathy.

I jabbed him with my finger. Not that my puny attempt to get his attention did much good. He might not be as big as Hayden, but he was solid.

"I spent hours every day with Rosie for the last days of her life. You visited exactly one time, Ken. And let's not forget that I left you when I found out you'd tried to bribe my pharmacist."

"Which I wouldn't have done if you'd been enough for me. But you insisted on being an icy bitch."

That hurt. Badly.

"You'll always be my biggest mistake." I turned to leave, but Ken's hand wrapped around my biceps, his fingers digging tight into my skin. He yanked hard.

"No, that musician was your biggest mistake," he hissed. "Made you look like a lovesick slut. Who'd want those leftovers?"

He'd hurt me, and he'd continue to pound on the spot. His triumphant smile lit his eyes, the pale irises darkening. Until Asher shoved him back. Hard.

I turned, wide-eyed, to stare at Asher.

"Why did you do that?" I asked.

"You don't grab a woman. Let alone speak to her like that." Asher tilted his head. "The receptionist is calling security." The girl, who was maybe twenty-four, was on the phone, her eyes open wide.

"Good. I'm suing you, Asher."

Asher folded his arms over his chest, his gaze dropping to the raised, angry skin on my arm. "I'd like to see you try," he said.

"I can't believe you shoved him," I said.

"Hanging out with riffraff," Ken sniffed. "I shouldn't be surprised. You were always beneath me, Briar."

"I can't believe he talked to you like that." Asher narrowed his gaze. "Just goes to show for all his calm God-itude, Kenneth doesn't know the first thing about women."

"We're not doing this," I said, stepping between them. I turned to Lia, begging her for help.

"Don't look at me," she said. "I wanted to hit him. What kind of man runs his mouth about a relationship when he doesn't have the whole story?" She glared, her gray eyes flinty. "Asshole."

Ken rounded on Lia. "I'm the asshole? You're supposed to be a writer. Surely you can engage your limited vocabulary to find a more descriptive word."

"*Asshole* connotes the most succinct description of my opinion," Lia shot back.

My arm throbbed nearly as much as my head. I placed my hand on Lia's arm. "Don't engage him. Please."

The lawyer, John Henderson, cleared his throat. Surprise trickled down my spine. I'd met him before—as Rosie's date. "Jeannette, have security show Dr. Brenton out. And Dr. Brenton? There were multiple witnesses, plus my video system. I'd think again about suing. You might want to think how it'll look to the hospital board to see you manhandling a woman who's spent weeks at your aunt's side."

He raised an eyebrow, waited. Ken clenched his jaw but stepped back away from me. Asher relaxed. Mr. Henderson turned his attention back to me, his smile warm.

"Lovely, to see you again, Ms. Moore. Won't you come into my office?"

"I'd like my sister and her boyfriend to come in with me."

"Of course," Mr. Henderson said, including Lia and Asher in his smile.

Lia grabbed my uninjured arm and pulled me into the lawyer's office. Asher trailed behind, the world's most talented bodyguard.

Mr. Henderson inclined his head and we stepped into his office. "I'm sorry, Ms. Moore. I didn't know Dr. Brenton would be here."

I rubbed the place where he'd grabbed my arm. "I'm okay."

"Glad to hear. So…" Mr. Henderson took his seat at the head of the conference table. He gestured to the rest of us and we sat, me on one side, Asher and Lia on the other. "Mrs. Douglas made a lot of changes to her will over the past few years. The largest was after she met you about three years ago."

I nodded, unsure what to say.

"She made some more during the last month of her life, and those might be contested. I understand from Dr. Brenton she was receiving large doses of narcotics to counteract the pain. That portion of the will may drag out. But you needn't worry. The bulk of your inheritance is untouchable."

I gaped. Lia leaned forward and gripped my cold fingers. "What, exactly, are you saying?"

Finding my voice, I said, "I loved Rosie for herself. I don't need her money."

Mr. Henderson smiled. "She knew that. Just as she knew you wouldn't do certain things without a nudge. So I'll jump right on in." He picked up his glasses and then handed me a copy of the will. I scanned the document quickly.

"Holy mcmoley." I couldn't have read that right.

"As you see, about a third of Rosie's assets go to you. Another third to her nephew, Kenneth Brenton, and the last third goes to the hospital's cancer wing. But Rosie wanted you to have *that* money—the money originally designated to the hospital—as well. To start a grief and counseling group through the hospital and the hospice center where she died."

I nodded, my throat tight. "I don't need that money."

"Well, the will's all legal, so the money's yours." Mr. Henderson smiled, quite pleased with the outcome. "You'll take home about six million after all the taxes. Death is an expensive business. The hospital will do better as it's a bequest."

"But...that's so much."

"She also left you her condo. I've talked to Dr. Reid—he's in charge of the cancer center at the hospital. He's happy to split the money with you for the counseling program. He's very excited about the potential there, actually."

"That's just...wow." I sat back in the chair, trying to process what he'd told me. I shook my head. "No, I don't think I can accept this."

Mr. Henderson leaned forward, his fingers linked. "Rosie worried you'd respond this way. She told me to tell you there was no one more deserving than you. If that wasn't enough, I was supposed to give you this."

He held out a white envelope. I let my fingers glide over Rosie's handwriting, taking a deep breath to steady my leaping pulse.

Slitting the top with Mr. Henderson's letter opener, I unfolded the single sheet of paper.

I want you to make others as peaceful during their last days as you

made me. And I want you to kiss that cute piano player back to his sens-
es. The way he looked at you. Whew! Brought back glorious memories.

No more whining, Briar Anne. You have people to help. Use my
money to do it. Please.

Rosie Douglas

P.S. I told John you can only keep the condo as long as you keep Prin-
cess. That cat loves you, and you know she hates everyone, including
me. Part of her charm. I expect you to keep her on the fresh fish diet
she's become accustomed to. You do know how to spoil a cat, and an old
woman. I love you, daughter of my heart.

I glanced up at the date. She'd written the letter five days ago.
The day after Hayden left.

"When did she change her will?"

"Right after you and Dr. Brenton stopped seeing each other. She
said now she could finally trust your judgment." I caught the twin-
kle behind the thick wire-rimmed glasses.

"Of course. And I'm happy to keep Princess."

Was I? I worried the tip of my thumbnail. I was. I loved the moody
fur ball, liked having someone greet me at the end of the day.

Glancing back down at the note, I stared at the words. Rosie
asked me to do this—something I really wanted. I slid the note
across the table because Lia vibrated with desperate need to know
what it said.

"Ken can't touch the will?"

"He's already trying to contest it, and he doesn't even know what
it says. Just what the papers reported about you. Lovely picture by
the way. I think Rosie would be touched."

I hugged my arm across my body, looking over to see Asher lean
in closer to Lia. Longing welled up inside of me; I wanted what Lia

and Asher shared. I wanted that with Hayden. But keeping him at a distance was the safe choice—the don't-get-hurt-again actions I'd become so good at over the years.

He'd told the world he loved me, but I didn't think he meant it. If he had, he'd be here with me now. When I needed him. Instead, he was with his band, touring the world, snuggling blondes. The ache built in my chest, an anchor of grief that wouldn't allow me to breathe, to think, clearly.

Lia's bright gray gaze met mine over the top of the papers.

"Dr. Brenton cannot win any kind of lawsuit," Mr. Henderson said. "I've made sure of that. I'll explain that to him when he comes in here in two hours. For our scheduled meeting."

We sat there in silence for a moment. Lia cuddled the papers in her hands. My sister was sensitive, always had been. Her ability to feel was what made her so good at writing her books, but it left her open to hurt. Doug, her first husband, never understood what made Lia tick, and he flailed her open because of her vulnerability. But with Asher…he took Lia's hand, the slide of their palms an intimate experience. When she tipped her head back against his shoulder, I turned away.

"Thank you, Mr. Henderson. I hope to see you at Rosie's funeral."

"Of that there's no doubt," he said. His voice was thicker, heavier.

I rose and held out my hand. He clasped it for a long moment, shaking with a firm but gentle gesture. Sadness crept over his cheeks and settled in deep.

"She talked about you," I said. "In her sleep. She always sounded so happy."

He nodded, his throat convulsing. "She refused to let me visit her. Said you were there, and she wanted my memories of her to be happy."

"I hope they were," I said.

CHAPTER THIRTY-FIVE
Hayden

"Ten till curtain," Harry yelled.

I moved to the back of the room, seeking as much privacy as I could, and called Briar. Early afternoon there now. Her meeting must be over.

"Hayden." She was out of breath.

"How'd the meeting go?"

"Tell you the truth, I'm in shock. Crap, hold on." There was a shuffle of the phone against fabric and then feet running. People were yelling. Crikey, Briar must be out somewhere. The media bothered her still. "Okay, I'm in the building now." Briar blew out a breath. "It's getting harder to avoid them. Rosie's funeral might well be a circus. She'd hate that."

"I want to be there. For you." As I said the words, I'd never been more certain of anything.

"Well, you're not," Briar said, always the pragmatist. Much as I loved that about her, the trait was currently irritating as hell. "Anyway, Rosie would be ignored, and it'll be the last time most of her friends get to say goodbye."

How to explain some of the realizations I'd come to? "I didn't understand how much Rosie meant to you, really, until I saw the picture that pap took of you splashed across every aggregator site. She's important to you. I should be there, helping you through this. I fucking hate that I'm not."

"Yes, and that went so well," she said. She'd rebuilt *her* wall. Not that I blamed her. Smart, especially considering my past actions.

I ran my fingers through the short hairs at the back of my head.

"I tried to work out the logistics with Harry last night. The concert runs late tonight. All I've seen is the concert hall. Looks like all the others we've been in."

"Aren't you at the concert venue right now?"

I wanted to talk about her day, not about the commitments keeping me from her. "Yeah."

"When does the show start?"

"We're going on in a few minutes. It's streaming live off our website if you want to watch."

"Oh."

So little and so much in that one word. "I'd like to know you're watching, Briar. Would you—" I swallowed. My breathing escalated. I forced the words past my lips. "Would you consider meeting me? I know you're busy right now, but we fly into JFK in a couple of weeks, winding our way across the country. I'll buy your ticket."

The silence stretched, filled with the recriminations Briar was too kind to say out loud. I'd offered this to her before. Then I'd left.

The words I'd been flagellating myself with for days.

"Thank you for asking," she said. "But I'm not sure us seeing each other again is a good idea. What we had…maybe it doesn't live up to the reality of our lives."

"We haven't even tried."

"The past few days have been an education," she replied.

I hunched further, my phone tucked into the nook between my shoulder and ear, unwilling to leave without getting some crumb of hope from her.

"I'll meet you at the airport. All incognito. I have my cap and sunnies. We'll go to Chinatown. I've always wanted to visit there. But it'll be more fun with you."

"You don't have to lie to me, Hayden. You told me going in that you'd leave. You told me you didn't want to do the relationship thing."

"That was before. Briar, I—"

"I don't want to be the butt of more bad jokes or be on the front of gossip rags when you leave again," Briar said. "For me, this isn't about getting attention. Some of the things they've said. Well, they hurt me."

Her words, the sadness and exhaustion behind them, they ripped me apart.

"Dammit, Briar, don't do this." My breathing was as harsh as if I'd sprinted five kilometers. "We're good together."

"Amazing. Maybe because we knew it would end."

No, I didn't want this to be all there was to us. I sucked in a big breath.

Harry's voice sounded from the doorway. "Hayden, you're on. Let's go, mate." I shook him off with a glare. Ets stood across the room, his arms crossed over his chest.

"I have to go. This convo isn't over." I dropped my hand and started walking toward the screaming crowd. I put the phone back to my ear. I wasn't sure if Briar was still on the line; I couldn't look because I knew I'd lose courage to say what I needed to.

"This here, these people don't mean as much as you, Sweet Briar."

I clicked my phone off and huffed out a breath, shaking the tension from my body.

"Let's get her done," I said.

"After the show, mate," Ets said, laughter in his voice. "And a few more besides."

I glared at my band mate. "I meant the show."

"You need to enjoy the moment, Hayden. Not many blokes get this chance. That Yank, she's just one woman in a sea of millions."

What Ets didn't understand was that Briar was the only one I wanted.

Three and a half hours later, I yearned for a long shower and a longer talk with Briar. She hadn't told me enough about her meeting with Rosie's lawyer. I wanted to know what time the funeral was. I wanted to make plans with her in New York. I wanted her. Period.

Backstage, I smiled; signed some pictures, napkins, and shirts well below the girls' chests; had more pictures taken of me than I wanted. But this was part of the gig—do for your fans so they stayed fans. Forget for a moment what I wanted, hell, needed.

I understood Briar's hesitation about this lifestyle. It wasn't anywhere near as glamorous as I'd expected. Less privacy, more grind. Not the best trade-off for her. I got that. But...I wasn't centered, whole, since I'd left her sleeping in my bed. I just hoped she needed me half as much as I needed her.

"We're heading back to the dressing room," Ets said. I raised my hand in a wave. "Found some hot girls to take your mind off that Yank."

I didn't want my mind off Briar. I'd finally found someone worth thinking about, and I planned to show her I was worth the risk.

I strode past our roadies, thanking them all for a job well done. They nodded, some high-fived me. Our bus was quiet. A shower, then I'd call Briar. Somehow I'd talk her into visiting me.

Halfway through washing my hair, the shower curtain opened.

"Get out," I yelled.

"I'd rather get you off."

A woman's hands slid over my naked shoulders; she molded her-self to my back. Her tits were firm, her sleek body rubbing against mine like a fantasy.

I opened my eyes, winced as soap slid into them. I turned my face into the spray, blinking until the soap cleared.

"Get out." I was in a tiny shower cube, in the clutches of some fan. A fan who should never have made it onto the bus.

"I'm going to show you a good time," she said. Her voice was husky. Probably sexy, but all I could think about was Briar. My con-nection with her was tenuous. Briar was already upset about the blonde—what was her name? Didn't matter. If this leaked, Briar would *never* give me another chance, not to mention Asher would break my hands. And I'd deserve the punishment and then some.

"Get out of my shower. Now." I turned my head to glare out of my left eye. The right one still burned from the soap.

The girl pouted sexy red-painted lips. Her mascara ran down her cheeks, and her pale hair was half plastered to her head. I didn't bother to look lower. Didn't matter. She wasn't the woman I wanted.

I scooted back farther into the corner as she stood on tiptoe, molding her body to mine, yanking my head down for a kiss. I exploded out of the tiny space. I wrapped myself in a towel before yanking open the bus's door to see Ets sitting there, pretty as you please, with a journo I recognized from our meet and greet earlier. My jaw clenched, hard, as I realized he'd set me up.

"I'm done," I said.

"Enjoyed your shower, then, mate." He laughed. He didn't have a clue.

The woman sauntered up behind me. She better have on a towel. She didn't.

I scooted away, my eyes never leaving Ets's face. He quit laughing. I couldn't believe I'd ever considered him my best mate.

"That was low, even for you. I quit." I stalked into the back, slamming and locking the door. Should've done that last time.

"Hayden, it was all in good fun. You need the relief of a good lay." I could still hear the amusement in his voice through the door.

I yanked on my boxer-briefs. "You have exactly ten seconds to get the journo out of here if you don't want him to hear what I have to say to you. And I was serious."

I pulled on my jeans and socks. I heard Ets say something as the bus door opened. I whipped my shirt over my head, sat on the bunk to pull on my shoes.

"They're gone," he yelled.

I sucked in a deep breath and headed out, giving Ets a hard glare as I brushed past him. Much as I wanted to slam my fist into his smirk, I resisted the urge. Barely.

"That picture or story gets back to Briar, and I'm going to fucking kill you. After you apologize to her for it."

"This is exactly why you need to screw another woman. The Yank's just some tits and an arse, Hayden. No different from any other woman."

This time I couldn't contain my anger. In a quick move, I had a fistful of his shirt and his body slammed against the side of the bus.

"She's not just some woman. She's *my* woman. And you not only topped as a band member, you blew past the line as a friend. You're a selfish wanker, and I don't want anything to do with you ever again."

I let go of his shirt and started to walk away.

"You can't quit." His voice went high with anxiety. "Fuck it, Hayden, you've *become* the band."

"I don't care. I'm done."

"What about the rest of the tour?"

"Should have thought of that before you tried to fuck up the *one thing* that is important to me."

I turned my back to Ets to see Jake and Flip walking toward us. "That's some serious yelling, mate. Might want to save the voice for our show tomorrow."

"I'm done."

"Whoa," Flip said. "What the hell are you talking about?"

"I quit," I hissed. "Ets can explain why."

"This have something to do with the wet chick crying and blubbering in German? Some journo was leading her off."

I wanted to slam my fist into the side of the bus. Instead, I settled for cussing loud and long.

"Mate, you can't just leave," Flip said, always logical. "There are too many people on this production. They're counting on you for their jobs. Including me and Jake."

Some of my anger drained. I'd disappoint the roadies and the rest of the staff with this move. Flip was a good bloke. He didn't deserve the drama from me. Still, I had to deal with the journo, sitting there, an evil glint in his eye, waiting to catch me with the groupie.

"I'm done. Especially with his shit." I pushed past them, turned back to look at Ets. He folded his arms over his chest, looking smug and frustrated all at once.

"You're a drongo, letting one woman lead you around like this. Once you get some perspective again, you'll see she's nothing special."

"Like Mila wasn't?" I shot back.

Ets's scowl deepened. "Yeah, that's right. Nothing special."

"I'd tread really careful now, mate," Flip said, arms unfolding to make fists at his sides. "You're making it sound like women are interchangeable, and neither Cynthia nor I appreciate that."

I straightened and glared back. "I told you, Briar matters to me. You fuck that up, you fuck me up."

Ets glared back, unwilling to back down. Not that he ever had. That bullheadedness got him to this level of fame—one few reached. But the pressure was dissolving the ties between us more quickly.

"Hayden," Jake said, looking back and forth between us. "Ets fucked up."

"Hey now," Ets said, his voice menacing.

"You brought in a woman he didn't ask for, and you brought the press into his personal life. You're going to fix this mess," Jake said, pointing his finger at Ets, who squared his shoulders, unrelenting.

"It was just in good fun," Ets muttered.

"No, you brought a journo here to tell the story about my wild shower sex. That I didn't have. Because I don't want that woman." I enunciated each word carefully.

"You're fixing this," Jake repeated. He stood in front of his older brother, arms akimbo, jaw set. "The way Hayden wants the situ fixed." Jake turned back to me, his eyes serious. "But you, Hayden, need to start thinking about the band. That's what we are—a group that, together, made commitments. Ets can be a complete horse's arse, but he's a talented one who's helped us get to this point in our careers. I'll make sure he fixes this, and then we finish our tour."

Jake held my eyes, and I held my breath. Finally, I nodded once.

271

"Keep him away from me."

Needing my space from Ets—from the whole band—I walked to the roadie bus. With everyone still packing up our gear, I had the whole bus to myself. Flopping onto a crappy couch, I counted the rest of the shows in my head. Forty-eight more shows. Nearly three more months. I groaned. No way I was going to last that long.

CHAPTER THIRTY-SIX
Briar

Abbi skidded around the corner of Simon and Ella's small living room, her socks causing her to slide like Tom Cruise in that one movie.

"Tell me you haven't been online this morning," she panted. She tripped over the edge of the carpet and plopped down on the couch next to me.

"I just walked into the house, Abs. Nice to see you, by the way."

"Aunt Bri, have you been online today?"

"They wrote something else about me?" I mumbled.

I'd been right to turn down Hayden's lukewarm request for us to be a couple. I didn't want to live my life in a fishbowl.

The press, Hayden's drama, none of that mattered. Rosie deserved today to be all about her, to see how much she was loved. I wouldn't let Hayden take that from her.

"It's not about you. Not really. Here, look."

Abbi tossed me her phone. She was practically bouncing in her seat when I glanced at her before I turned my attention back to the screen.

It was an article about Hayden's band. The original was from some German paper I didn't follow. My eyes widened as I read.

"You've got to be kidding me," I whispered.

I grabbed my phone from my purse and powered it up. Between my mom and the media constantly calling, I rarely left it on anymore.

Four texts from Hayden. I sucked in a breath and opened the first.

Don't believe the crap in the German paper. Ets is about to sort it.

Confused, I nibbled at my lip. The article said Murphy Etsam and Hayden were in an altercation after the show last night, but the American version glossed over the reason. Dread crept into my stomach.

I clicked on the next message.

Ets sent the woman in to meet me. I want to call you so badly, but you're finalizing the plans for Rosie's funeral. Just know I didn't do anything. I wouldn't do that to you. I meant what I said. And I sure as fucking hell didn't ask for her to be there.

Wow. Hayden sounded…concerned. These words were from the man I'd spent time with in Seattle.

The third text listed the Berlin time as 5:00 a.m. I wondered if Hayden slept at all last night. *R u asleep? Did an interview with the reporter before we left Berlin this morning. Please read it. Please call me.*

I pressed the phone icon before I could talk myself out of it.

"Briar."

His voice—just his voice—killed me. "Hi," I breathed.

"You read the interview?"

"Only the part printed on the gossip site Abbi gave me."

"I meant what I said there. You're the woman I care about. The *only* one. I miss being with you. Like we were in Seattle."

I glared at Abbi, who shrugged before getting up to leave. Lia's voice answered something Abbi said. I hoped they'd stay in the kitchen.

"Hayden, we don't live on the same continent. You haven't stayed in one country for more than three days. And that was only because of your mom."

"My mum was the reason I came to Seattle. I stayed for you. I never should have left you either. This tour is killing me." He

274

sounded tortured. Wrong as it was, a little thrill trickled past the dread sitting icy in my stomach. "I didn't want to say the words on the phone. Not the first time. I told you I wanted to court you. I have it all planned out in my head, and this just isn't meeting the criteria for the romance you deserve."

"Like what?" Sure, I knew I sounded breathy, but I didn't care. I wanted a love affair. The kind Hayden and I started here.

"I want to dip you back over my arm and kiss you better, longer than you've ever been kissed. Better than our night at The Edge-water. I want to hold you in my arms as we take a boat down the Seine. I want to dance with you on the cobbles in London. I want to stand on the top of the Statue of Liberty with you, and yell to the whole world that I love you, Briar."

"Holy shit."

"You didn't believe me before? Not quite the response I expected."

From what little I'd overheard of the conversation with his mother, Hayden had been hurt, many times, by people who were supposed to love and care for him. No wonder he'd run away from his feelings.

"I'm moving in to Rosie's condo. She left it to me."

"Again, not really what I wanted to hear."

The static crackled across the line. Our breaths mingled, synchronizing just as they had when we'd been sated, ready for sleep.

"I don't know what to say, exactly."

"Nothing's been right since I left you."

I cracked. I couldn't let him think I was *that* uncaring. "Send me your itinerary for the next few weeks. I'll see what I can do."

"You'll meet me on tour? Crikey, I want to see you."

"I…"

"I'd like you to meet Jake and Flip."

I tucked my hair behind my ear. No mention of Ets, the only band member he'd talked about when he was here. Much as I wanted to ask, I didn't want the guilt of being the wedge between them.

"We live nearly a day apart. The logistics of this arrangement are ridiculously not in our favor."

"I know what I'm asking, Briar. But if you could meet me—there are things I want to say to you."

"Besides screaming from the top of the Statue of Liberty?"

"Well, yeah. Besides that. But telling you I love you was the most important."

"When you left, I was crushed." I paused, my heart fluttering in a hummingbird's insane rhythm.

"Hurt me, too. But I was focused on doing the right thing then. Turned out to be the exact wrong decision. I should have told you how I felt. I should have trusted you as much as you trusted me."

"Hayden, this isn't the time—"

"See. There isn't a good time. We're on different continents, trying to have our own lives, but I don't want separate lives. I want a life with *you*. I haven't been happy since I left our bed."

"Hayden?"

"Sweet Briar?"

I blew out a breath. "I fell in love with you." I hung up before he could respond.

"What did he say?" Lia settled on the couch next to me. She wore a smart black dress, her long auburn hair pulled up into a loose chignon. Lia pulled off understated elegance like she was born to it.

"The funeral starts in an hour."

She raised an eyebrow. "Abbi said you called him."

"Ugh. Fine. I did. He wants me to meet him on tour. New York is his first stop in the States, but he...he talked about Paris." I swallowed, still gripping my phone hard. "The last time I talked to him, before today, he said he'd meet me at the airport, take me to Chinatown. We didn't do that here."

"That's not why you look that pale. Spill, Bri."

I stared down at the phone, my head buzzing with the words. "He said he loved me." My voice was soft, as if the very air itself could destroy the memory of his words.

Lia leaned back, a smug smile on her face. "Did he now? To just you. Excellent."

My eyes shot to hers. Her smile grew and her eyes glowed. She took the phone from me, and even though I grabbed for it out of reflex, I let her set it on the coffee table.

"He can't mean it," I said. "Maybe it's just for press for his tour. Jackaroo, specifically Hayden Crewe, is the hottest thing in music because of our affair."

Lia's smile grew broader. "You lived a whirlwind romance. It is a little like a Cinderella story. Who doesn't love that fairy tale?"

"Me. I like reality—the boringness of two people just rubbing along together, content."

"Because your relationship with Ken worked out so well. That wasn't love, Briar. The real deal is bigger than either of you. It'll give you the highest high, better than you can ever imagine, because of the connection that's so deep it's impossible to unlink. You know that. That's what Dad felt for Mom."

"And look where that got him," I huffed.

She tipped my chin so I had to meet her eyes. "It's what I feel for Asher, and he returns those feelings. Love can work out. You've already let him back inside." She placed her hand just over my heart.

"I want to see him, make sure he means it."

"No, I know you, Briar. You want him to prove he won't do anything stupid again. Something that will hurt you."

I stood and began to pace, thinking about how I'd felt when I'd read Hayden's note. When I'd been bombarded by the media with questions about our breakup.

"Of course I do. He broke me, Lia."

"I asked Dad about his relationship with Mom once."

I stopped midstride, just like she knew I would.

"Right before his last deployment." Lia smoothed the hem of her dress across her knees. "He told me that he could never regret loving Mom. Not because he got us out of the deal." A ghost of a smile slid over Lia's mouth. "That's what I expected, some platitude about us being awesome. Instead, he told me the eleven years with Mom were the ones where he lived out loud. As big as he could. And that was all we could ever wish for."

"What does that mean?" I asked, confusion and frustration bubbling through my stomach.

Lia raised an eyebrow. "Maybe it's time you figured that out."

———◆———

The funeral service ran long because more than fifty people stood up at the podium, reliving their favorite Rosie moments. As I listened to John Henderson speak, the night I'd met Rosie bubbled up in my mind.

I'd come as Ken's date to the cancer charity function, a cause I planned to write about for next day's paper. Since Ken was the leading oncologist on the team, his office helped set up the fundraiser for the new cancer facility the hospital wanted so desperately. We were in the Terrace Room at The Edgewater, the doors open to let in the light breeze blowing in off the sound. I'd been standing near our table, talking with a colleague from the much larger Seattle Times newspaper. He'd been there to cover the event, and I'm sure he knew who Rosie was when she walked over.

"Are you here with Dr. Kenneth Brenton?" Rosie had asked.

I'd affirmed, giving my colleague an apologetic what-can-I-do look. He'd shaken his head, chuckling as he wandered off.

"Is Kenneth someone special?" Rosie asked.

I clutched my glass of white wine in both hands. "I'm not sure yet. We've been out a few times." I'd shrugged, noncommittal. I didn't plan to share my relationship status with a nosy older lady I'd just met.

Rosie had studied my eyes, exposing my secrets. I'd forced my gaze to stay locked on hers and finally she smiled, transforming her face.

"You have spunk. There's hope for you yet."

"Excuse me?"

"What do you love best in the world, dear?"

I'd opened my mouth, snapped it shut.

"Ken told me you helped set up this event. He said you wanted more awareness for the need for early cancer detection."

"That's true. It's important. I like the idea of giving back." I'd sipped my drink, glancing around the room. "This may not be the most efficient way to do it, but events like this attract reporters. And that helps build awareness. Harder to do when we're tackling all cancer instead of a specific kind."

"I like you. My husband would have, too. He's been gone these ten years. Lung cancer, bless his soul."

Pulling myself out of my thoughts, I stared at the huge bouquet of calla lilies behind her casket. Hayden had sent those. A sweet gesture for a woman he'd met only once.

Rosie wouldn't have any patience for my fear. She'd wanted everyone to *live*. Maybe that was the point Lia had tried to make earlier.

When my turn came to speak at the podium, I didn't bother with the notecards I'd spent most of the night scribbling on.

"I only knew Rosie for about three years," I started. "She was my surrogate mom, confidant, and good friend, all rolled into one… without the strain of actual family." I waited for the titters to die down before I continued. "I learned a lot from Rosie. She taught me that sometimes being strong meant giving in." I dipped my head toward Lia who did that raised-eyebrow thing. "She taught me to trust my instincts first, last, and always. And, most importantly, she taught me about love. That it doesn't have to be blood. Love can bind you to someone special you meet toward the end of your life. Rosie was one of the best people I've ever known, and I'll miss her cheating at canasta."

I smiled as John Henderson laughed, wiping his eyes.

"But mainly I'm thankful we had the time we did together. Much as I wish it were longer, knowing Rosie brought contentment into both our lives. That's something I've promised her I'll continue. With her generous funds, I plan to start the Rose Douglas Foundation, which will help families dealing with cancer and terminal illness get the counseling and support they need."

I paused, needing a moment to collect myself. Emotion filled Ken's eyes. Yeah, even Ken mourned Rosie. She was just that charismatic. My eyes swept out into the sea of people there. I brought them back to my mom, her gaze intent on me, her mouth bracketed with wrinkles she'd developed in the last year or so, when she buried her second husband. She wiped her cheeks with a handkerchief my half brother Noah handed her.

"I can't think of a better legacy for Rosie. And I'm so thankful to be part of her future. To continue to share the love she spread so abundantly through our community."

I took my seat next to Lia. "Nice speech," she said.

"Thank you for being here for me. I think I get what you meant. I mean, what Dad said to you."

She wrapped her arm around me. "So are you going to go?"

I sucked in a breath. "Yes. But I'm really scared. What if…what if it's like Ken?"

The people around us stood, filing out toward the cemetery. Mom and our half sister, Preslee, headed toward us.

"You have to trust, Briar. Otherwise you're going to be so lonely. Look at what Rosie accomplished by opening up to others. Look what Asher and I have because I took the leap."

Mom stopped in front of me. "Lovely speech, Briar."

"Thank you. Rosie deserved it."

Mom smiled but her eyes were sad. I hugged Preslee, surprised—as I always was—that my half sister was a full-grown woman. She reached up, touching her close-cropped, dark hair. "She was lucky to have you in her life," Preslee said, her voice as soft and lovely as the rest of her.

I shook my head. "I was the lucky one. You have the key to the condo?" I asked.

Preslee nodded, her pale green eyes sparkling. "Yes. I stopped by before coming here." She grinned. "I took your advice and went to the fish market first. Princess wound through my legs as soon as she smelled what I'd brought her. I patted her head while she ate, but I didn't want to press my luck."

"Smart," I said. "That cat has very distinct opinions."

"We'll let you go to the reception," Mom said. "It should be nice."

"You don't want to come?" I asked.

Mom shook her head. "The boys went to bring the car around." Mom looked around the large space, her eyes settling on the coffin. "I'm not much for funerals. Brings back memories I wish it didn't."

After a moment's hesitation, I embraced my mother. "Thank you for your help."

She patted my back, her eyes gleaming when she stepped back. "Not a thing, honey."

Lia's eyes tracked our mom and Preslee as they walked away. "I never know what to expect with Mom. I'm glad she helped put this together, though."

"Going to bury the hatchet once and for all?" I asked.

Lia snorted. "Maybe. But that's between Mom and me. I like Preslee, Nate, and Noah. The twins are really protective of both Mom and Preslee. It's sweet."

"Preslee was happy to help with Princess."

Lia pulled out a large white envelope. "Here."

"What this?"

"Backstage pass and Hayden's hotel information."

"What? How did you—"

"Asher's been busy," Lia said with a wink.

Tears filled my eyes and I threw my arms around Lia's shoulders. "Thank you."

CHAPTER THIRTY-SEVEN
Hayden

A travel day was worse than a gig day because I didn't have anything to focus on except my inconclusive conversation with Briar. I'd called about chartering a private flight to Seattle but I couldn't make the twenty-plus hours of flight time work, not with a two o'clock rehearsal tomorrow I couldn't miss.

Flip and Jake were right. I owed them my best for the remainder of this tour, especially since the song I'd played in Prague was such a viral hit, and our fans loved that we were adding more to it with each performance. But that didn't mean I wasn't frustrated by the situation.

Interesting how Flip, the most inscrutable of our group, turned out to be my rock. The best mate I'd always craved. And Flip, being that mate, wasn't going to leave me alone to think about Briar as she struggled through Rosie's funeral.

"Whatcha say? Let's go see what Amsterdam has to offer," Flip suggested as we gathered our bags from the carousel. Flip, Jake, and I opted to fly instead of spending the day on the tour bus. The decision made everyone happy, because Ets was entertaining twenty-two-year-old identical twins on the bus. From what little Jake said, the girls were screamers. I couldn't imagine a worse way to spend the seven-plus hours between locations than listening to Ets getting it on.

Jake hoisted his bag onto his shoulder. He'd been even quieter than usual, but I was glad for his company.

"I want to see the Rijksmuseum," he said.

"Really?" Flip asked. He put on his sunnies, heading through the speed customs we'd VIP through—one of the benefits of superstardom.

"Yeah, took 'em ten years to renovate it. I read it has heaps of the Masters."

"I read about that," I said. "Reckoned to be one of the best museums in Europe. I'm game."

"Let's get our gear checked in and we can head over," Flip suggested.

He nodded toward our driver, who walked us to a large, sleek SUV. I liked riding in these way better than limos, which felt pretentious and wasteful. With no other choice, I relaxed, looking forward to the afternoon.

"I want to try out some of the beer here," I said. "Isn't this the birthplace or something?"

"Dunno," Jake admitted. "The guys from uni were more interested in the legal pot and sex."

"I bet." Flip laughed. "I'm steering clear of both of those. Cynthia would have me by the balls. Can't imagine your Yank would like those pics much, Hayden."

I shook my head, a small smile forming. "I've no plans to find out about any of it."

"You two are doddery. Soft," Jake said.

"Hey, you could've stayed with your brother," Flip responded. "I'm sure one of those girls would've been happy to entertain you, too."

Jake shook his head. "It's getting old. All the partying and easy sex. I'm ready to see some of the world. You know, get the most out of our time on this tour." His gaze slid to mine. "Something tells me things are going to change when it's over."

I leaned back into the soft leather, refusing to rise to the bait. "So whose paintings are we going to look at?"

"Rembrandt, Vermeer. Some van Gogh. I want to stand in front of *The Night Watch*. One of my favorites we studied."

"That's right! Your degree's in art something." Flip pouted his lips together in a kissy duck face. "Wanker."

"Don't give him shit," I said. "Mine's in music composition. Worked out well for us. You're just jealous you didn't get the cert."

Flip shrugged. "I've got the cash to see the real deal painting now. Maybe even buy it if I wanted. Seems like that's a pretty big win."

———◆———

The rest of the day sped past, and I fell into bed. Exhaustion mixed with the five different beers I'd managed to try between dinner and now. I dialed Briar's number again, the tenth time in the past few hours. She'd texted me about an hour after our talk, letting me know she'd have her phone off during Rosie's funeral. I frowned when it once again went to voice mail. Surely, with the funeral starting at 10:00 a.m., it should be over by now.

I went to the gossip sites. Their information about Briar's doings was better than mine. According to the web, the actual funeral was over, but the large group—nearly five hundred people attended Rosie's funeral—had gathered at The Fairmont in downtown Seattle. An all-day affair, then.

I sent her a text.

Hope the day went smoothly. Thinking about you. x

I stared at the screen for many minutes before I plugged in the charger and set it on the nightstand. When I woke in the morning, I'd have a message from her. I hoped.

———•———

I woke up late the next morning and reached for my phone. A grin started to form when I saw I had a text from Briar, but the budding happiness faded quickly when I realized it wasn't a message I wanted to see.

Today was hard. Turning off my phone. Just need some time. I'll be in touch. Soon.

No. She was supposed to call me back. Something more than the bullshit lines I reread, trying to make sense of.

I checked my phone the rest of the morning as I went through my usual routine. Her response frustrated me enough to warrant a run down by the canals instead of staying inside. Signing the hundreds of autographs on the way back to my hotel made me late, and I raced through my shower. I arrived at the venue fifteen minutes late—a feat considering I'd barely returned to the hotel before I was supposed to leave. Good thing we were only a short walk—and an even shorter car ride—from the venue.

"Nice of you to join us, Hayden. Now we can finally get started." Ets's words pushed me further over the edge.

"Sorry. Went for a run and got mobbed."

"Sure it was rough having women rub against you. Did you file a suit for molestation? Is that what took so long? You're not the only member of this band, dickhead."

I didn't bother with words. I lunged. Jake and Flip got between us quick enough. "Cool it," Flip said. "We've only got a few hours before the gig, we've got to start sound check. Pull it together."

I stomped over to my piano and went through our pre-performance checklist.

Four hours later, I slammed into the dressing room, angry with the compromise I'd made on "Between Breaths." I flopped on the couch, arm over my eyes. I was supposed to use this time between practice and the actual show to eat, nap, or meditate, but I was too restless.

Briar hadn't told me she loved since the night before I left her. She'd said she'd *fallen in love* with me. That could be past tense.

Maybe she couldn't get beyond my bloody stupid behavior. She hadn't agreed to meet me in Paris, London or New York. She hadn't said anything about us, really.

Maybe it was time to let go of that dream.

CHAPTER THIRTY-EIGHT
Briar

I stood out front of the Seven One Seven, impressed by the old-world charm.

The place was small, barely big enough for the band. My heart pounded as I approached the black door, pulling my suitcase behind me. Inside, I slid my sunglasses up onto the top of my head and walked to the front desk. Time to test my plan.

"Hi," I said when I reached the concierge.

"Good afternoon," the sleek brunette said, her smile professionally inquisitive, but recognition widened her eyes. Being chased by cameras finally had an upside. Her brass name tag read Lotte.

"I'm here to check in," I said with a bored look. At least I hoped it was. My heart raced faster than it did when I ran sprints.

"I'm sorry for your inconvenience but we have no rooms."

I tapped my sunglasses on the counter. "Oh, no. I'm checking in to Hayden's room," I leaned forward to whisper with a smile.

Lotte smiled politely and typed on her computer. "Mr. Crewe didn't leave any instructions for us to allow anyone up to his suite." She shook her head.

Well, there went the easiest route. I kept my smile in place but my heart rate ratcheted up and sweat gathered at the back of my neck. I pulled my phone out.

"I'll just text him to clarify the confusion. Does he need to come back from the Melkweg to sign me in? That's not his normal routine. Well, I hope it doesn't throw him off his performance tonight." I nibbled at my lower lip.

"I wouldn't want to inconvenience Mr. Crewe," the girl said, clearly at a loss. I kept my head bent over my phone.

"I understand. Let me just finish this and we'll get it all cleared up," I said, my fingers flying over the screen.

Lotte set a key card in front of me. "Pleasure to have you staying with us, Ms. Moore." I lifted my head to see the girl flash a smile, her dimples dancing. "Mr. Crewe will be happy, I believe. He's been…restless," she finished with a shrug.

"Ah. Didn't he get to run? That helps."

"The fans mobbed him by the canal."

I frowned. "He doesn't like that part," I muttered to myself.

"That is why I didn't ask for his autograph." Her cheeks deepened from pink to rose. "Though I would like one, if possible."

I snagged the card off the counter and grabbed my bag. "I'll see what I can do," I said. "Which room?"

"The Room at the Top. Up the stairs. That suite offers the most privacy and the best view of the city." She nodded toward the narrow flight tucked across the lobby.

"Thank you, Lotte. Are you working tomorrow?"

She nodded. I smiled, hoping neither of us would be in trouble. "See you then."

"A pleasure, Ms. Moore."

Hayden's room was nice, but they always were. Not overly big but the beamed ceiling added ambience. I stood at the window for a few minutes, soaking up my first view of Amsterdam, before heading to the shower. I needed to wash off the plane ride and take a nap so I was ready for the night ahead.

Clean, but only mildly more awake, I pinned up my damp hair, wanting fat curls to flow down to my bare shoulders. I was sure Hayden would like running his fingers through them. As I sat on the bed, fatigue threatened to pull me under. I yawned hard, tears gathering in the corners of my eyes. Jet lag was no joke, especially on top of days of little to no sleep. I should call Lia. At least text her.

I'd set my purse on Hayden's desk. I walked to it and pulled out my phone, shooting off a quick note. Lia responded immediately.

I'm going to need all the details.

I smiled and dropped my phone back into my purse. I missed and it landed on some of Hayden's papers. Picking up my phone, my eyes caught the top sheet.

It was some sort of itinerary. Seattle. From Berlin. That was scratched out. Brussels was listed below. The date was in three days.

A name—probably the company owner or a pilot—was under the jetliner's name, all scrawled out in Hayden's slanting script. Picking up the paper, I pressed my other hand to my chest.

He'd scheduled a flight back to see me. On the only open two days in his schedule for the next six weeks, he'd planned to fly across the Atlantic and the entire US to see me. He'd told me he wanted me in his life. Here was the proof that he'd work hard to make that happen—on my terms.

I set the paper down, smoothed my hand over it. We'd talk our relationship through, he and I. We'd work through his confusion and my feelings of betrayal. Because my relationship with Hayden was once in a lifetime.

I yawned again, my jaw popping. Four hours until I needed to be at the venue. I slid into Hayden's bed in just my panties and a cami. I inhaled his scent, already more at peace than I'd been in days.

———◆———

I woke to a light tapping on the door. "Ms. Moore? You didn't answer the wake-up call."

"Crap!"

I scrambled from the bed and ran to the door, opening it just a little. "Thank you," I murmured.

"You are most welcome. Anything else I can help you with?" Lotte asked, hands folded demurely in front of her.

"Nope. All good."

I flew into the bathroom to wash my face. I'd slept longer than I'd anticipated, leaving me less than thirty minutes to get to the venue.

I quickly added some mascara and a touch of lip gloss before pulling on my backless silk top. I wiggled into my skinny jeans and slid on a pair of beige wedges. Unpinning my hair, I despaired I didn't have the time to style it better.

I grabbed my purse and hustled out of the room.

The walk to the Melkweg would have been much more fascinating if I weren't so anxious. I should've waited for Hayden at the hotel, talked to him there, in private. Or just called to let him know I wanted to fly out and be with him. He'd invited me to New York…I didn't have anything to worry about.

I owed him a grand gesture. He'd told the world he loved me, and I'd returned his feelings with skepticism and fear. I wanted to show him I was willing to embrace his fame, all of him.

Cameras flashed as I walked up to the window, showing them the all-access pass Asher had gotten through his record label. Knowing the right people made this process so much easier.

I put the lanyard around my neck and worked my way through the mass of bodies, some talking, some drinking, many wearing way less clothing than I was. I took a deep breath and headed toward the side entrance. Time to see Hayden.

I pulled out my phone and texted Lia, needing some support. *I'm scared shitless. Not sure I can do this.*

She'd been waiting for a message from me based on how quickly my phone lit up with her reply. *He's the one who told the world he loves you. Claim your man.*

I tucked my phone back into my small purse and lifted my chin. I walked up to the first official-looking man I found. He was big and broad, probably a member of the security team. I flashed him a smile but he didn't so much as blink.

"I'm looking for Hayden," I yelled over the current band.

"Who isn't?" the guy growled.

I showed him my pass and he pulled me forward by the lanyard, a scowl deepening on his face as he turned it toward the light. "Haven't seen one of these." He glared at me. "Wait here."

He moved to take it off, but I stopped his hand. "It's mine. I got it from my—" How did I categorize Asher?

He whipped it off my head, and I winced as the lanyard caught in my hair. "No, sweetheart. When it comes to an all-access pass, only the band and record executives decide who gets 'em."

Shit. I couldn't get any closer to the band, and he knew I knew it. Smiling, the security guard pushed forward and was swallowed by the crowd.

Unsure what to do, I followed. Well, sort of. I couldn't move past the crowd like the security hulk did, and most people weren't as willing to let me through.

The guy disappeared through a set of doors. I fidgeted. Would he come back? I didn't know.

A man said something to me, probably in Dutch. I shrugged.

Pointing to the stage then my ears.

He gave me another once-over and then walked on, sucking on his beer.

The song ended and still I stood there. The opening band bowed and the lights came up. I pulled out my phone and texted Lia. *Some security guard took my pass. I don't know what to do.*

She didn't respond.

People swirled around me, laughing and chatting. The door that the security guard passed through opened and another guy came out. Dark hair, lots of tattoos. Hooded, cynical eyes. Then I recognized him: Jackaroo's guitarist, Murphy Etsam.

He beckoned me over. People turned to look at him, some of the girls gasping and calling his name. He ignored them all, eyes on me.

"Briar?"

"Yes. Hayden calls you Ets."

I started to put out my hand for him to shake, but he crossed his arms and leaned against the doorframe. My spine stiffened as he did a once-over, starting at my feet.

"Can't say I think you're that special."

"You don't have to," I said, my eyes narrowing. "I'm here to see Hayden."

Ets smiled, but it didn't reach his eyes. "That's the rub of it. Ben found *me*. And I'm not letting you in."

I raised an eyebrow but my heart slammed against my ribs.

"You're a cool one, I'll give you that." He leaned forward. "But you've fucked with Hayden's head. He can't keep it in the music. That's because of you, and I don't like what you've done to him."

In all the possibilities I'd considered, this wasn't one of them. I knew the situation between Hayden and Ets was strained, but I didn't think he'd try to stop me from seeing Hayden.

"Look, I don't want to cause any problems between you," I started. My phone beeped and I resisted the urge to look at it.

"You already have. Everything was fine before he went to Seattle."

"Are you really going to try to stop me from seeing Hayden?"

"No. I'm not trying. I'm doing. He's sandwiched between two groupies and looks happy as a clam. So turn around and go home."

He shut the door in my face. I blinked, disbelief warring with anger and shame. The shame won and my face burned. People saw that—heard him talk to me that way. My phone beeped again. I pulled it out.

Lia said simply, *Text Hayden.*

But—two groupies? Of course I knew how easy it was to get sex. Still, he'd told me he loved me. Last time Ets pulled something like this, Hayden stayed up all night to ensure he told me his version of the story.

I'd believe him. Hayden wanted me here.

I pulled up his name. *I'm here, at Melkweg. I wanted it to be a surprise, but Ets just shut the side door in my face. Maybe because you told him to? If you want me to leave, I will.*

"You're Briar. Hayden's Briar." I turned to find a young girl looking at me.

"Excuse me?"

"You're Hayden's girlfriend. Why didn't Ets let you backstage?"

The girl's friend asked her a question, eyeing me. She answered, and the groupie's gaze turned apprising. "Marie wants to know if you can get us backstage passes."

I shook my head. "The security guard took mine," I said. My chest ached.

"Why would the security guard take your pass?"

I glanced over and saw a growing group of people surrounding me. Someone snapped my picture. Another flash.

"Why aren't you backstage with Hayden?" someone in the crowd called—probably a reporter.

"Did you break up with him because he was cheating?" another asked.

"Are you angry he didn't come to your friend's funeral?"

"Do you like to do threesomes?"

The questions shot at me, so rapid-fire they landed over each other, hard to tease apart and understand. More flashes as more people took my picture. I was hemmed in, surrounded. I pressed against the wall. Stupid move, and I regretted it immediately. The crowd leaned in, pressing closer. The camera flashes caused my head to ache.

"Please, back up. I need some space."

"What brings you to a Jackaroo concert?"

"Did you and Hayden get married in Seattle?"

"Back up!" I yelled. One of the men grabbed my arm.

"Look this way," he said.

"Let go!" The fear, anger, and frustration overwhelmed me.

Coming here was a mistake. A big one. I whirled around and ran straight into the security guard who'd taken my pass. I stumbled back, trying to keep my balance, but my purse slid off my arm, its contents spilled onto the floor. The security guard gripped my biceps to steady me. More flashes. More intrusive pictures. I couldn't even begin to imagine what the papers would print this time.

"Don't touch me," I said, close to hysteria. "This is your fault."

"Look, lady, you need to calm down."

"Don't tell me to calm down." My hand dashed at the tear sliding from my eye. "I just traveled five thousand miles to see my boyfriend and you took away my pass."

"What are you talking about?" He sounded shocked.

"You took away Briar's pass?"

"Did Hayden tell you to do that?"

"When did you break up with Hayden, Briar?"

I dropped to the ground and picked up my purse, shoving back in my phone, my passport, lip gloss, and my hotel key card.

Ben snatched the card from me, turning it over. "Only the band's staying at this hotel," he said, eyes fixated on the card.

"I know that." I snatched the key card from his hand and managed to duck out from under the crowd hemming me in.

"When did you check in to the hotel?" a reporter next to me asked.

"How long are you staying with Hayden on tour?"

I couldn't breathe. Flash. Flash. This was worse than anything I'd dealt with before. Flash. I bolted toward the exit.

"Hey! You can't leave now."

Oh, yes, I could, and I was. Albeit slowly. The crowd was larger, maybe triple the size of when I'd arrived. Moving back through the melee was nearly impossible. I couldn't even begin to imagine the headlines for tomorrow's papers, but with the crowd of reporters here, I knew I'd be humiliated. Again. Especially now that Hayden hadn't answered my text.

He'd made his point.

I'd misunderstood. Somehow, I'd gotten our relationship wrong. *Sandwiched between two groupies.*

An image I'd never, ever get out of my head. I swiped at another tear. So much for my grand gesture.

Finally, I could see the exit. I sucked in another breath. My credit cards and passport were tucked into my purse. I'd go home, crawl into bed with Princess, and never get out again.

CHAPTER THIRTY-NINE
Hayden

"Maybe he's being told off about all the passes he's handed out," Flip said, raising his chin to indicate Ben and Ets, who were in the hall backstage. I saw Ets take a pass from Ben before he glanced in at us then walked down the hall toward the side entrance of the venue.

"Picking up another woman, more like," Jake said, his voice laced with disgust. "Mila leaving like that hurt him, sure, but he's become a complete man-whore."

I shrugged. "Keeps him from bothering me. You haven't seen my phone, right?"

"You already asked. No," Flip answered.

I sighed, running my fingers through my hair. I'd never gone this long without checking my messages, the sites.

I grabbed a bottle of water from the table. We'd be on in about fifteen minutes. Once I got back to the hotel, I'd call Briar again. I needed to hear her voice, for her to give me a reason to continue to fight for us.

The local band opening for us, an indie group called Berg, filed into the room. "People listened to us," Jonah, the lead singer, said.

"Well, that's kind of the point." Flip chuckled.

"We've been to plenty of gigs where the audience didn't even show until the main act went on. This was better."

"Until that girl started screaming," Topi said. He shook his head. "I don't like the idea of a woman being molested. The crowd really hemmed her in."

"Here?" I asked, throwing my empty bottle into the trash. "Did security get involved?"

"One of your security guards was talking to her, but she was upset. Cameras were all over her. Pretty thing."

"Tall," Jonah said. "Her dark hair was nice in those big curls. Looked a bit like your girl from the papers." Jonah raised his chin toward me.

"Couldn't have been. She's in Seattle," I said.

"Glad the show went well for you guys," Jake said.

I stretched, searching the room once again for my phone. Suspicion nagged me. I glanced back toward the door. "Where's Ets's bag?" I asked.

Jake pointed. I went over and opened it. Sure enough, my phone was there, buried under his picks, a T-shirt, and a box of condoms.

"Your brother is a complete wanker," I said, rising. I turned on my phone and walked toward the door. "He and I are having words."

"He took your phone?" Jake asked. "Shit. I'm coming with."

"Hayden, don't do anything stupid, mate. The press is out there," Flip said.

I glanced down, a thrill running through me when Briar's name popped up. I read the message as I walked.

"Bloody hell," I yelled, and started running.

"What now?" Jake asked.

"Briar's here. Ets wouldn't let her backstage." Jonah had said the screaming girl looked like Briar. Crikey. "If she's hurt…"

Rounding the corner, I nearly plowed into Ben.

"I didn't recognize her," he panted.

"You met Briar out there?"

He nodded. I sidestepped around him and started running.

"She's crying. I couldn't get her to come back. She headed toward the front exit."

"Bloody hell," Flip shouted.

Exactly. I burst through the doors, Flip following close behind, out into the venue, and immediately saw the group of reporters near the groupie door. Aw, hell. They'd mobbed her. The crowd turned as one to stare at us. Girls started screaming and bodies pressed forward, touching. I craned my neck.

"Briar!" I bellowed. My voice was drowned out by the screaming.

Flip grunted, cursing. "I'm going to the stage."

I nodded once, pushing my way through the grasping hands, panic pressing hard against my chest. "Briar!"

My shirt ripped at the shoulder, fingernails scored my arm. I kept pushing forward. My eyes scanned the crowd, and I kept yelling for her. This, even for Ets, was too far. She'd been crying. Fear built in my chest, pushing out.

"Briar Moore, if you're still here, Hayden is trying to find you."

Ah, Flip was on the stage. Good.

"Anyone seen Hayden's girlfriend?" Flip asked. "She's tall, dark hair, blue eyes."

Realizing I wasn't out to socialize, people began to step back, letting me through. Everyone craned their necks, searching for her mink-brown hair.

"Briar!" I bellowed.

I scanned the sea of bodies but kept pushing toward the exit. Ben said she was heading toward the taxi station when he'd come backstage. She might already be gone.

I was most of the way through the auditorium now. My insides curdled. She wasn't here.

Then I saw a glimmer of that mink brown I missed so much. Yes! She walked back into the building. Her dark hair rioted around her head in thick ringlets, her long, athletic legs clad in tight jeans that showed off her trim thighs. As I got closer, her pretty pink lips parted in surprise. Her eyes were damp, the lashes clumping together.

I pushed around a guy in a hoodie and a girl in a tiny red dress and then my palms were on the soft skin of her cheeks. I bent my head, my lips settling over hers.

She opened her mouth, and her taste rushed over my tongue. I moaned, wrapping one of my arms around her hips and pulling her tight against me as my other hand speared into her hair. I kissed her and kissed her, drunk on her essence.

Finally, I was whole.

"All right now, Hayden. You have a different kind of show to put on tonight." Flip's voice. Through a mic. Right-o. I was on the floor of a music venue surrounded by at least two thousand people. Flip stood on the stage, smirking.

This wasn't the place for the kind of kissing I needed, much as I wanted to continue. With one last moan, I pulled back slowly, loving the way my lips clung to hers.

"You're here," I said. My voice was raw, pulsing with lust.

She blinked up at me. I wiped my thumbs under her eyes, clearing away the smudged mascara.

"Supposed to be a surprise."

I leaned my forehead against hers. "The best one." Unable to resist, I placed a soft, chaste kiss at the corner of her mouth. She shivered.

"Ets said you were with two women," Briar said, her voice uncertain.

"How could I be? All I can think about is you."

I pulled back and the crowd around us roared its approval—stamping feet filled the auditorium. Some people whistled, others catcalled. I didn't have to look to know Briar's face was suffused in color.

"This turned out to be more challenging than I'd expected," she said as she snuggled into my side. I smiled, everything clicking into place. This, now, this wasn't a moment I'd forget.

"Stick with me, love. I'll keep life interesting."

"You always do," she said, tipping her face back to smile at me. I kissed her again and the crowd clapped and screamed.

I glanced around, unsurprised to see reporters closing in around us. Briar raised her eyebrow a little at my gaze and sighed.

"They surrounded me," she said.

"We didn't get much of a story," one of the men grumbled.

"Love doesn't sell many newspapers," another said.

"Why can't someone get high? Or smash things. We need another Liam Gallagher. He was interesting."

Briar shook her head, a wry smile flipping the corners of her mouth. "Thank God. I plan to be really boring for a long time."

"I'm as boring and in love as they come," I said, kissing her under her eye, in my spot.

The crowd began to roar, "Briar's song! Briar's song!"

The chant got louder, more demanding. I pulled her forward, toward the stage. Briar balked, shaking her head frantically, but I kept pulling her up toward the stage. I boosted her up onto the raised platform and followed. I grabbed her hand and bowed deep, laughing when Briar curtsied.

When the noise reached an even higher level, her eyes sparkled and her mouth twisted up in a mischievous grin.

"This is kinda fun," she said.

"I'll make a performer out of you yet."

She rolled her eyes, the grin growing on her face. "That's a no."

I positioned her on the end of the piano bench, farther from the crowd. I shucked my button-down, shaking my head when Harry offered another. I threw the ripped shirt into the screaming crowd. Briar's big blue eyes widened as I untucked my black T-shirt before sliding onto the piano bench next to her. "Never stripped onstage before," I said with a wink. "Or played with a woman on my bench."

She smiled, her eyes as soft as her mouth. "I missed you," she whispered as I positioned the mic.

"The song is called 'Between Breaths,'" I told the crowd. Picking up Briar's hand, I pressed a kiss to her palm. "And this one's for you, love."

Being onstage with Briar here was a different kind of high. Flip hit his drum kit hard and I smiled. Jake raked through his chords, charging in on his bass while Ets held a long, powerful note. I leaned into the mic, singing the words I'd been holding in.

The guys revved on my energy and it spilled over into the crowd, feeding back to us. This was what a concert was supposed to be.

CHAPTER FORTY
Briar

After the song, I slipped off the piano bench and headed to the side. Hayden's gaze followed my progress, but his fingers never missed a key or a note. I shook my head, and he winked. So I blew him a kiss.

"Sorry about earlier, Ms. Moore." The security guard who'd taken my pass rubbed his hands over his bald head. "Hayden's going to kill me, no doubt there. At least fire me." He shrugged. "I didn't recognize you."

Nice eyes. Light brown. Not as rich as Hayden's.

"What's your name?"

"Ben Carr."

I extended my hand. He took it carefully, and I knew he wondered if I'd yell or bite or something equally as horrible.

"Nice to meet you, Ben."

His thin lips curled up, sardonic and apologetic all at once. "You don't mean that. But I appreciate the thought anyway."

He let go and stepped back. I realized why when I noticed Hayden glaring at him. I crossed my arm over my body, clasping my far elbow.

"Why don't you tell me more about the situation?" I asked.

"Not much to tell. Your tag—or at least one like it—black markets for about ten G's. The girls who get 'em think they'll automatically get one of the guys to, er, you know, do stuff together."

I bit back a smile. "They expect sex?"

He swallowed hard, his whole head turning red. "Most of the time."

"So your job is to keep the groupies from the band."

"In a nutshell."

"I'm not a groupie," I said.

"No, ma'am. That's why Hayden's going to kill me."

"Ets said Hayden *was* with groupies," I said.

Ben snorted. "Hayden hasn't been interested in a woman since he came back from Seattle. That's another reason why I figured your tag was black market." He shook his head. "I shoulda realized it was you. I'm so sorry."

I turned back to watch Hayden, relief at Ben's confirmation easing the last of my concerns. "I'll worry about Hayden as long as you keep the other women away from him."

"He does a good job on his own."

I smiled at Ben's reply. Harry, Hayden's manager, came over and offered to take me to the front row, but I declined. I stood there for the rest of the concert, happier each time Hayden glanced my way. The band nailed their songs, and they came off the stage euphoric.

"Best show yet!" Flip said, man-hugging Hayden, Jake, and even Ets. Jake's smile was wide, guileless, but Ets...I shivered as a cobra-like darkness uncoiled in his eyes.

"Good show," I said to Hayden.

"Better with you here." Hayden kissed me near my eye, in that spot that drove me wild. I shivered and laid my head against his sweaty chest. He nodded his thanks when Harry handed him a fresh T-shirt.

The fans were screaming, worked up into a frenzy from the last few fast-paced songs. Need filled the space, a sharp hunger for more of their talent. They'd go back out in a minute, and I'd be right there, watching and listening.

"It was excellent," Flip agreed. "Right, Ets?"

"Like Flip said, best show we've put on yet," Ets said on a sigh. "Hayden was on fire."

"Which is why you're not going to take his phone or try to undermine his relationships anymore," Jake growled. "Because if you do, I'm leaving the band, too."

"You wouldn't," Ets said, eyes narrowing.

"I would," Flip said. Arms crossed over his chest, eyes dark and hard, Flip was intimidating. "Hayden's made it clear he's staying for us—Jake and me. So the question is, are you going to get your head out of your arse and start paying attention to the people around you?"

"Right-o." Ets snapped his mouth shut, nodded twice. He turned to Hayden and me, took a deep breath, and met my gaze. Then he lifted his head to face Hayden.

"I was wrong. I shouldn't have messed with your relationship or your girl."

Something made me wonder if this was all about jealousy. No, I didn't think so. I could tell Ets had been hurt. Badly. It was something in those blue-gray eyes.

Hayden tightened his arms around me. "You stay away from Briar. Me, too, and we'll be fine. I told Flip and Jake I'd finish out the tour. But don't push your luck."

Ets dropped his head. "Got it. Let's finish this. I need a drink."

He walked back onstage, picked up his guitar, made faces at the audience. The consummate performer. Hayden grabbed my wrist and pulled me down a hall.

"Where are we going?"

"Somewhere private," he growled.

"You have to go back on!" I struggled to keep up with his long strides. He led us to the back of the building and through the large metal entrance doors.

As soon as the doors shut behind us, his body pressed against mine. I'd missed the feel of his chest, the broadness of his shoulders, the way he pushed his thigh between my legs, pinning me in place with such ease.

"Hayden, what's this about?"

"I told you, I have important words to say to you. I don't want to wait. I don't want you to doubt me. Not again."

"What do you want to say?" I asked. I loved looking at his face. I pushed a damp caramel wave off his equally sweaty forehead.

He leaned in, pressing kisses to the tip of my nose, my jawline, below my ear. I gripped his forearms for support. "That I love you. I need you. I think about you all the time. I need to tell you about my mum. Why my dad and I left Seattle. Why I love the piano. You're the one I want to share that with."

"You'll travel for your job. I don't want you to change for me, Hayden."

"I won't. Not sure I could, really. But, fair dinkum, Briar, you make me *want* things. And whatever I have to do to make that happen, I'm all in."

"Even with an old woman like me?" I asked. The comments about our age difference, all twenty months of it, were cruel. Toward me. I was too old for someone as attractive and talented and famous as Hayden Crewe, so said the media.

"My dad was more than thirty years older than my mum. Granted he died before her, but only by a couple years. And they didn't have the best of relationships. Okay, they're a bad example. But what I'm saying is relationships come in lots of different flavors. For me, you're it. You fill me up and make me love living."

He pressed a kiss to my nose and I smiled, snuggling my cheek into his chest. I couldn't remember the last time I'd been this content. Probably because I'd been too young to remember.

"Rosie left me money. A lot of money."

"Yeah? That's great."

"I want to set up a support group in Seattle for people like you—who are struggling to deal with a loved one's death."

Hayden nuzzled into my neck, nipping my earlobe. "You'll be amazing at that. Suits you."

"I can get my degree from any university, and I will, as long as I can be near you. We can talk about my plans more. Later. But I wanted you to know I don't mind about the paparazzi as long as I get to be with you."

"Sweet Briar, I just professed my undying love. Of course you get to be with me. Always. That's all I want." He stroked that callused thumb down my cheek, over my chin, resting it there, right in the small cleft. "I love you." He leaned forward, his lips a mere breath from mine.

I slid my fingers up into his hair, tugging his mouth down to mine. "I love you, too. God, I love you so much." And I kissed him the way I'd been dreaming about: long and deep and so perfectly slow.

"Hayden, you're on. Oops! Sorry, mate," Harry's voice was sheepish. "You gotta get back out there."

Hayden's arms slid from my shoulders, down to my waist, farther down to my butt, which he cupped in both his hands. "I will. When I'm finished kissing my girlfriend." He glanced at Harry.

309

"Go away."

"They're all waiting for you."

Hayden leaned in, his lips a whisper over mine. My head shifted back, giving him better access.

"No running off with one of the roadies while I'm singing for my tea."

I frowned. "I'm pretty sure they'd give you a beverage if you need a drink."

He blinked. "Supper. That's what you Yanks call it. I'm going to sing for my supper. You'll wait for me?"

"Always," I sighed. Hayden took my hand and led me back out, down the hall.

"Knock 'em dead," I yelled over the din of the crowd as I released my fingers from his.

He winked at me before he turned into the glare of lights. Squaring his shoulders, he took a deep breath.

"Hayden?" He glanced back at me. I blew him a kiss. "For luck. I want an expensive tea."

His smile, this real one he rarely let others see, was slow, devastating. I melted.

"For you, Sweet Briar, anything."

ABOUT THE AUTHOR

With a degree in international marketing and a varied career path that includes content management for a web firm, marketing direction for a high-profile sports agency, and a two-year stint with a renowned literary agency, Alexa Padgett has returned to her first love: writing fiction.

Alexa spent a good part of her youth traveling. From Budapest to Belize, Calgary to Coober Pedy, she soaked in the myriad smells, sounds, and feels of these gorgeous places, wishing she could live in them all—at least for a while. And she does in her books.

She lives in New Mexico with her husband, children, and ginormous, piano-hating Anatolian Shepherd, Mozart. When not writing, schlepping, or volunteering, she can be found in her tiny kitchen, channeling her inner Barefoot Contessa.

ACKNOWLEDGMENTS

There are so many people I need to thank. This journey wasn't an easy one. First, my husband, Chris, and my parents. Your support made this possible.

Jeffe, I love our bubbles dates and all the knowledge you've shared over the years. I'm so very blessed to call you a friend. Your kitties aren't bad either. And, no, Izzy is *nothing* like Princess.

Taylor, your thoughtful comments were insightful and so very helpful. I'm so glad we've had the opportunity to work together.

Juliette, thank you, thank you, THANK YOU for all the help with the Aussie-isms. And for reading such an early draft and giving me hope there was, indeed, something special in this story.

My LERA friends, thank you so much for your generosity and support.

Clarissa, thank you for an amazing cover. I love it.

Nicole, your thoughtful edits made this book shine. I cannot thank you enough. I've so enjoyed getting to know you and now count you a dear friend as well as a kick-ass editor.

Sara, your careful read-through caught the final timeline issues. Thank you so much and I hope Bumbershoot was super fun!

Erin, you amaze me with your ability to create such strong back-cover copy. My books are stronger because of your efforts. Thank you.

And to my readers, thank you, thank you, thank you for reading. You're the best! Be sure to say hello on Facebook or Twitter. I'd love to "meet" you all.

ALSO BY ALEXA PADGETT

Sweet Solace, Book One in the Seattle Sound Series

She Knew Him When

When they first met, she was far too young—seventeen, and already in love with the man who would break her heart. Asher Smith was an up-and-coming songwriter, but he knew better than to show his fascination. He wrote a song for Dahlia. And then he moved on. His whiskey-rough voice made him a star, even as fame extracted its price.

He Never Forgot Her

When she sees Asher next, Dahlia Dorsey is the widowed mother of a teenager, a reclusive writer. She's given up on happy endings—she can't even script them for her characters. But a moonlit beach and the touch of an old friend turn loose her pain and her desires, whether she's ready or not.

They're Risking It All

Dahlia's career is on the rocks. Asher's family is falling apart. Neither can chase a passing attraction. But for two souls wounded worse than they can admit, the connection between them is a balm too precious to refuse—and a thrill too exhilarating to resist...

The Spirit Seducer, Book One in the Echo Series

A god undone by prophecy. A warrior strong as the earth. And the woman who will decide their fate…

The dream comes every night: A warrior clad in leather and wielding a spear, fighting off demons with the heads of jackrabbits and pumas. Defending her.

Echo Ruiz knows it's ridiculous. There's no one in Santa Fe less likely to need defending. Thanks to the migraines, she's confined to her mother's house. Her Native American Studies classes are online, and she hasn't made a new friend in a decade.

Until her twenty-first birthday party, when trickster Coyote himself shows up. An hour later, Echo is on the run from the power-hungry god. Her headaches are gone. Her mother is a hostage, and she's been thrust into a mirror-world of deadly loveliness to fight or die.

Her dream warrior? He's as real as the sweat on her skin. His name is Zeke, and he remembers a lot more about Echo than she does about him. So does her best friend, Layla, who has secrets Echo's never guessed.

But if Echo wants to defeat Coyote—if she wants to survive—she'll have to discover the way herself. Because that's one ending the legends have never told…

The Magician's Ruins, Book Two in the Echo Series

The portals to the underworld are unguarded, and demons roam free in the Southwest. To return the world to balance, Echo Maria Ruiz must survive enough trials to meet with the Magician in his ruined city and learn the secrets he holds. Secrets like the location of her best friend.

Alone and unprepared, Echo must trust Honani, her spirit guardian, and Zeke, the handsome, mysterious warrior who carries her on the back of his motorcycle, battling demons and monsters at her side. In her darkest moments in the Magician's ruins, Echo discovers betrayal lurks, and her warrior may not be *her* hero after all.

Read on for a peek at Ets's story, HOLD YOU CLOSE!

CHAPTER ONE
Mila

Fourteen months ago, I tossed away my entire life. For him. Murphy. He didn't know any of it, and, finally, I was coming to terms with the fact he probably never would.

He didn't want to see me, never would again. His song, "She's So Bad," made that abundantly clear.

I fingered the ticket in my pocket and pulled out the copy of the letter I hadn't wanted to send. Because I hadn't wanted us to be over. But my life sure as certain wasn't a fairy tale, and I wasn't going to get a happily ever after.

I walked down the narrow, hard-packed dirt path, ducking under the thick limb of a gnarled tree. The last few days proved even harder than I anticipated—wasn't the first year supposed to be the hardest?—but the visit to Me-Kwa-Mooks Park was nonnegotiable. I needed the soft sound of water to ground me, give me a reason to move forward. Problem was, water, the beach, reminded me of Murphy. Even this gray Seattle version, so different from our Sydney favorite with its soft, white sand and surfers dotting the water.

I settled in on the narrow strip of sand, gazing out over the tumbled gray boulders and the fog-riddled green-gray water. I bawled my eyes out, but even the overflow of emotion didn't alleviate the building knot in my chest. I patted my other pocket. Thank goodness I had my trusty little bottle of Xanax, the only reason I'd get through these next few days.

Pulling out the ticket, I read the date. He'd be here in two weeks, performing for sold-out crowds at Key Arena, and the more intimate Showbox. That's the ticket I held now. Probably a complete waste of eighty dollars, but I needed to see him. Just once more. I'd mailed the original letter to his mother earlier today, knowing she'd make sure he got it when he returned home at the end of their tour. Ten days until she received it, give or take problems with customs. Two weeks, tops, and this chapter in my life was closed. Unfinished, but over.

Maybe—finally—I could move on. I rested my elbows on my knees and looked out over the water. Seaweed clung to the boulders, driftwood littered the dark brown sand. I wrinkled my nose. Nothing like the beaches we used to frequent years ago when our future was bright, shiny, perfect. How wrong I'd been. How stupid to think I'd ever—ever—escape from the nightmare my mother had caused.

My phone rang.

"Mila!"

Mum's voice sent me back into a tailspin. I might love my mother, but that didn't mean I trusted her. She'd let me down too many times. She was part of the reason I'd moved.

"I'm thinking of coming for a visit. I've never been to America."

And my stomach tanked even further. "That's okay, mum. I'll get out to visit you." Lie, lie, lie. I'd never set foot in Australia again. I'd made that promise on my first—and last—trip to the cemetery to visit my son.

She made a disgruntled sound. "You've said that for the last year. And last time we Skyped, you were so thin! It's those crazy hours you work."

"I like my job," I said, standing. No point in sitting here enjoying a view when my mum's chatter had already destroyed the moment.

"I don't know how you could. You haven't been home for a visit in years. I barely know what you do."

"Because you're not interested."

"Of course I am. Jordan asks me all the time."

At the sound of his name, I stumbled. The phone slid from my fingers but I managed to catch it before it hit the dirt.

"You didn't tell him I was here, did you?"

"Now, why would you worry about that?" Her voice was all innocent. She'd blinked her eyes, I'd bet. I hated that look because it meant she'd done something royally stupid. Or insane. Like the time she'd married a man fifteen years older than she was. The bloke was a rancher with a cattle station out in the Western Territory. Their affair lasted long enough for us to travel to his godforsaken stretch of red, dusty land before my mum dug in her heels, insisting he take us back to "civilization." He'd dropped us in Sydney, disgust shining from his eyes.

That summed up my childhood—one flighty mistake after another. At least the mistakes didn't hurt anyone. Until Jordan. But he wasn't my mum's mistake. More like *her* mum's.

"Mum," I said. I backed away, planning to dart back into my car and…what? Hyperventilate? Call the police because I was scared?

"Don't be like that, Mila." Impatience laced her tone. Her mouth must be puckering in that annoyed moue she tried hard not to let settle over her near-perfect skin. "Jordan loves you. And anyway, why would he care about your boring old doctor job in the Pacific Northwest?"

"You told him I live here?" My voice went from too loud to too

quiet. I couldn't breathe. I clutched my keys and purse like they could hold me erect.

Allowing my mum to visit was the *worst* idea. Danger smeared this situation. At least she only knew I was in the Northwest. I'd never given her the precise location, fearing she'd rat me out. I glanced around the deserted Seattle beach. My private sanctuary destroyed with fears of being accosted. Dragged from the safety of my life. Raped.

"It's been *years* since you made up those silly accusations, Mila. Nothing came of it and Jordan's forgiven you. Let it go."

Actually, it had been twelve months and twenty-one days since my last run-in with Jordan Jones. I dropped a small pill into my .open mouth and swallowed. Thirty-one minutes and the relief would begin to trickle through my system. I closed my eyes.

"See? A lifetime. I'll make the flight arrangements today. Should I fly into Seattle or Spokane? Maybe Vancouver? Portland?"

Sweat burst across my skin. Subtlety wasn't my mother's strong suit. It was obvious Jordan had asked her to fish for more information. I grabbed a tree branch as I passed by, holding it tight in my hand as my knees weakened.

"Oops! I'm late for my next appointment. I'll touch base with you soon." I hung up the phone before my mum could respond. I'd turn it off completely but I needed the reassurance of being able to call 911 in under five seconds. My legs gave out completely and I plopped onto the ground, my breathing ragged and my eyes stinging with the tears I wouldn't shed.

My mum hadn't believed me then. Not when I was eighteen and scared. Not when I was twenty-one and jaded. And definitely not when I was twenty-six and so broken, I never would have been able to put myself back together if my best friend, Noelle, hadn't collected my sorry self and forced me onto that airplane.

That my mother would actively help Jordan seek me out again, even after I'd moved halfway around the world, told me how little she'd ever cared for me.

But she didn't know where I lived, and I wasn't about to tell her.

Anyway, I was being silly. Jordan was in Sydney. I kept tabs on him through social media. Well, actually Noelle was the face of the accounts. I couldn't be that close to him, not even via the binary code of computers.

I released a shaking breath and forced my legs under me. No way my mum would bring him here. I sucked in a breath and released it slowly. My legs were stiff but I managed to stand and walk to the car. I settled into the supple leather seat. Immediately, I locked the doors and slid the key into the ignition. Shoving the car into reverse, I refused to acknowledge that my hands trembled or my breath came in shallow pants.

I was safe. Thousands of miles away from Jordan Jones. There was no reason to panic. No reason to worry.

I pulled over onto a side street and let the shivers take hold of my body. Finally, the medication kicked in and I leaned my head back against the seat, closing my eyes as I forced my tensed muscles to relax.

My mum's phone call brought it all back. All the ugliness I'd been trying so hard to put behind me.

I'd wanted to go back to Perth for the anniversary of his death, but I couldn't gather enough courage. Plus, I'd reasoned, Murphy was in Europe. Not much chance of me running into him there. And that's what I needed: a chance meeting.

To tell him the truth.
To apologize for killing his child.

www.ingramcontent.com/pod-product-compliance
Lightning Source LLC
Chambersburg PA
CBHW070628260626
47161CB00007B/2626